There was a light on in the glass-fronted refrigerator. Three shelves had been removed to make a place for the six-layer cake. Susan stopped dead and took a breath.

It was spectacular. She moved forward to admire it more closely and her foot slid on something lying on the floor. She looked down and gasped. The tiny bride and groom from the top of the cake lay together on the scuffed brown linoleum. They had both been decapitated. . . .

By Valerie Wolzien
Published by Fawcett Books:

Josie Pigeon mysteries:
SHORE TO DIE
PERMIT FOR MURDER

Susan Henshaw mysteries:
MURDER AT THE PTA LUNCHEON
THE FORTIETH BIRTHDAY BODY
WE WISH YOU A MERRY MURDER
ALL HALLOWS' EVIL
AN OLD FAITHFUL MURDER
A STAR-SPANGLED MURDER
A GOOD YEAR FOR A CORPSE
'TIS THE SEASON TO BE MURDERED
REMODELED TO DEATH
ELECTED FOR DEATH
WEDDINGS ARE MURDER

WEDDINGS ARE MURDER

VALERIE WOLZIEN

FAWCETT GOLD MEDAL • NEW YORK

A Fawcett Gold Medal Book
Published by The Ballantine Publishing Group
Copyright © 1998 by Valerie Wolzien

http://www.randomhouse.com

Library of Congress Catalog Card Number: 97-94701

ISBN 0-449-15035-6

Manufactured in the United States of America

First Edition: April 1998

10 9 8 7 6 5 4 3

For Elisa Wares,
a kind and thoughtful editor

PROLOGUE

IT WAS A NIGHTMARE.

The aisle of the church seemed to grow longer with each step. It was darker than usual, almost gloomy. The bouquets of spring flowers decorating the ends of the pews were skimpy and wilted—and the greenery looked remarkably similar to the poison ivy that lined the country lanes in Connecticut—but maybe none of the guests was allergic.

Susan was beginning to think it had been a mistake to include Clue in the wedding party. The golden retriever seemed to be more interested in sniffing the carpet than in leading the bridal party down the aisle carrying a basket of flowers in her mouth. Maybe that accounted for their slow progress.

She glanced at her son. Chad was escorting her on his arm, a scowl on his usually cheerful face. Susan nervously tripped on the edge of the taffeta runner and glanced down at the floor. Red Converse high-tops! Why was Chad wearing red Converse high-tops with his tuxedo? Red was not part of the color scheme she and Chrissy had been sweating over for the past few months. What would their guests think?

She looked around. The pews were overflowing and she didn't recognize a single face. Her grip on her son's arm tightened. "Chad," she whispered urgently. "Who are these people? Your father and I didn't invite these people!"

"That's the groom's side of the church, Mom. They're his friends and his family."

Susan stared. These people were the invited guests of the man her only daughter was going to marry? They didn't seem to know how to dress for a formal afternoon wedding. They were . . . well, they were casual, she told herself—hell, they were downright sloppy, she decided, becoming more than a little upset. And look

1

at that! The groom's mother was wearing a black leather motor-cycle jacket with the words BORN TO BE BAD painted across the back and a skull and crossbones underneath. That certainly did not blend with her delicate color scheme. Had any of her friends noticed? What were Jed's mother and her parents thinking? What would Kathleen and her family say? She glanced to the right.

The right half of the church was empty!

"Chad!" She didn't bother to whisper this time. "Where is everyone? Where's our family? Where are the neighbors? Where's your father's boss?"

Her son shrugged. "Guess you finally flipped this time, Mom. Looks like you forgot to mail half of the invitations to Chrissy's wedding."

It was a nightmare. The only thing she could do was wake up.

ONE

SUSAN WANDERED INTO HER KITCHEN LOOKING FOR A CUP OF coffee and found a roomful of relatives.

"It doesn't look like your nap did you much good," her husband remarked, getting up from the kitchen table and offering her his seat.

"I had a bad dream," she muttered, running her hand through her hair as she accepted the steaming mug.

"Only twenty-six hours until the wedding. Once you start to walk down that aisle, you'll be able to relax and have fun," Jed's mother, Claire, promised, slathering a piece of semolina bread with a thick layer of duck and truffle pâté before popping it in her mouth.

"I guess you're right," Susan said. "Where did all this come from?" she asked her husband, staring at the lavish spread covering her English pine table.

"Just stuff I found in the refrigerator. Everyone was hungry so I just looked around," he explained proudly, and looked down at the plate in front of him. "This paste is interesting. I don't think we've had it before, but you really should buy it again. It's great." He followed his mother's example and ate a huge chunk of pâté.

"Jed, may I speak to you for a minute?" Susan smiled at her mother-in-law and the good-looking gentleman sitting by her side as she spoke. Claire's companion was enjoying a huge container of caviar.

"I don't know how people can stand that stuff," Susan's mother commented smugly. "It's dreadfully fishy and probably costs a fortune. I always think a nice smoked salmon from my fish man would do equally well, and it would be much cheaper." She gave her daughter a pointed look.

"We all love caviar, Mother," Susan said. Although the way

Claire's date was digging into the tin, no one else would be enjoying any today. She tried to make her voice sweeter. "Jed, I really do need to talk to you."

"Sure, honey, but . . ." He had his head in the refrigerator.

She gave up on sweetness. "Right now, Jed!" She stalked from the room, waiting until they were alone in the hall to continue. "Jed, that pâté should be good," she insisted as the door swung closed behind them. "It costs almost forty dollars a pound."

"You paid forty dollars for that stuff . . ." he began, in the same half-incredulous, half-angry voice he had been using for the past few months.

"Jed, your daughter only gets married once. You know I want everything to be perfect!" She offered her standard answer before he finished his standard complaint. "Besides, that's not what I want to talk with you about. You shouldn't be serving that food now. It's supposed to be waiting in the refrigerator until this evening. You're eating up all the appetizers I was planning to serve to Stephen's parents before we go to the rehearsal dinner tonight!"

"I thought the refrigerator was unusually well stocked," he admitted. "But don't worry . . ."

"Don't worry? Jed, what am I going to offer Stephen's parents? I invited them to meet here an hour before we all go over to the church. Jed, we talked about this—it's on the schedule and everything!" she added, referring to the printed sheets of paper that, for the past month, had been hanging beside the medicine cabinet in the bathroom they shared. Of course, the plans had changed many times, and crossed-out phrases had begun to blend with more recently written words, making them difficult to decipher—but that wasn't the point now. "Jed, what are we going to do? Everyone's going to be here and we won't have anything to serve them. Stephen's parents will think we're rude—at the very least."

"Maybe Kathleen can help out. She's in the living room and . . ."

He didn't get a chance to finish. Susan dashed into the living room, barely missing four large boxes stacked in the hallway. "Kathleen! Thank goodness! You'll never believe what Jed has done! Could you possibly do me a favor?"

Kathleen Gordon put the object she had been examining back on the mantel. "That's why I'm here. I figured you might need someone to do last-minute errands today so I asked Jerry to take the kids to the zoo for the afternoon—he's been promising to take them for months—and I came on over. What do you need?"

Susan's relief was so great that she collapsed on the couch—and leapt up immediately as a sharp pain informed her something was amiss. "What the . . . ?" She pulled a heavy brass pipe, about a foot long with a ceramic ball on one end, out from underneath her.

"What is that?" Kathleen asked, sitting down.

"Mystery Wedding Gift Number Three," Susan muttered, scowling at it. "One of my great-aunts sent it. The card said she has had one for years and has no idea how she could live without it. But she didn't mention what she uses it for."

"And you have three of them?" Kathleen asked, amazed.

"No. It's just one of the three gifts that we can't identify. There's this thing, of course." She waved it in a circle in the air. "Also a set of cast-iron flat pans with quarter-inch high circles set into them. Chad thinks they're to make identical pancakes, but I can't imagine anyone being quite so anal retentive. That was Mystery Gift Number Two, and then yesterday a very odd package arrived, marked, 'Number three of four.' It contained a bag of large bolts."

"And packages one, two, and four weren't delivered?"

Susan sighed. "I hope not. Because if they were, they're lost for sure. And I'd much rather the delivery service made a mistake than someone in this house. Especially since . . ."

"Especially since what?"

"Since the package came from Stephen's parents. Mr. and Mrs. Canfield."

"They do have first names, don't they?" Kathleen asked.

"Of course they do. Barbara and Robert. Barbie and Robbie. Barb and Rob. Something along those lines. Do you believe I don't even know what to call them?"

Kathleen chuckled. "Is that the only reason you have trouble saying their names?"

"I know. I'm being silly, aren't I? I haven't even met these people and I don't like them."

"But you said Chrissy was so happy when she visited them."

"Chrissy had a wonderful time. She loved them. She loved their house. She loved their swimming pool. She loved their weather. I think she would have been happy to stay in California for the rest of her life."

"So what does she call them?"

Susan grimaced. "Mom and Dad." She noticed the grin on her friend's face. "Okay," she said, her lips crinkling into a smile, "I admit it. I'm jealous. I never thought of my only daughter as being part of another family—of calling anyone else Mom." She leaned against the back of the couch and closed her eyes. "I think I'm going to have a nervous breakdown."

"You've been saying that for the past three months and you look fine to me. And you only have to hang in there awhile longer. This time tomorrow . . ." Kathleen glanced at her watch. "What will be happening this time tomorrow?"

Susan looked at her watch and frowned. "Chrissy's bridesmaids should be here. They're supposed to be putting on their makeup and getting into their gowns around now."

"Around now? Are you telling me that you didn't give them their minute-by-minute itinerary?"

"I'm not that compulsive," Susan insisted.

"Not usually, but . . ."

"But what? I think I'm being wonderful. Everything I've spent months planning is going wrong and I haven't started screaming yet. I have a house full of guests, more coming for cocktails, and the refrigerator is almost empty."

"What happened to all the food the Hancock Gourmet delivered yesterday afternoon?"

"It's vanishing as we speak."

"All that expensive caviar . . ."

"Yes. Jed passed it out in the kitchen as an impromptu lunch while I was napping. His mother is gobbling down the pâté as though it were going out of style, and my mother is complaining about the caviar tasting fishy." She sighed loudly. "Mothers!"

Kathleen laughed. "You say that just the way Chrissy does—" Then she added quickly, not wanting to offend her friend, "—and the way my daughter will probably say it when she gets older."

"Chrissy's been complaining about me?"

"Chrissy is wonderful," Kathleen insisted. "She knows how hard you've worked to make this wedding perfect. She not only knows it—she appreciates it. And that's not true of many twenty-one-year-olds."

"Not many twenty-one-year-olds would become engaged on St. Patrick's Day and then expect to be married—complete with a large, formal wedding—less than three months later."

"What's so special about St. Patrick's Day?"

Susan shrugged. "Green beer?"

"Somehow Chrissy doesn't strike me as the green-beer type."

"Chrissy doesn't seem quite as consistent as she used to be," Susan mused, a worried expression on her face.

"What do you mean?"

"Well, take this wedding for example. Some things about it haven't surprised me at all. I mean, it's just like Chrissy to ask a friend from one of her design classes to make her a gown instead of going to Saks and buying one off the rack. It's creative and original and makes things just a bit more difficult than going the conventional route. It was also her idea to hold the reception at the old Yacht Club—she's loved that building since she was a child. She used to talk about how she'd like to live there when she grew up. I just hope it isn't dreary. It's an awfully dark building. . . ."

"There were an amazing number of florists' vans out front when I passed by. I didn't know there were that many in Hancock."

"I think Erika brought in every truck from every single one of her stores. She and Chrissy have been poring over plans to decorate that place and the church for weeks and weeks. You know, Erika's been absolutely wonderful. Do you think she and Brett are planning on getting married sometime soon?" Susan asked, momentarily distracted.

"I have no idea. They do seem pretty inseparable these days. I ran into them at the Inn the other night and they were planning a vacation together."

"Sounds serious."

"Maybe they were talking about Bermuda like Stephen and Chrissy," Kathleen suggested. "I love it that they're going there! Such a traditional place for a honeymoon."

"That's one of the things that bothers me," Susan burst out. "Chrissy isn't the type to want to go to Bermuda for her honeymoon. She should be walking the hills of Tuscany or Umbria. Or maybe a romantic little inn in Scotland. Or . . ."

"Did Stephen insist on Bermuda?" Kathleen asked gently.

Susan sighed. "Yes. And having his fraternity brothers as ushers—because they're all the same height."

"None of that sounds so terribly awful to me."

"It's not awful. It's just not like Chrissy."

"She loves him. He's different from her. She'll adjust. He'll adjust. In fact, you could see this marriage as a successful blend of Chrissy's imaginative, artistic lifestyle and Stephen's more traditional leanings. Think of it this way, Susan. You'd be more worried if she were marrying a free-spirit potter from RISD than a young man starting work on his MBA at Wharton, wouldn't you?"

"I suppose so," Susan said doubtfully. "I like Stephen, and Jed is nuts about him. It's just that I worry. I'm not even sure what I worry about."

Kathleen patted her friend on the shoulder. "You're allowed to worry. Your only daughter is getting married tomorrow. You wouldn't be human if you weren't at least a little worried.

"You know what I'd like to do?" Kathleen continued.

"Go out and buy lots of expensive munchies so Chrissy's future in-laws will have something to go with the champagne Jed is serving this evening?"

"In fact, I'd be happy to do that. But could I just get a peek at the wedding gown first? Chrissy's been talking about it for months and . . ."

"It's not here."

"Susan, the wedding is tomorrow. Where is it?"

"I don't know." Susan sighed loudly. "That's just one of the smaller problems. You see, the young woman who agreed to design and make the dress has been studying in Europe her spring semester, so she made the dress over there. You wouldn't believe how difficult it has been to plan all this—Chrissy and this girl have been airmailing fabric swatches back and forth across the ocean on an almost weekly basis. I thought everything was settled—the drawings were wonderful—and then this young woman just happened to meet a young man who just happened to take her to meet his family in Milan—where she just happened to see this fabric in a store window, fell in love with it, and was inspired to design a different dress. And since then the packets have been FedExed back and forth across the

Atlantic like nobody's business. Chrissy has described this dress endlessly, but I haven't seen a sketch and I really have very little idea of what it is going to look like and I'm just hoping it's . . ." She stopped and glanced down at her watch. "That it's going through customs at Kennedy Airport right about now, in fact."

"How is it going to get here?"

"The last I heard, Stephen's best man is supposed to be picking it up and driving like a bat out of hell to Connecticut. I keep thinking of things that might go wrong. The dress getting lost. The plane being delayed. The flight canceled. Hijackers. A bomb. I'm getting a little carried away, aren't I?"

"I think so. But knowing you, I'm sure you have an emergency plan ready to go into action."

"A rotten one. I pulled my own wedding dress out of the attic."

"Good idea."

"Bad idea. Chrissy would hate the dress. Remember, I was married in the Sixties. My dress is white cotton with an Empire waist and—would you believe this—little cotton sprigs of daisies sewn around the hem. I carried daisies, too. I felt young and charming. My mother hated the whole look. I think we fought about that right up until I walked down the aisle." She smiled.

"What are you smiling about?"

"I was just remembering that day. Jed and I didn't have much money, but we decided to spend a long weekend at an inn by the ocean in Rhode Island. The brochure showed a huge Shingle Style building, lovely and romantic, but we got there late at night and we were both exhausted, and instead of charming, it just seemed musty and old. I thought I was going to break down and cry, but when we went up to our room, I discovered that Jed had arranged for two huge bouquets of daisies to be placed on either side of the bed. I knew everything was going to be just fine when I saw them."

"But the dress . . ."

"Is old-fashioned and filthy," Susan added. "I wore it as a Halloween costume once, remember?"

"That's right! Your pregnant bride outfit! I loved it!"

"But can you see Chrissy walking down the aisle in a dress many of our friends and neighbors would remember like that?"

"Definitely not. So what is Plan B?"

Susan frowned. "Well, Chrissy has an old white tennis outfit or two hanging in the back of her closet . . ."

"Your daughter is so beautiful she could walk down the aisle in an old bathrobe and look lovely," Kathleen said, as the phone rang.

Susan picked up the receiver and spoke a few words before a large smile spread across her face. "Thanks . . . No, don't worry. It's easier for me to pick it up than to give you directions—and I was going to be checking things there this afternoon anyway. Just hang it in an out-of-the-way spot. And thank you so much." She hung up, her grin widening.

"The dress has arrived?" Kathleen guessed.

"Yes. That was the best man. He got lost on the way here and he happened to pass by the Yacht Club when he was looking for a phone. The florists' vans were parked out front so he dropped in and called. He's going to leave the dress there. You know, Jed can handle the group in the kitchen. Want to go pick it up with me?"

"Love to. Why don't I drive?"

"Great. There are a few phone calls I should make on the way."

TWO

"Ow!" Susan flinched as she shut the door of Kathleen's Jaguar.

"I gather you haven't seen a doctor about your shoulder yet?" Kathleen asked, starting the car and steering out of the driveway.

"I haven't had the time . . ."

"But you're still carrying that monster purse. Susan, it couldn't possibly be doing you any good. The first thing any doctor is going to do is insist you use something smaller."

"This purse is essential!" Susan fondly patted the pile of scuffed forest-green leather lying at her feet. "I'd be completely lost without it. Everything is here. All my lists. The addresses of everyone we've hired for the wedding. The responses to the invitations. Fabric samples . . . well, I guess I could throw those away now. But everything else is absolutely essential. I couldn't live—"

A shrill ring interrupted their discussion.

"Not to mention your phone," Kathleen added, as Susan scrounged around in the bulky satchel, pulling out the tiny black cell phone.

Flipping the phone open, Susan answered on the seventh ring. "Damn."

"They hung up?"

"Yes."

"If it was important, they'll call back."

"I guess so. I sure hope it wasn't the caterer. There was some question about getting the soft-shell crabs for the appetizers. Of course, we could switch to calamari, but some people are still a little squeamish about eating squid. And they were concerned about the smoked salmon for the quenelles . . . Irish or

Scottish . . . or some small company in Alaska that has just started production . . ."

Kathleen, who had been listening to Susan ramble on like this ever since Chrissy had called her parents from California to announce her engagement, tossed in a few reassuring words. "Susan, those kids who bought the Holly and Ms. Ivy's building are working their butts off to make Chrissy's wedding a success. They know this event is the best publicity they could ever ask for."

"They're wonderful chefs, but they haven't had much experience running anything this big and—"

"Susan, you were thrilled with the plan they made for the dinner tomorrow . . ."

"Yes, but—"

"And Jed seemed equally thrilled that their bid was so reasonable."

"Maybe too reasonable . . . ?"

"Look, any catering company that is run by people who care about the difference between Irish and Scottish salmon is bound to produce a fabulous meal."

"I guess, but—"

The conversation could have gone on forever if the phone hadn't rung again.

This time Susan was more prepared. She had the phone flipped open and answered before the third ring. "Hello? Oh, Chrissy . . ." She put her hand over the tiny receiver. "It's Chrissy," she explained needlessly to Kathleen before resuming her conversation.

"Where are you, honey? Uh-huh. But . . . Are you sure that . . . ? Well, if you think . . . Okay, but . . . I . . . Chrissy? Chrissy?" Susan snapped her phone shut. "She hung up on me!"

"Prewedding jitters," Kathleen suggested.

"She just muttered something about her dress and hung up."

"So the dress has arrived, and Chrissy's seen it, and you have one less thing to worry about."

"I suppose that's possible . . ." Susan admitted, wondering if she dared relax just a little. There was so much that could go wrong.

"So is Chrissy at the Yacht Club?"

"I don't know."

"You asked . . ."

"She didn't answer. She was just babbling about how it was essential that the Canfields be driven from the church to the rehearsal dinner since there was some sort of screwup with their rental car, and Stephen said something about his father—or maybe she said his mother—having absolutely no sense of direction."

"How are they going to get to the church?"

"I haven't the foggiest. Maybe a taxi. We arranged for a limousine to pick them up at the airport and bring them to the Inn, but they were planning on renting a car once they arrived in Hancock. Jed spent hours last Sunday drawing a map of the town with everything marked out for them. It's waiting for them in their suite at the Inn."

"Wow. You really are organized, aren't you?"

"Well, I thought we were. But now all these last-minute things are cropping up. Like, where is the dress? And what has happened to the car the Canfields rented? And there are probably a dozen other things that I don't even know about going wrong right at this very minute."

"Well, not here," Kathleen said, parking her car at the end of the line of almost a dozen vans. Six were painted with the logo of Stems and Twigs, the chain of floral and natural products stores that Erika Eden, special friend of the chief of police, owned. Two were from Hancock Fine Wines. (Which, despite its name, did stoop to selling hard liquor.) The rest were from the catering company.

"'Fabulous Fool'?" Susan read slowly, trying to make out the elegant gold script on the sides of the dark green vans.

"I think the last word is 'Food,'" Kathleen said. "But look at that," she added, before Susan could panic.

"The awning?" Susan stared down at the shimmering silvery-gray tunnel that led from the street, down the stairs, and across the sidewalk to the entrance of the Hancock Yacht Club.

"Underneath the awning."

"Balloons . . . tiny, silvery, transparent balloons . . . but it looks like there's something inside them." Susan got out of the car as she spoke.

"Hmm . . . But what?" Kathleen followed closely behind.

"Flowers—peonies and hydrangeas! And streamers of ribbons! I've never seen anything like them!" Susan cried.

"You sure haven't. They were invented for your daughter's wedding reception. What do you think?" Erika Eden walked down the pathway toward Susan and Kathleen. Even dressed for work in charcoal gray leggings, black suede sandals, a large white shirt, and huge tortoiseshell glasses pushed up in her cap of curly black hair, she looked distinctive and chic.

"They're wonderful," Kathleen exclaimed.

Susan had just noticed the huge metallic pottery urns sitting on each step and lining the walkway. In each, white clematis vines climbed up to the top of the awning from a base of blowsy peonies—one of her favorite flowers. Tiny silvery stars twinkled amidst the vines and seemed to fall to the floor from the urns.

"Tomorrow the awning will be draped with bunches of lilacs . . . three varieties: Leon Gambetta, Krasavitsa Moskvy—both double-flowered pastels—and Primrose, which is a wonderful creamy white. They're all spending the night in a specially built refrigerator at my wholesaler in the city so they will be absolutely fresh tomorrow."

"You're sure they'll be here in time?"

"I'm sure they'll be absolutely beautiful—and the scent!" Kathleen, a knowledgeable amateur gardener, enthused.

"Do you want to see what we're doing inside? It's not finished yet, but . . ."

"Of course!"

"I think I'd better talk with someone from Fabulous Food," Susan said, glancing through the glass panes on the double French doors into the Yacht Club.

"They've set up their main preparation area downstairs," Erika explained. "Right now we're building arches that will be covered with more lilacs over each of the doors, so it might be easier if you went in through the doors down there."

"I will," Susan said, heading down the outdoor stairway to the bottom floor of the building.

The Hancock Yacht Club had been built almost a hundred years earlier, when the coast of Connecticut was a chic resort area. It had seen more than its share of regattas and parties before the club dissolved. The large three-story building on Long Island

Sound had fallen into disrepair during the Fifties. Since that time it had been a private club, a Chinese restaurant, an aerobics studio, a French bistro, a preschool for gifted children, an Italian trattoria, a "mini-mall" of independent antique dealers, and a Japanese sushi house. Its dark woodwork and heavy stone walls had been featured in numerous commercials, three horror movies, and a rock video. Recently restored to its former elegance, it was rented out by the owner for weddings and other large parties.

Chrissy had always loved the building, Susan remembered, as she trotted down the wooden stairway leading to the ground floor. Three young men were coming out of the doorway, clasping large boxes labeled WINE BALLOONS in their arms.

"Aren't you going the wrong way?" Susan asked, grabbing the door as it swung closed behind the last man.

"Not really," he explained. "Wine and champagne glasses upstairs. Coffee and espresso cups down here."

They were gone before Susan could ask any more questions, so she headed on inside. Over the years, the various restaurateurs had all located their kitchens here, and although the food for the reception was being prepared in Fabulous Food's kitchens, it would be served from here. Susan recognized Jamie Potter, one of the seven new co-owners of the catering firm, peering into a large commercial Traulsen refrigerator. The young chef was muttering to herself.

"Hi, Jamie!"

"I don't know who you are, but if you're here to tell me more bad news, please go away," came the tense response.

Susan was immediately on the alert for another crisis. "What sort of bad news?" she asked.

"Who the hell?" Jamie Potter swung around quickly, spilling a pint of what looked like heavy cream on the floor. The irritated expression on her face changed to what almost passed as polite interest when she realized who her visitor was. "Mrs. Henshaw! I'm so glad you're here. I have a few things to talk over with you, if you have a moment."

Susan didn't have time to do what her mother always called "shilly-shallying around." "What's wrong?"

"Nothing. Absolutely nothing."

Susan suspected a lie, but she didn't say anything.

"There have been a few last-minute changes in the menu—due to the availability of some items," Jamie added in a more businesslike voice.

"Such as?"

"Well, we got wonderful soft-shell crabs. And the Alaskan salmon was so beautifully smoked that there was really no choice when we got to the fish market. But the wholesaler we use offered us the most incredibly fresh, tiny little Toulon clams—I'm afraid we couldn't resist. I'd love to serve them raw with just some lemon juice, but I didn't know how you would feel about raw shellfish. Our distributor has an impeccable reputation and—"

"You mean you're adding to the appetizers?" Susan asked. This was a problem?

"Yes. Also, there was some . . . what did Sean call it? *Fougeru.* That's it. *Fougeru.* It's a soft French cheese only made this time of year and wrapped in fern fronds. I've never tasted it, but he's the expert and he says it's wonderful. I thought since Chrissy was having such beautiful flowers, and everything was so fresh and special, that you wouldn't mind if I replaced the Brie with *Fougeru.*"

"Of course not. You know best." Susan had, about a month ago, realized this was one of the best answers she could come up with. Jed always said to hire good people and then leave them to get on with their work. She ground her teeth, determined to keep images from this afternoon's dream out of her mind. "What else?"

"Nothing. Although I should admit something to you."

"What?"

"Well, I was a little hurt when you didn't ask Fabulous Food to provide the wedding cake . . ."

"I know, and I really would have preferred it if you had done the baking and decorating," Susan said honestly. "But this woman I know has just gone into business for herself. Her first husband was murdered and then the second man she married turned out to be a rat, and she recently got a divorce. And then she practically begged me to let her make Chrissy's cake, and Chrissy thought it would be okay—they worked on the design together—and so I . . ." She had a terrible thought. "Is it here? Is it awful?"

"No, that's what I wanted to tell you. The cake is in the refrigerator in the back room. The woman with the headband—"

"You mean the woman who made the cake? Her name is Kelly."

"Oh, that's right. Well, we had a nice talk. She finished the cake about an hour ago. I just wanted to tell you how wonderful it is. I'm going to have to ask her to teach me some of her techniques."

"Where's this refrigerator?"

"Right through that doorway. There's a little pantry and a . . ."

But Susan wasn't going to take the time to hang around and listen for directions. She felt she had been browbeaten into asking Kelly to make this cake and she had been worried about it ever since. She jogged through the short hallway to the storage room, wondering only if the slight tinkling sound from the box she bumped into indicated breakage, but not stopping to check.

There was a light on in the glass-fronted refrigerator. Three shelves had been removed to make a place for the six-layer cake. Susan stopped dead and took a breath.

It was spectacular. She moved forward to admire it more closely, and her foot slid on something lying on the floor. She looked down and gasped. The tiny bride and groom from the top of the cake lay together on the scuffed brown linoleum. They had both been decapitated.

THREE

"OH, DON'T WORRY. I STEPPED ON THEM WHEN I WAS working. But it doesn't matter. I brought them along as a joke. Chrissy and I have been kidding each other about putting a bride and groom on top of her cake for the past few weeks. Then they fell on the floor, and I had my hands full, and then I forgot to pick them up later. . . . Well, what do you think about it?" There was a short pause while both women transferred their attention from the figures on the floor to the creation inside the refrigerator. Kelly nervously adjusted the velveteen headband she wore and waited for Susan to answer.

Susan heard the insecurity in Kelly's voice and rushed to reassure her. "It's the most beautiful cake I've ever seen."

Kelly smiled modestly. "You don't really mean that."

"I do. I really do." And she did: the cake was truly a work of art. Tiers of rich fondant were topped with amazing decorations. Tiny wildflowers peeked from deep green moss on the bottom layer. Swirls of celadon vines climbed around the middle layers, culminating in small wisteria blossoms. The top two layers were covered with white peonies streaked in red. Susan, busy trying to think of an appropriate comment, had a terrible thought. "You're sure nothing is poisonous, aren't you? I mean, I wouldn't want anyone to get ill at the reception. . . . Why are you laughing?"

"Susan, you've been involved in too many murder investigations—you're suspicious of everybody. Besides, everything on this cake is fake! Everything is made from either frosting or marzipan. I know—I made them!"

Susan leaned closer. They were. Fabulous and fake. Perhaps she should schedule an appointment with her eye doctor right after consulting someone about this pain in her shoulder. "They're beautiful and amazing. This is the most incredible cake ever. No wonder Jamie said she wanted to find out how you did it."

Kelly smiled. "I know she's interested, but I'm hoping I can convince her to hire me to make cakes for Fabulous Food. Susan, this could be what I've been looking for—a career in baking. Do you think I'm nuts to try to go into business?"

Susan remembered the time and energy this woman had once flung into social events like her annual Christmas cookie exchange and shook her head. "I think you're the perfect person to make a success out of a business like this one. And, if this cake is an example of your work, you've got it made."

"Really?"

"Really."

A knowing grin spread across Kelly's face. "You didn't think the cake would be this good, did you?"

"Well, I—"

"You came all the way here to check me out," Kelly reminded her. "And you must be awfully busy today."

"That's not why I'm here," Susan said honestly, suddenly remembering the goal of her mission. "I mean, I did want to see how the decorating was coming. And it's always fun to look at the caterer's setup. But actually I have to go look for Chrissy's wedding dress. It was supposed to have been delivered here. I think," she added less certainly, remembering Chrissy's call.

"You had the store deliver her wedding dress to the Yacht Club?"

"Not a store. It's actually being flown in from Italy—"

"Heavens. From Italy? At the last minute? Susan, you've been to Italy. It's a beautiful country, but so disorganized. You must know about the strikes they're always having. And the dress isn't here yet? Don't you think you're cutting this a little close?"

"Believe me . . . Oh, damn this thing," Susan cursed as she fished around in her purse for the ringing phone.

"Hello? Oh, Chrissy! I'm so glad you called back. Don't hang up until you tell me about . . . What? Are you sure? That's not possible! Yes, I know, but . . . Well, honey, I don't think . . . Are you sure? Then . . . But . . . I . . . Chrissy! Don't you dare hang up until I . . ." Susan looked down at the silent phone in her hand. "I don't believe it."

"I gather she hung up."

"Yes. I don't believe it," Susan repeated, flipping the phone closed, putting it down on the zinc-topped table in the middle of the room and scrounging around in her purse once again.

"Something's wrong," Kelly guessed.

"Chrissy's fiancé's parents seem to have disappeared."

"You're not kidding, are you?"

"No, they were supposed to be picked up at the airport and delivered to Hancock, but according to the limousine driver, they never appeared."

"Were they on the plane?" Kathleen stood in the open doorway, her arms full of silky white lilies.

"Oh, Kathleen, I was wondering where you were. Chrissy called and—"

"And said the Canfields have disappeared. I know, I heard you telling Kelly. Is there anything you want me to do?"

"Chrissy wants me to call Brett and ask him to find out if they were on the flight. Do you think he could do that?"

"He could try, but airlines usually don't give out that information. They will tell you if someone bought a ticket, but not if they were actually on the plane."

"But the police—"

"All Brett can do is try," Kathleen repeated. "Why don't you go upstairs and ask him?"

"He's here?"

"Upstairs with Erika."

Susan headed for the wide stairway which connected all three floors of the Yacht Club.

"Susan, be careful," Kathleen called out. "There are piles of stuff on the landing at the top of the stairway! You don't want to trip and get hurt right before the wedding . . ."

Both Kelly and Kathleen were on their way to the stairway before the echo of the crash had vanished.

Susan was sprawled in the middle of a pile of boxes. "I'm fine. I'm fine," she insisted, before anyone asked any questions. "But I don't know about these things."

"No problem. That stuff was all waiting to be loaded back into the vans," Erika assured her. "Just empty flower cans, spare greens, frogs, and stuff like that."

"You're damn lucky you didn't break your neck," Brett said dourly, joining the group that had gathered around Susan.

"Brett, I was looking for you!" Susan cried out. "The Canfields are missing!"

"Aren't they the groom's parents?" Erika asked.

"Funny, I thought it was the groom who was supposed to be shy about appearing at his own wedding," Brett said.

Susan rolled her eyes. Why men she would have considered modern and somewhat liberated seemed to think it was perfectly acceptable to make sexist jokes about weddings . . . "The limo driver told Chrissy that they didn't show up at the airport. I was wondering if you could find out if they missed their flight."

"Where are they coming in from?" Brett asked.

"California. They live in the Santa Clara Valley. . . . I guess they were flying out of San Francisco. At least that's where Chrissy flew to when she visited them."

"Hey, is Mrs. Henshaw still up there?" someone yelled up the stairway.

"Yes, I'm here. Who wants me?"

"Your daughter."

"Chrissy! Chrissy! I'm up here," Susan yelled.

"No, she's not here. She's on the line. I think you left your phone on the table downstairs. . . ." A young man dressed in the unmistakable uniform of a chef jogged up the steps, Susan's cell phone in his hand.

"Oh . . ." Susan reached for the phone. "Chrissy, don't you dare hang up until . . . Oh, thank goodness! Where were they? What? They . . . What? Chrissy, they were going to come for cocktails before the reception, so what . . . ? Chrissy!"

"She hung up on you again?"

"She hung up on me again."

"But it sounds like the Canfields have arrived," Kathleen said.

"Yes. They came in on an earlier flight and rented a car at the airport. Chrissy said something about a convertible. . . . But that doesn't matter. Apparently they've been in town for a few hours."

"Well, it sounds like everything is just fine," Erika offered.

"No, it isn't!" Susan protested. "Chrissy is with her future father-in-law and they're going to be heading for some art gallery in Greenwich . . ."

"Where is Stephen's mother?" Kathleen asked.

"I don't know, but that doesn't matter. What matters is that Mr. Canfield is supposed to be coming over to the house for drinks before the rehearsal and Chrissy didn't even give me a chance to tell her the time . . ."

"She knows the time," Erika said. "She even has a little printed schedule of the entire weekend tucked in her wallet."

"Wow! You are more organized than I thought!" Kathleen cried.

"I didn't print out a schedule," Susan protested, wishing, in fact, that she had done just that.

"Her fiancé did," Erika explained. "Chrissy showed it to me. She seemed to be very proud of it, in fact."

"Chrissy? Likes being on a schedule?" This didn't sound like the harum-scarum daughter Susan had been nagging to and fro for years.

"She's growing up," Kathleen suggested, knowing what Susan was thinking.

"Sure. I guess so, but—"

"Did she mention the dress?" Kathleen asked.

"No. And I didn't see it downstairs. Maybe . . ." Susan looked around the large room as though hoping to spy a mannequin dressed in white silk materialize out of the ozone.

"I didn't see it on this floor," Kathleen added.

"No one has delivered a dress since I've been here," Erika said. "You can ask the kids I've got helping me, but they're pretty responsible. I think they would have mentioned a delivery to me right away."

"Oh, no."

"But, on the other hand, we've all been pretty busy. A deliveryman might have dropped it off and no one would have noticed."

Susan closed her eyes. "It was the best man who dropped it off. And it could be anywhere."

"Look, let's go through this place systematically," Kathleen suggested. "Then, if we don't find it, at least we'll know one place it isn't."

"Yeah, because if it isn't here, it could be almost any place in the world," Susan said. "You don't think the best man decided to try to take it to my house, do you?"

"We don't even know it isn't here," Kathleen pointed out.

"And we don't have that much time to look," Susan said. "I have to get to the hairdresser and you—"

"I'm going to go find the best appetizers in the state and buy them all for you," Kathleen said. "Don't worry. But first, let's go look for that dress."

"Fine. I'll check out the third floor and you—"

"I'll go down and we'll meet back here," Kathleen said.

"And I'll search this floor," Erika added, as the other two women hurried off to the stairs.

Susan scurried up the wide wooden stairway to the third floor of the Yacht Club. Three distinct areas had been planned for Chrissy's reception. The main floor was covered with tables, and dinner would be served there. The ground floor was for drinks and dancing. And the third floor was where dessert and coffee would be served (after the cake was cut by the bride and groom below). Like the other floors, this large room opened onto a balcony which hung over the water of Long Island Sound. (Erika and Chrissy hoped the metallic balloons that lined the three balcony ceilings would send the doves, pigeons, and seagulls who called the place home on a short vacation.) There were restrooms on one side of the room and a stone fireplace set in an inglenook on the other. The shiny oak floor was covered with an antique Samarkand. The carpet was covered with lots of comfortable upholstered couches, grouped into seating areas.

Two young men from Fabulous Food were busy tinkering with a large Italian espresso maker in one corner of the room when Susan arrived. They were surrounded by cardboard boxes, none of them the size or shape to hold a full-length gown. The young men turned toward her and Susan smiled weakly.

"Have either of you seen . . . ? Oh, thank heavens, it's here!" Susan was so glad to see the large plastic dress bag that she swooped down and almost embraced its crinkly surface.

Then she realized what a mistake she was making. The plastic was old and ripped. And it was too short and skimpy to hold a wedding dress.

"Uh, that's my tux, lady."

She looked up at a young man whose embarrassed face seemed vaguely familiar.

"I know you," he cried. "You're Chad's mother, aren't you? Your husband coached my soccer team when I was in junior high. That's my tuxedo you're hugging, Mrs. Henshaw."

Susan looked down at the bundle in her arms. "I . . . uh, I thought it was something else."

"I'm working here for Chrissy's wedding," he explained. "This is an internship for me. I'm studying at the French Culinary Institute in the city. I brought my tux to change into tomorrow afternoon. The tux you have in your hands," he explained.

Susan dropped the garment bag onto the couch. "You haven't happened to see another bag like this around anywhere, have you? Well, not exactly like this. Big enough to hold a gown." And, hopefully, in a lot better shape, she added to herself.

"No, but there's a huge box in the ladies' room. I suppose it might have a dress in it. But it's probably not what you're looking for. It was air-freighted from somewhere in Italy. . . ."

The door of the ladies' room was closing behind Susan before his final words were out of his mouth.

FOUR

"So IT ISN'T THERE EITHER," ERIKA SAID, LOOKING UP AS Susan walked slowly down the stairway a few minutes later. "Don't worry. I'm sure it will turn up."

"Yeah," Susan agreed almost absentmindedly. "I suppose it will."

"You took so long I was ready to come up and see if you needed help," Erika added.

"I was . . . just talking with the young men up there. One of them used to be on a soccer team Jed coached," Susan explained.

"You stopped to chat?" Kathleen had a puzzled expression on her face.

"He's a nice young man," Susan muttered.

"Yeah, I was up there with them earlier this morning. Good kids." Brett Fortesque had rejoined them.

"Brett, I don't suppose you saw anyone carrying a large box or bag earlier?" Kathleen asked. "Chrissy's wedding dress is missing."

"No, but I could ask around."

"Kathleen, there's no reason to bother Brett about something like this," Susan interrupted. "I think we can handle it ourselves. In fact," she added, perking up a bit, "we should get going right now."

"Whatever you say," Kathleen agreed, starting for the door. She still wore a puzzled expression.

Susan muttered a good-bye or two and followed her friend, almost running into Kathleen when the other woman stopped abruptly once they were alone together.

"So what was that all about?"

Susan looked blank. "What do you mean?"

"Look, you leave the room in a panic about the wedding dress

25

and you come back in some sort of trance, almost uninterested in the dress. What is going on?"

Susan glanced back over her shoulder at the closed door and then pulled Kathleen farther away from it. "You won't believe what I found," she whispered.

Kathleen looked at her friend intently. "Tell me."

"There's a body. A dead body," she added, when Kathleen didn't respond.

Kathleen was silent for a moment before asking the next logical question. "Whose body?"

"I don't know. I've never seen her before." Susan frowned. "I'm sure about that. I may forget names, but I recognize faces. She's a complete stranger."

"Where did you find this woman's body? What did those kids upstairs say? Why didn't you tell Brett, or call an ambulance, or . . . Susan, let go! You're hurting me!"

Susan loosened her grip on Kathleen's wrist. "Kathleen! No one must know about this! No one!"

"Susan, are you nuts? You find a dead woman and you don't tell anyone . . ."

"No one else must know. She's hidden—"

"You hid the body?"

"I didn't hide her body. Someone else hid her body. I just found her!" Susan looked back over her shoulder again. "Look, let's just get away from here and I'll tell you all about it."

Kathleen frowned and thought for a moment. "No, I'm not leaving. It will be too difficult to explain to Brett why we did that. We can talk in my car for a bit—it's private, and Brett might understand that you were so overcome with shock that you needed a few minutes to calm down before you reported this to him—I hope."

Susan had other plans, but she hurried back to the Jaguar with Kathleen.

"So where did you find this woman?" Kathleen asked, when they were seated in her car.

"In the ladies' room on the third floor. She was lying in Chrissy's dress box. On the couch. That is, the box is on the couch and the woman is in the box. You see," she added, realizing she wasn't explaining anything very clearly, "I went into the ladies' room looking for Chrissy's dress. And I was thrilled when

I saw a huge cardboard box on the chaise longue in there. It was big enough for a dress—for two or three dresses, in fact—was addressed to Chrissy, and had been air-freighted from Milan, Italy. I assumed it was the dress, of course."

"Of course. Was it sealed?"

"Well, it had been taped shut, but someone had already cut the tape. There was twine tied around it in two places. I untied it." She stopped.

"So you untied the twine and opened the box."

"Yes. And found this woman lying inside."

"I gather she didn't die of natural causes."

Susan thought for a moment. "I can't imagine that she did. I didn't look all that carefully—I didn't touch her or anything. I just assumed someone killed her here and then put her in the box. . . ."

"Now wait a second. How do you know that this poor woman didn't die in Italy? And then her body, which was to be shipped back here to her family, was misdirected here?"

"The box is addressed to Chrissy in care of the FedEx office at Kennedy Airport. Kathleen, do you think it could have been accidentally mislabeled or something?"

"It's possible."

"But if she was killed in Italy, wouldn't she have been . . ." Susan paused. "What's the word . . . preserved before she was shipped?"

"You mean embalmed. I would assume so."

"She doesn't look like a body ready for a funeral. She's pretty pale and all."

"Believe me, embalming has nothing to do with making the body pretty. A makeup person would have done that here—if there was to be an open casket at the poor woman's funeral."

"I suppose it's possible. . . . Maybe you'd better take a look."

"Yes."

"But you have to promise not to say anything to anyone. Okay?"

"But . . ."

"Kathleen, tomorrow is Chrissy's wedding day. She doesn't have her gown, but she does seem to have a dead body. If this is handled wrong, it could ruin everything. Please."

"Look, just let me see this body and—"

"Great. If anyone asks why we're back, we'll say I left something upstairs."

"Fine."

But no excuse was needed, as everyone seemed to be too busy to notice their return. Susan and Kathleen hurried through the Yacht Club and up the stairs to the ladies' room. The young men, still setting up, didn't even glance in their direction. "There it is," Susan said needlessly, pointing at the box as the bathroom door swung closed behind them.

The ladies' room was large, but not so large that anyone in it could possibly not notice the big brown box lying on the chintz couch in one corner of the room. Kathleen hurried over to it, and using a handkerchief from her purse, she opened the top and peered inside.

Susan looked around Kathleen and down at the dead woman. "I'm sure I don't recognize her," she repeated.

Kathleen studied the body. "There hasn't been time to embalm the body. I'll bet she's been dead for less than a day. Maybe a lot less. Strangled."

"Really? Strangled?" Susan, looking closer, saw the line of bruising under the blue and white batik scarf around the woman's neck. "Yes, I see what you mean. I didn't see that before. She was murdered, wasn't she?"

"Definitely. We'd better get Brett before he leaves. He needs to know about this right away."

Susan grabbed her friend's arm before she could leave. "Kathleen, you can't do that!"

"Susan, don't you dare say what I know you're going to say!"

"Kathleen, we can't tell Brett about this. It will ruin Chrissy's wedding day. Her only wedding day. You know how important that is to a young girl."

"So what do you plan on doing? Hiding the body until after the ceremony? Finding the murderer yourself in the midst of the festivities . . ." Kathleen took a good look at Susan's face. "Oh no! Susan, you're not thinking about that! Tell me you're not thinking about that!"

"Kathleen, listen to me. We don't know who this woman is, do we?"

"No, but . . ."

"She might be someone connected with the wedding, right?"

"It's possible, but . . ."

"Oh, my God, maybe I do know who she is!" Susan pushed Kathleen aside and stared down at the body. "At least who she could be. What do you think about the clothes she's wearing?"

A multicolored silk batik tunic hung over slim raw silk slacks, and elegant high-heeled sandals completed the dead woman's outfit.

"She looks nice. Casual. Maybe sort of artistic—you know, the aging-hippie look, assuming the aging hippie happens to have a non-hippie type income . . ."

"How old do you think she is?" Susan asked, still staring intently at the dead woman.

"Around fifty, maybe a little more, maybe a little less. She has wrinkles around her eyes, but she may have been one of those women who spent hours in the sun when she was young."

"Like in California?"

"I suppose . . . You think you know who she is?"

"Chrissy's future mother-in-law!" Susan announced dramatically.

Kathleen squinted down at the body. "Well, her hair is the same blond as Stephen's hair, but I think hers is dyed. I suppose she's old enough to be his mother. You said you hadn't met the Canfields. Did you see a photo of them or something?"

"No, but look. She's the right age. She's chic, but casual and sort of liberal—you know, like she's from California—and . . . um . . ."

"Too bad her murderer didn't pack up her purse and tuck it in beside her," Kathleen suggested. "Then we could have looked in her wallet for an ID."

"That's a good point. We don't know where she was killed, do we?"

"We don't know anything, Susan. And it's not our job to find out."

"It's my job to give Chrissy a wedding day she'll always remember. And I'm talking about good memories, Kathleen."

"And how does a murdered mother-in-law fit in with your plans for this festive occasion?"

"Oh, God, I don't know." Susan sank down on the couch beside the box and put her hands over her eyes. "I just know I have to try to make tomorrow a wonderful day for Chrissy—" She was interrupted by a hammering on the bathroom door.

"Hey! Everyone all right in there?"

Susan grabbed Kathleen's arm. "It sounds like Brett!" she hissed.

"We're fine. Just taking care of some small female problems," Kathleen called back. "We'll be out in a few minutes!"

"Great! I'm heading back to the station. If I don't see you again until the reception, have a good wedding, Mrs. Mother of the Bride!" Brett called through the door.

"Ha. Ha." Susan suspected her laughter sounded artificial. "See you tomorrow!" she called out, then turned to Kathleen and hugged her. "You didn't say anything! Thank you! Thank you!"

"This doesn't mean I'm necessarily going to help you hide this body," Kathleen insisted.

But Susan knew it did, in fact, mean just that. She sighed her relief and then giggled. "Small female problems? What in heaven's name does that mean? Hot flashes? Labor pains?"

Kathleen grinned. "Who knows? But you know how men hate any suggestion of that sort of thing. He certainly wasn't going to ask more questions. Why are we standing here talking? Susan, what are we going to do about this woman?"

"She is a problem, isn't she?" Susan agreed, looking down at the body. "I guess we'll have to wait until everyone is gone this evening to move her...."

"Move her?"

"Well, we can't hold a reception without letting women use the ladies' room, and I don't think we want our guests confronted with a dead body every time they come in to put on more lipstick or use the john."

"Maybe we could find a large roll of wrapping paper and wrap her up like a wedding present and stand her in the corner of the room."

"Do you think that would work?" Susan asked, excited until she got a good look at her friend's face. "Oh, you're kidding, aren't you?"

"Yes."

"Of course ..." Susan continued to stare at the body. "She probably isn't Mrs. Canfield. She might not even be connected with the wedding party.... What's that thing hanging out of her pocket?" Susan leaned over for a closer look, but didn't touch any part of the body or the box.

Kathleen used her handkerchief to pull the piece of paper from the pocket. The women examined it together.

"Is this what I think it is?" Kathleen asked.

"It is if you're thinking it's an invitation to the wedding tomorrow."

Both woman silently stared down at the stiff envelope.

"Look, the small RSVP card was never returned," Kathleen said, peering inside.

"Well, I guess this woman, whoever she is, will not be at the wedding tomorrow," Susan said slowly. "If there is a wedding tomorrow, of course."

FIVE

"DO YOU THINK SHE'S SAFE WHERE SHE IS?" SUSAN ASKED, AS Kathleen's antique Jaguar XKE roared out into the heavy Saturday afternoon traffic.

"I don't know what else we could have done with her," Kathleen said, glaring up at the driver of a green Land Rover. "What is wrong with these people? Doesn't she realize she's blocking my view? Does she think her damn car is transparent?"

"Maybe we should have tried stuffing her behind the couch . . ." Susan mused, when Kathleen didn't answer her first question.

"Susan! She wouldn't fit behind the couch. She wouldn't fit under the couch. We did the only thing we could do. We'll just have to hope it works." Kathleen used one hand to tuck her blouse back into her sleek slacks. After a few minutes of panic, they had decided that the body must be hidden—at least until she could be moved. And she would have to be moved before the reception tomorrow afternoon, they both realized. But first things first, Susan had insisted. Where to put the body?

The door in the ladies' room led to a slop closet equipped, unfortunately, with a large, deep soapstone sink. The only way the dead woman would fit in there was to remove her from the box and plop her in the sink. Without speaking, the women agreed that was a terrible idea. Susan, who had once claimed to have spent at least a month of her lifetime in lines waiting to get into ladies' rooms, had come up with the idea of standing the box on one end and dragging it into a booth, propping it against the toilet, and then hanging an OUT OF ORDER sign on the door. "After all," she had explained, "no one will think anything about it. Those signs are practically as standard a part of the decor in most ladies' rooms as sinks and toilets."

It had been a struggle, but they'd managed to stand the box on end, making sure it wouldn't come open by tying it with a long length of peach silk (possible fabric for the mother-of-the-bride dress before Susan found one ready-made at Bloomingdale's) from Susan's commodious purse. The same purse had provided a roll of masking tape (necessary to attach balloons to her mailbox to identify her home to guests this weekend) that they used to hang the note on a sheet of paper torn from Susan's Filofax (a week sometime in July—Susan figured that if she lived through the wedding, she'd spend at least a month in bed).

"We'll go back tonight after the rehearsal dinner and move her when no one's around," Susan announced.

Kathleen didn't answer.

"You think I'll change my mind and tell Brett about her, don't you?" Susan asked, once again scrounging around in her purse.

"To be honest, I don't see how you're going to be able to avoid it. Look, what's going to happen when Mrs. Canfield doesn't show up for the rehearsal? Are you going to just pretend you don't know what happened to her?"

"But maybe the dead woman isn't Stephen's mother."

"You did send her an invitation, didn't you?"

"Yes . . . just to show her what they looked like . . . Oh, my goodness! That's why the RSVP card wasn't returned—the Canfields certainly wouldn't have done that. Oh, Kathleen, it is Stephen's mother!"

"Maybe, but don't get hysterical until we actually know something."

"You're right." Susan glanced down at her watch. "Can you drop me off at BeBe's?" she asked, mentioning the name of the most popular hairdresser in the county.

"I thought he was coming to your house tomorrow morning to do your hair as well as Chrissy's."

"Nope. Chrissy insisted on doing her own hair, so I thought I'd have mine done today and look decent for the entire weekend—I hope." She glanced up at the sky. Those couldn't possibly be rain clouds to the northwest! But Kathleen was talking.

". . . timing."

"Excuse me? I guess I wasn't listening," Susan admitted.

"I was just wondering how you planned this afternoon to go."

"Well . . ." Susan pulled a notebook from her purse as she

spoke. "Let's see . . . I'm late for the hairdresser—I was supposed to be there at one-thirty. I'm not just having my hair done, I'm also doubling up for a manicure and pedicure—I know no one except Jed is going to see my toes in the next twenty-four hours, but I couldn't resist . . ."

"And after the hairdresser?"

"Well, I wanted to get a facial, but I decided a nap would be just as good for me, so I gave myself an extra hour—of course that was over a month ago."

"So?"

"So I took it away a few weeks ago and put in . . ." She paused, squinted at her notebook, and continued, "It looks like time with Mother. But that's not possible. I couldn't have actually planned to spend time with my moth— Oh, no, that's Jed's mother I'm supposed to be with—she asked me to spend some time with her and I suggested tea at that nice little place downtown. She wants to discuss the present she's giving Chrissy and Stephen."

"What is it?"

"What is what?"

"What is she giving them?" Kathleen asked.

"I haven't the foggiest." Susan frowned. "But I gather it's a big deal. She and Chrissy have always been close, and you know how Claire can be."

"Very enthusiastic," Kathleen suggested tactfully.

"Highly likely to go over the top about almost anything," Susan corrected her friend. "So I really don't want to miss our meeting. If she is so concerned about the gift she's giving them that she wants to speak to me about it, I'd better hear what it's all about."

"Can't Jed meet her without you?"

"Nope. Jed wasn't invited. Just me. Which is part of the reason I'm worried. Claire knows Jed would have no trouble telling her a gift is inappropriate so she comes to me first—"

"You know, you're just as capable of saying no as Jed is."

"Not to his mother. It's always easy to say no to your own mother, but when was the last time you told Jerry's mom that she was wrong about something?"

Kathleen grinned. "You're right. So what good does going to this tea do, since you're just going to agree with whatever Claire suggests?"

"Well, I'll know what's coming and I can warn Jed about whatever it is. Then he'll take care of it all," Susan said, her voice more doubtful than her words implied.

Kathleen chuckled. "Maybe. As I recall, stopping an enthusiastic Claire is like stopping an avalanche."

Susan smiled. "True, but once Jed is involved, it won't be my problem anymore."

"So what do you have on the schedule after this tea party?"

"If I leave the restaurant before four-thirty and the traffic isn't too bad, I should be home by five. Just in time to change my clothes and put the finishing touches on appetizers to go with the champagne we're serving, and before we all head over to the church for the rehearsal—that is, once you buy the food."

"Don't worry. You'll have the best munchies money can buy," Kathleen assured her, before asking, "Are all the members of the wedding party invited to your house for drinks?"

"They all were invited, but they all declined. Chrissy and Stephen are going to see some sort of spiritual advisor that Stephen's parents know, the bridesmaids are spending the afternoon at that day spa in Greenwich, and the ushers . . . well, I have no idea what the ushers are doing, but I figured I wouldn't ask. I know Chad has something planned, but I don't know what."

"A date with that girl he's so smitten with?"

"What girl?"

"Susan, you must have seen him riding around town on that silver BMW motorcycle with that sexy blond goddess driving. I heard she's French—everyone's been talking about the two of them down at the Field Club."

"And I don't know anything about her," Susan admitted. "I've been so wrapped up in plans for the wedding that I guess I just wasn't paying attention the way I should have been." She frowned.

"Susan, the young woman is not only rich and beautiful, but she's a sophomore at Harvard. I don't think you have to worry about any sort of bad influence here."

"He'll be getting married next."

"Don't be sad about it."

"Oh, I'm not!" Susan assured her friend. "I was just wondering if, once the kids were both out of the house, I could talk Jed into taking a long trip to Europe. Like one of those canal trips through France. Or China! I've always wanted to go to China!"

"But first you have to get your hair and nails done," Kathleen reminded her, pulling up in front of the green-and-white striped awning that led into BeBe's shop.

"Oh, my goodness, we're here. I still haven't decided whether to wear my hair up or down. What do you think?"

"If BeBe's the genius everyone says he is, you don't have to worry. It will look wonderful either way," Kathleen assured her. "I'll be at your house around five to help set up for cocktails, okay?"

"Oh, Kathleen, I don't know what I would do without you," Susan cried. She thought Kathleen muttered something about her moving bodies by herself before the long Jaguar roared down the street in the direction of the Hancock Gourmet. Susan straightened her shoulders and tried to avoid looking at her reflection in the door of the salon. Well, she thought, hair up or down, she was bound to look a lot better when she left there.

Susan was greeted enthusiastically by the woman behind the front desk and taken to a small room at the rear of the shop. "First your manicure and pedicure. Then the wash and then BeBe will be ready for you!" the young blonde explained, as she dropped a pile of magazines into Susan's lap and glided from the room.

Susan's usual hairdresser had recently gotten a divorce, quit her job, and moved to a salon in the city, so Susan had never visited this particular place before. That it was classier than her normal shop was obvious in the choice of reading material—not only were the issues of *Vogue* current, but they were exclusively foreign editions. Susan picked up British *Vogue* and flipped through the glossy pages. There was a beautiful bronze dress that would have done wonderfully as her mother-of-the-bride dress. . . . But she stopped herself as she remembered that she had made that particular decision, and a beautiful dress was waiting in her closet that very moment.

But the thought of dresses led, of course, to Chrissy's gown, and Susan was wondering about its whereabouts when two young women entered the room, each carrying a large pink tray.

"Hi, I'm Rita."

"And I'm Meredith," the other girl introduced herself. "We're your hands and toenails. Now, did you bring a piece of fabric or something we can match?"

Susan thought about the rejected fabric swatches unraveling in the bottom of her purse. "But why do you need . . . Oh, you mean that my nails should match my dress."

"It's up to you. Some women seem to prefer a contrasting color. Or some go a shade lighter or a shade or two darker. The lighter shades make your fingers appear longer and the darker shades are very dramatic. Of course, there's the French manicure . . ."

"Just clear polish with white underneath the tips of the nails," Susan said, catching onto something she understood.

"But that's a rather Eighties look, don't you think?"

"Maybe a light silvery peach . . ." Susan suggested, thinking of the color of her dress.

"Which one?"

Susan stared down at the tray of tiny bottles extended before her. There were probably two dozen colors of polish that might be described as peach; an equal number were probably apricot, and as for iridescents . . .

"This one is nice," Meredith offered, picking up a pot. "It's called Rosa Rubiate. Or maybe this one. Seashell Sienna. Or maybe Moonlight Moss."

"I've always liked Damask Dream. Of course, there's really no reason why your toes need to match your fingers—or your dress either. I have one client who always wants her toenails to match—or at least coordinate with—her underwear."

Susan didn't have all day—and she didn't want white polish on her toenails. Besides, she did, after all, have a bottle of nail polish remover in her dressing table. She reached out and grabbed a tiny bottle, the color of a pale pink peony. "This for my fingers," she insisted. "And this . . ." She picked one at random. "This one for my toes."

"It's a little greenish . . ."

"That's fine. I plan to do a lot of walking on grass tomorrow," Susan explained illogically, leaning back in her chair and closing her eyes. This might be her only chance to rest all day. Not that she could possibly relax when she had no idea where the wedding gown had ended up—to say nothing of the dead woman in the box. . . .

She woke up because someone was giggling.

"I don't think I've ever heard anyone snore quite that loudly."

"Shh. You know the rule—never offend a customer. You know who this is, don't you?"

"Chrissy Henshaw's mother. Chrissy was a year ahead of us in high school."

"Yeah, I remember. The guy I was dating my junior year once told me he thought Chrissy was the most beautiful girl in the world."

"Thrilling for you."

"Yeah, men are such scum. I should have realized it then instead of having to get dumped twice when I was almost at the altar before finding it out."

"Well, Chrissy is getting married. That's what this manicure is for," one of the young women announced.

"Then maybe she'll be finding it out for herself soon enough."

Susan opened her mouth to protest this condemnation of her future son-in-law, but the manicurist's next words made her shut it again.

"You know, I heard something very interesting about this guy Chrissy Henshaw is going to marry—something about a commune."

"What? Is he involved in some sort of religious cult?" the other woman asked.

Yes, what? Susan wanted to ask, when there was no immediate answer.

"I heard that he was—"

"Are we done, ladies?"

He might be the best hairdresser in the state, but he sure has rotten timing, Susan thought, glaring at the man reflected in the mirror before her.

SIX

"YOU LIKE?" BEBE SPUN HER AROUND AND FLIPPED THE PINK silk pongee drape off her shoulders in one movement. Susan peered in the mirror. Soft waves framed her face while an elegant French twist swirled around the crown of her head. She looked . . . she stared again . . . she looked like she was wearing someone else's hair!

BeBe seemed to sense some hesitation. "Of course, when you have had time to put on your makeup . . ."

"Oh, yes. It's wonderful," Susan gushed, realizing she had been so concerned about what the manicurist had been starting to say about Stephen—which led her back to wondering about the identity of the dead woman—that she hadn't concerned herself with a more immediate worry: Exactly how much was she supposed to tip this man? She'd planned on charging the visit, but surely she didn't write the tip on the tab the way one did in a restaurant.

"Perhaps the French twist was a mistake? Perhaps you would rather have worn your hair down?"

Susan realized BeBe was interpreting her silence as disapproval. "No, this is wonderful! My hair has never looked so sophisticated or so elegant!" That wasn't saying much, she realized.

"You will wrap it in a length of net overnight." It was a demand. The artist preserving his work.

"Of course." Now where was she going to find a length of net? Even her purse failed her there.

"And just use your fingertips to push it into place in the morning before the wedding."

They both looked down at her elegant nails. They were certainly worthy of such a job.

"Yes. Yes, of course, I will. Thank you." Susan rummaged in her bag.

"You will pay Tiffany at the front desk."

"Yes. Yes, of course." Susan edged toward the doorway. "Thank you," she repeated.

"Your bill is made up for you already."

"Yes. Of course." And with a final thank-you flung over her shoulder, her face burning with embarrassment, she fled the room.

"How much do I owe?" she asked the elegant young woman who had greeted her over an hour before.

"We don't take plastic."

"You don't *what?*" Susan stared down at the gold card in her hand as though she'd never seen it before.

"We do not take credit cards. Cash or personal checks. That's BeBe's rule. And the check must be approved ahead of time," she added quickly, before Susan could get the foolish idea that they trusted the likes of her in a place like this.

Susan straightened her shoulders and lowered her voice. "Of course, I have cash," she announced. "If you will just tell me how much I owe . . ."

Maybe there was water blocking her ears from the shampoo. "Excuse me?"

It wasn't water. It was the truth. Thanking the gods for sending her to the bank yesterday afternoon, she handed over most of the money in her wallet and headed toward the door. Only to remember Kathleen had dropped her off; she needed a ride if she were going to go anywhere.

"Do you mind if I use the phone? I need to call a taxi."

"We can call one for you." The receptionist was going through the pile of twenty-dollar bills Susan had handed her with a frown on her face.

"Oh . . . I forgot the tip," Susan said, recklessly pulling the rest of the money from her wallet and handing it over. She'd use the twenty dollars she kept in the pocket of her purse for emergencies to pay the cab driver. "If you'll just make that call, I'll wait outside."

"Of course."

Susan hurried out the door, relieved to be alone.

The receptionist was efficient, and as Hancock was a fairly small town, the taxi arrived before Susan had a chance to call home to see if there was anything she could stop and pick up on the way. She was settled in the backseat of the local taxi company's Lincoln Town Car before it occurred to her to spend the time making a few phone calls to dig up some information about the last time Mrs. Canfield had been seen. She flipped open her cellular as she riffled through her address book. Then she dialed the Hancock Inn.

The driver's mirror was adjusted in such a way that she could admire her new hairdo as she spoke. Her hair looked so good, so perky, so . . . so young. She frowned. Too young? "Oh, yes, hi. I'd like to speak to the registration desk please." She turned her head to the left and squinted. There was a small tendril hanging down next to her ear which disguised the slight droop her chin seemed intent on making. That man was a genius . . . "Yes. Hi, I'd like to inquire about a guest staying there. A Mrs. Robert Canfield . . . Yes, I understand you have to respect the privacy of your guests, but . . . Yes, of course, I would feel the same way, but . . . Yes, but . . . But . . . But . . ." Susan finally gave up and allowed the woman to explain at length the Inn's policy regarding their guests' right to privacy. When she ran down, Susan asked another question: "Is Charles there?" (referring to the owner of the Inn). "Yes, I'm sure he is busy. It is a very important wedding," Susan agreed, as the driver turned on to her street.

She leaned toward the front seat. "It's the white colonial in the middle of the block, on the right." She really had to get those balloons tied up, first thing.

"The one with the driveway full of cars?"

"Yes. No, I'm not talking to you," she said to the woman still on the other end of the phone call. "I'm sorry. I'll have to call back . . ." She shut her cellular and dropped it into her bag.

"You having a party?"

"My daughter is getting married."

"Hey, are you Chrissy Henshaw's mother?"

"Yes, I—"

"Don't you remember me, Mrs. Henshaw? I took Chrissy to the junior prom. . . . Lance Dancer. You know my parents."

"Of course, Lance. I didn't recognize you. The last time I saw you, your hair was somewhat longer, wasn't it?"

"Somewhat longer and somewhat greener. I was going through

a late punk stage. But I've gotten over that. It was just an adolescent phase. You know."

"What are you doing now?" Susan asked, breaking a pearly pink nail on something at the bottom of her purse as she searched for her wallet.

"Well, I graduated from college and thought about going to Europe for a while or maybe bumming around down in South America. I was a cultural anthropology major, you know."

"I didn't remember, actually. So how did you end up driving a cab?" she asked, remembering that she'd spent her emergency money a few days ago.

"Oh, I'm just doing this for the summer. I finally made up my mind. I'm going to go to law school in the fall. Got to go where the money is, you know."

"So I've heard." From half of Chrissy's friends, in fact. Whatever happened to the good old days of liberal arts majors and plans based on idealism, she wondered when she had the time—which she didn't now. Now she had other problems. "I . . . I don't have any money with me. I spent it all at the hairdresser."

"Oh, yeah. I thought you looked different."

Susan noticed that he said different, not good. "I can go into the house and get some money." If anyone had left any in the drawer by the door where they kept bills for tips and the like. The Henshaws had been making the employees of the U.S. Postal Service, United Parcel, FedEx, and the like rich for the past few months.

"Why don't I just write you a bill and send it?" he offered.

"Would you? I'm awfully busy. . . ."

"Sure. You just pay a ten percent surcharge for the service."

So much for generosity. Susan smiled. "Of course. And thanks for suggesting it." She got out of the car, and after repeating her thanks, hurried up the sidewalk to her house. The door swung open as she arrived and her son Chad barged out, almost knocking her over.

"Chad!"

"Hi, Mom. I'm late."

"But I was just going to ask you to tie the balloons to the mailbox."

"We're decorating the mailbox for Chrissy's wedding? Does Dad know about it? He was just complaining to Grandmother about how much you paid those gardeners to plant all the flowers around the house."

"I . . . he . . . which grandmother?" She wasn't sure whether she preferred her husband complaining to his mother or to hers, but it still would be interesting to know. "And where are you going?" she asked, as her son stepped off the porch.

"Mo-omm."

"If you would get the balloons that are in the garage and tie—or tape—them to the mailbox, I won't ask you to do anything else."

"You will, you know."

Susan looked at her son's slightly too long hair and cheerful face and grinned. "Yeah, you're probably right, but if you hurry you might be able to vanish before I make another request."

"Okay. The balloons are in the garage, right?"

"Yes. There's tape in my purse if you need—"

A star on the freshman soccer team at his university, Chad was out of hearing range before the words were out of her mouth.

Susan entered the door intent on finding her husband—so intent that she did not notice a silver BMW motorcycle roar up in front of her house—so intent that she fell over the pile of boxes stacked just inside the front door.

"You should be more careful, dear. Some of those gifts have FRAGILE stamped on them." Claire stopped on her way down the front hall stairway to offer this suggestion. There was a long garment bag in her arms. "And from Tiffany's, too!"

"And Cartier," Susan added, looking down at the packages by her feet. "Maybe we should put them in the living room with the rest of the gifts."

"I was about to do that. I was taking the dress—"

"Chrissy's wedding gown has arrived!"

The relief Susan felt was to be short-lived.

"I was talking about my dress for the rehearsal dinner tonight," Claire corrected her. "Of course, I bought a dress for the wedding, but I just couldn't resist this one when I saw it at Neiman Marcus. . . . Are you telling me Chrissy's wedding dress has been misplaced?"

"Yes, I haven't even seen it. I think it's here—it was coming from Italy and then the best man picked it up at the airport and brought it to the Yacht Club, but no one seems to have seen it."

"Of course, it has arrived. I saw it in her room just a few hours ago."

Susan ignored the box that fell on the floor as she dashed upstairs to her daughter's room.

It was a mess. Each year Chrissy had come home from Rhode Island School of Design with piles of art projects and assignments, her own and her friends'. What had started out as a charming young woman's room had begun to look like an artist's storage closet by the time she was a sophomore. Two more years had increased the disorder and then, less than a month ago, Chrissy had topped off everything by moving in all her belongings from her dorm room. The sprinkle of wedding clothes and presents had only been frosting on a very disorderly cake. But there was only one spot in the entire room where a wedding gown could hang. Susan stared at the brass hook centered high on the back of the closet door. Empty.

"I think Stephen's mother wanted to see it. She must have taken it over to the Inn."

Jed's mother appeared in the doorway by her side.

"You saw it?" Susan asked.

"Of course, Chrissy was showing it off down in the kitchen just a while ago. Where were you?"

"At the hairdresser." Hadn't Claire noticed?

Apparently she had. "Yes. I . . . I thought you were going to leave it down for the wedding—not that it doesn't look absolutely lovely the way it is, of course."

Of course. Susan just smiled—a little weakly. "Tell me about the dress. What does it look like?"

"Susan, I thought Chrissy was exaggerating, but she wasn't. It is the most beautiful wedding dress in the entire world!"

Gushing, her mother-in-law could only be described as gushing—which told her nothing. "But what does it look like?" Susan persisted.

"Well, it's long and just skims her body at the bodice then it flares out to the ground."

As if that didn't describe about half the wedding dresses in the world! "So what's the fabric like? Is it as unusual as the girl making the dress insisted?"

"Yes. It's . . . it's white, of course. But there are highlights of blue . . . some green . . . a little silver and bronze. . . . It is incredibly beautiful, but very difficult to describe." Claire sat down on Chrissy's bed, apparently thinking she had done just that.

Susan decided it was time to get to the crux of the matter. "Where is it?"

"Oh, I thought I just told you. Chrissy took it with her to see her in-laws."

"What?"

"She thought they would like to see it—especially her future mother-in-law. . . . You know, I am so glad she and Stephen's mother get along so well. I think the relationship of the mother-in-law and the daughter-in-law is sometimes so difficult, don't you? I have friends whose daughters-in-law have done some terrible things. Such terrible things, I cannot tell you . . ."

"I guess . . ." Susan wondered just where this conversation was leading.

"I know I'm terribly lucky Jed married someone—"

"Susan, I've been looking all over for you." Her mother had arrived.

"I was at the hairdresser," Susan said, wondering if anyone was going to notice this fact without her mentioning it.

"Yes, that's nice, dear," her mother said, looking around Chrissy's room. "It's not here, is it?" she asked.

"What's not here, Mother?"

"The box. The box Chrissy's wedding dress was shipped in. I've been looking all over for it. I was going to throw it away—this house is getting very messy, Susan. And all this wrapping material is going to be a real problem unless you start taking care of it."

"Oh, you don't have to worry about that," Jed's mother announced. "The dress wasn't in a box when Chrissy brought it home. And I loaned her the plastic bag from my dress to carry it over to her future mother-in-law's. I just happened to have an extra garment bag with me. I like to be prepared for emergencies."

Susan's heart dropped. "You said she was going to the Inn?" Susan asked.

"Actually the Field Club," her mother answered. "I think she was meeting her future father-in-law there."

"I don't know about that. I thought Chrissy said something about Mrs. Canfield needing the wedding dress at the Inn—

although I can't possibly imagine what for. I was actually thinking of heading over to the Field Club myself. I'd like to use the weight room for a few minutes," Claire said. "Where is your daughter dashing off to now? She just arrived home a few minutes ago."

"Susan, where are you going?" her mother called out as Susan headed down the stairs.

"To the Field Club."

"But, dear, you have guests coming in less than two hours. And you were going to change your clothes, weren't you? And if you're heading in that direction, maybe you should take Claire along with you. . . ."

"I think Claire will want to spend more time there than I do. I'll be back in just a few minutes. There is something I have to check out."

Susan hurried down the steps, not waiting to hear more. Her hair didn't matter. Her clothing didn't matter. Even the dead woman in the stall at the ladies' room in the Yacht Club didn't matter. She had to find Chrissy.

SEVEN

SHE JUST MISSED HER. CHRISSY WAS FINE, APPARENTLY. THE front right fender of Susan's Cherokee was smashed, and there was a large fieldstone dislodged from the hundred-year-old pillars that marked either side of the driveway into the Field Club, but her daughter was just fine. It paid, Susan reminded herself, to keep things in perspective.

"Women drivers! I shoulda known it was a woman driver when I heard the crash into the post. Lady, do you know how many years these posts have been standing here? And no one has run into them except women drivers. There was that Mrs. Swenson who used to get drunk while her husband was out on the links—ran into that exact same post at least half a dozen times. And then there was Mrs. McNaughton—she hit the post one morning when she was driving a huge station wagon of kids coming in for swim team practice. Scared the life out of the little mites, it did. And then there was . . ." The club's character, Scotty the gardener, took off his hat and leaned closer to the windshield. "Ah, Mrs. Henshaw, I didn't recognize you with your hair all fancy like that. You just missed your daughter. . . . Ha, ha." He laughed at his own joke. "You missed seeing the lassie and you just missed running into the car she was in. Get it?"

Susan bent her lips into a smile. "I certainly do, Scotty. You don't happen to know who was driving that monster car my daughter was in, do you?" Her asking was just a formality. Scotty was the unofficial gatekeeper of the club. He knew everyone who went in and out, who they were with and, if possible, what they were doing with that person. The joke around the clubhouse was that if Scotty ever wrote his memoirs, half the club would be in divorce court.

"You mean the one you almost hit?"

"I mean the one that almost hit me!" Susan responded. "That huge car . . ."

"Antique roadster, Mrs. Henshaw. Don't see too many like that anymore."

"Okay, that antique roadster almost smashed into me. If I hadn't turned quickly—"

"And smashed into the post."

"And smashed into the post, I would have run into that . . . that man."

"That man is your daughter's future father-in-law. I guess that makes him your future . . . ah . . . your future in-law, too."

"The driver of that car was, uh . . . Bob Canfield?" Susan asked.

"Canfield, yes. Bob, no. Let's see, what did he tell me to call him? Something kind of interesting, if you know what I mean."

She didn't. And she didn't care right now. "Do you have any idea where he was taking my daughter in such a rush?"

"Said something about a jewelry store downtown . . ."

"Starr's?" Susan asked, naming a popular store, while she put her car in reverse.

"Yes, but don't be in such a hurry. Seems to me he also mentioned the Yacht Club, the Presbyterian church, and that little Italian bar on the river. Seems to me they just had a drink inside the clubhouse. Would be a sad thing if a nice young girl like your daughter married into a family of alcoholics."

"Giovanni's? They mentioned going to Giovanni's?" Susan asked. Was her daughter being escorted around town by a drunken driver on the day before her wedding?

"Yes. And maybe they were going to meet Mrs. Canfield there. What's her name again?"

Not wishing the world to know that she wasn't aware of how her future in-laws wished to be addressed, Susan ignored the question. Besides, if Chrissy and Mr. Canfield were planning on meeting Mrs. Canfield, didn't that imply that Mrs. Canfield wasn't the victim—unless they didn't know she was dead. . . . It was too confusing. "I'd better go find them," was all she said.

"I'll make sure the bill for the repairs is put on your monthly statement." He looked at the pillar with a frown on his face. "The last man to rebuild that pillar retired and moved to Florida. Going to be hard to find workmen to do that type of work. Probably costs a lot these days."

"It doesn't matter," Susan assured him through clenched teeth as she drove off, leaving a spurt of gravel in her wake. It really didn't matter—if Jed were right, they were going to have to declare bankruptcy immediately after the wedding anyway.

She was busy considering the layout of Hancock and didn't notice when she ran over the stone she had just dislodged from the wall. The church was nearby and that would be her first stop. Then the Yacht Club. If she hadn't caught up with them by that time, she would corner them at Giovanni's. She turned her car in the direction of the church, glancing at the gold Rolex on her wrist.

She had almost an hour and a half before her guests were to arrive, but she was due for tea with Claire in . . . She slammed on her brakes, taking a deep breath and praying she was in time to avoid hitting the white sedan of the chief of police.

She only fully recognized the vehicle as she gently smashed its bumper. Both cars came to a full stop, still touching, and Brett Fortesque hopped out of his car.

"Susan, are you all right?"

"Yes. I'm fine. Ahh . . . I'm in a hurry, Brett."

"Susan, I could see that. You came around that corner like . . . well, too damn fast. You could have been in a serious accident."

"I have to find Chrissy. She's with Stephen's father. They're on their way to the church—or the Yacht Club—and maybe that little Italian bar downtown." She knew she sounded like an idiot, but she really didn't have time to stop and chat. "Brett . . ."

"Look, I'll escort you to the church if you want. Or we could split up and I could go to the Yacht Club while you go to the church. We'll both look for Chrissy. But you have to slow down. You don't want to have an accident—another accident—and ruin Chrissy's wedding day."

Susan tried not to think about the body that was just waiting to ruin Chrissy's wedding day. Brett wouldn't ignore that the way he was choosing to ignore the connection between their cars. "Thanks for the offer, but I can manage," she lied.

"Well, it shouldn't be difficult to find them. Chrissy sure is marrying into an interesting family, isn't she?" he said, heading back to his own car.

"She sure is," Susan agreed, starting up her car and wondering if she was going to even meet these people before they became intimate with everyone else in town.

But that wasn't her problem now. Her problem was to head off Chrissy and Mr. Canfield before they started to wonder where Mrs. Canfield was. Not that she had any idea at all what she would say when she ran into them. Glancing in the rearview mirror at Brett's car receding in the distance, she pressed firmly on the accelerator.

"Get Me to the Church on Time" is what she would have sung if she had been in the mood to sing. But she wasn't.

In the mood to sing, or on time.

The Presbyterian Church of Hancock was a large brick colonial that occupied a spacious block in a residential area of the town. It was surrounded by discreet landscaping and lots of macadam for the parking convenience of its membership. There were a half dozen cars in the lot. None of them was the extravagant roadster that had passed by her at the club. Susan frowned and gently pressed on the brake. Maybe she should just take a few moments to see if everything was ready for the rehearsal tonight.

The appearance of Erika in the open doorway at the rear of the church made up her mind for her. Susan turned into the lot and drove over to the doorway. Erika came out to greet her.

"I've done lots of weddings over the years, and you win the Best Mother prize—you're organized and you check out every little detail. There are people in the business of putting on weddings who don't do it as well as you do. Come on in and look around. Chrissy's planned something wonderful—I don't think it will ruin the surprise if you see it a few hours early."

She couldn't resist. What difference would a few minutes make? She parked her car and hurried into the church.

The interior of the church was as austere as its exterior. The cream walls and white woodwork were accented by golden chestnut rails around the pews that matched the wood of the pews themselves. Brass organ pipes rose behind the altar and pulpit. Windows of bubble glass marched along the walls. There was a U-shaped balcony across the back of the room. Sunday's decorations usually consisted of a large floral arrangement on the altar. At Christmas and Easter this was augmented by bouquets placed on windowsills. Many brides also chose to decorate the panels on the ends of the pews. Chrissy, on the other hand, had had other ideas.

Each of the dozen windows was topped by an arch of flowering white lilacs. Each sill was covered with green moss from which tall white Japanese irises sprang toward the light. Copper candelabra displayed thick flaxen beeswax candles in the middle of each sill. The altar was decorated in a similar manner, except that purple irises and dozens of candles had been added to the mix. The ends of the pews were hung with bunches of deep purple peonies. Large copper cauldrons of mixed peonies stood at the rear of the room, ready to be put into place after the rehearsal ended. And, finally, the balcony was draped with boughs of lilac.

It was incredibly elegant; Susan could hardly believe her eyes. And she had a question. "Erika, I don't think we paid you enough for all of this. I don't want to take advantage of our friendship. . . ."

"Don't think about it for a second. Chrissy and I designed this together and I'm thrilled by the way it's turned out. You just paid for the raw materials. The rest is gratis—it's going to be the centerpiece of my book. Chrissy will even get her first professional designing credit."

"That's right, I'd forgotten you were working on a book."

"The photographer is coming to watch the rehearsal. And as soon as Chrissy and her party practice their walk down the aisle, he'll set up the lights and we'll start taking photos. I hired someone local—I hope he knows what he's doing," Erika said, picking a stray leaf off the floor. "We're going to be here half the night as it is. I probably won't get a chance to do more than take a nap before starting to get myself presentable for the wedding tomorrow. Fortunately, I don't have to go back to town. We have permission to leave the vans in the lot until we clean this all out tomorrow evening."

"This is the most beautiful place I've ever seen," Susan said, feeling tears well up in her eyes. "Erika, thank you."

"Don't thank me. That's one talented daughter you have. I just hope she doesn't give up her art work when she gets married."

"So do I." Brought back to reality by thoughts of the future, Susan realized she couldn't hang around here anymore. She had to find her daughter—and her daughter's dress—and her future in-laws—and in less than half an hour she was to meet Claire at the new tea shop downtown. "I'd better get going," she muttered, but Erika had detected a problem with one of the arches and was urging an employee up a ladder to fix it. Susan hurried back to her car.

The Yacht Club was only about ten minutes from the church. Susan figured she could make it in six—or seven—easily.

Unless she was stopped for speeding. Cursing under her breath at being caught in the speed trap near the high school that every single person in town knew would be there on warm days, she pulled over and forced her lips into a smile.

Which faded when she realized the face of the officer walking up to her car was not at all familiar.

"Was I speeding, Officer?" As though she didn't know it!

"I'm afraid so."

"You know, I'm a good friend of Brett Fortesque," she began.

"Lady, ask any cop. Everyone who speeds is a personal friend of the chief of police. Everyone."

"But it's true!"

"Still gonna cost you seventy-nine dollars—unless you're close personal friends with the judge. Can I see your license?"

Susan broke another nail while opening her wallet. "Damn it!" She handed him her license.

He glanced at the photo. "Doing your hair a little different these days, aren't you?"

Finally, someone noticed.

"This photo must have been taken quite a few years ago—"

"Three months!"

"Really?"

Susan got the impression that he considered her at least a pathological liar, if not a serial killer. "Really. Could we just get on with this? I'm in a hurry."

She wouldn't have thought it was possible for him to move any slower, but the man had hidden talents. She gritted her teeth and clenched her fists—and broke another nail. "Damn it!"

"You know there are laws about abusing an officer."

"What's going on here, Officer Setzer?"

Susan breathed a sigh of relief. Brett Fortesque was better than the Mounties any day. "Brett . . ."

"You really do know the chief of police?"

"Well, someone has to, Officer Setzer," Brett reminded the young man, a smile flickering across his handsome face.

"So you want me to tear up this ticket?" The policeman looked down at the pad in his hand.

"I think, in this case, a stern talking-to will do," Brett said.

"I thought that was protocol just for teenagers."

"Wayward teens and Mrs. Henshaw. It's my fault. I probably forgot to brief you on some of the idiosyncrasies of life here in Hancock. We try not to give tickets to the mother of the bride until after the ceremony."

"Look, I appreciate all this," Susan said impatiently. "But, Brett, I really have to go to the Yacht Club."

"Fine. I'll give you a police escort. I got a call about two minutes ago. I was just on my way there."

And she thought she'd had problems a few minutes ago. "You got a call to go to the Yacht Club? Do you know what the call was about?" she asked.

"Not really. Some sort of emergency, was all I was told," Brett said, heading back to his car.

What sort of emergency, Susan wondered to herself, was a dead body?

EIGHT

Susan drove with her fingers crossed all the way to the Yacht Club, her head whirling with questions. Had someone found the body? Who had found the body? What was going to happen now that someone had found the body? Was it possible to proceed with the wedding even though Mrs. Canfield was dead? Was she dead? Was there some sort of place she could go to have a nice quiet nervous breakdown? And why, if someone had discovered the dead woman, wasn't the Yacht Club surrounded by police cars? She swung her car around and parked out front, just tapping (she told herself) the minivan already there.

"Good thing Jeeps and minivans have the same height bumpers," Brett commented, joining her on the sidewalk in front of the club.

"I barely touched it!" Susan protested.

Brett just raised his eyebrows and accompanied her into the building.

"Mrs. Henshaw, am I glad to see you!" The young man who had been setting up on the third floor was sitting on the stairs, a cell phone in his hands. "We've got a problem. . . ."

Susan took a deep breath and braced herself. Here it came.

"I called the plumber about that stopped-up toilet upstairs and he won't come out until he knows who's paying—you or the guy who owns the building."

"Stopped-up toilet?" Brett repeated the words.

"Yeah, we were supposed to check out the entire floor before we took our lunch break—late, but, you know, we're busy— and so I went into the ladies' room and one of the cubicles . . . booths . . . whatever you call the places where the toilets are . . . Anyway, it has an OUT OF ORDER sign on the door, and Erika said to make sure everything was perfect. So I called the plumber that my parents use. And he said—"

"Did you go into the stall to see what the problem was?" Brett asked.

"No, I . . ."

"Why don't you go back and see just what the problem is. Maybe it won't take a plumber to fix it," Brett suggested.

"No! No, Brett. I . . . I was up there earlier and checked out everything!" Susan realized she sounded a little hysterical and tried to lower her voice. "Believe me, it won't help anything if you go into that stall." Well, that much was true. "And why don't I just call the plumber Jed and I use? He can do the work and then bill us." And, with luck, he would be as late in coming as he usually was, and she wouldn't have to worry about the body being found until the end of the week—at the earliest.

"You'll have to pay weekend rates," Brett reminded her. "And keeping the fixtures in order probably is the responsibility of the owner of this place."

"Brett, with what we've spent in the past few months, it won't even be noticed," Susan said truthfully.

"Why don't I just go up and take a look—"

"Brett! No!"

"Why not, Susan? I'm a cop. There's nothing in that bathroom that I haven't seen before."

"But, Brett . . ."

Saved by the bell. Brett's two-way radio started to squawk, and he responded quickly. "Yeah."

Susan held her breath.

"Okay. I'm on my way. The emergency here was a false alarm."

Thank heavens. "Thanks for all the help. I'll just call my plumber," Susan added to the young man. "You don't even have to go back in there—just leave everything to me." She didn't wait for his reply, running up the stairs two at a time.

"Mothers," she heard the young man say disparagingly to someone. "They get so upset about everything. You'd think no one had ever gotten married before."

Susan ran into the ladies' room and headed right for the occupied stall. She pulled the door open and breathed a sigh of relief. The body was still there. But not, she decided, for long. Her heart wouldn't survive another panic like the one she had just experienced. She had to move the body. But where? She looked around the room as though expecting to discover some new hiding place she and Kathleen had overlooked.

No such luck. She had no choice. She was going to have to get it—her—out of here. But then what? Much as she would like to dump the woman in Long Island Sound and forget about her, she knew she couldn't possibly do that. She wasn't a large woman, but the box was bulky, and there was no way it would fit in the back of Susan's Cherokee. She peered out the small window down at the street. Three Stems and Twigs vans were still lined up at the curb. What was it Erika had said about leaving them parked in the lot by the church and not cleaning them out until after the wedding? The rear doors of two vans stood open, and Susan could see they were both filled with plastic garbage bags and odds and ends left over from the arrangements.

She leaned away from the window and straightened her shoulders. If she were going to do it, she might as well get it over with. She marched back to the toilet stall. Summoning all her strength, she yanked the box to the floor, hoping it was sturdy enough to withstand its next trip. She slid it along the floor toward the doorway, where she stopped, took a few deep breaths, opened the door, and peeked out. She was alone on the third floor. She knew that if she thought about it, she would lose her courage, so she shoved the body out the door, across the large room, and down the stairway.

Her luck held; no one was in sight. Most of the employees of Stems and Twigs had finished their afternoon's work here and had gone on to the church. Fabulous Food sounded like it was having some sort of private party in the basement; loud laughter floated up the stairs. Great, now no one would hear her. Saying a silent apology to the dead woman, hoping she was a mother who would understand the necessity of what was happening to her, Susan tugged the box down the stairs.

Susan didn't know what Chrissy's gown was like, but someone in Italy sure knew how to pick out a nice strong box. When they arrived at the bottom of the stairway, she counted two smashed corners and another broken nail as the only damage done by the trip. Just a couple dozen more yards to go to the door. She tugged at her burden and . . .

"Hey, Mrs. Henshaw, you shouldn't be doing that. You're too old . . . I mean, you don't want to damage your back before

Chrissy's wedding tomorrow, do you?" Two large hands grabbed at one corner of the box.

Susan, wondering how long she could live without her heart beating, spun around to look at the speaker. "Wha . . . ? Oh, Tom, it's . . . uh, it's nice to see you!" Tom Davidson, ace reporter (well, only reporter) for the local cable television station was at her side. She realized she sounded rather overenthusiastic, but she was relieved to find him standing behind her rather than someone more threatening—like a member of the Hancock police department.

"Let me help you carry this thing," he offered.

"Oh . . . well, thank you." Why look a gift horse in the mouth?

"Do you think this will fit in your Jeep? What's in it anyway?" the young man asked, resting the package up on one shoulder and pushing his permanently unruly hair back with the other hand.

"I don't . . ."

"Know, huh?" he finished her statement incorrectly. "I suppose people don't necessarily tell the mother of the bride what they're sending as a wedding gift, do they?"

Susan stared at the large box. "No, they definitely do not." She was more than a little relieved by his incorrect assumption. "And you're right. This isn't going to fit in my car. I was going to put it in one of Erika's vans—then it would be out of the way and someone could drive it over to my house late this evening . . ."

"No need. I'd be happy to drop it off."

"I appreciate the offer, but I don't think it will fit in your VW Bug," Susan said, remembering the beat-up little car Tom was so proud of.

"Oh, I traded that in a few months ago. There just wasn't enough room for my equipment. I've got a new van—you'll see. It's parked right out front. This thing will fit like a charm. And I can drive it over to your house right after I get done at the church."

"Are you talking about my church? What are you doing there?"

"Making a video and doing still photos for Erika Eden. She's hired me to tape the decorations that she and Chrissy designed. Then she'll be able to use it for publicity and advertising. And the photos are for a book she's writing."

"I didn't know you did that."

"I'm trying to broaden my base. The networks don't seem to be clamoring for my services, so I'm branching out. Maybe I'll go into advertising . . . or something." He ended less positively than he had begun.

"I thought you loved the news business," Susan said, trying to hold up her end of the box and, perhaps, distract his attention from its contents.

"Yeah, well, it's not all that it was cracked up to be in the textbooks. I went to college thinking I would become the next Edward R. Murrow and then found out that everyone was interested in stories that last only a couple of minutes. It's discouraging."

Susan certainly agreed, but this was not the time for a serious discussion. On the other hand, it was a pretty good time for a monologue—something she had noticed most men were good at when they were asked the right question. "What do you think about the blurring of news and gossip?"

"A disgrace. A threat to democracy. And you know what this is going to mean in the long run . . ." He was off and running.

Susan was pleased. All that was necessary was for her to mutter an "uh-huh" or two when he paused for breath and nod indignantly as they pulled the box down the stairs and out to Tom's new van.

"Well, here we are!" Tom interrupted himself to wave toward a navy VW van parked right in front of the Yacht Club.

"Oh, I didn't know they were making these things anymore," Susan commented, wondering if her back was going to survive lifting the box into the rear of the van.

"It's only new to me. It's an eighty-seven. Not bad, huh?"

"It's nice," Susan said, peering through the window into the back of the dented and rusting VW bus. She noticed some Grateful Dead stickers on the rear windshield and wondered briefly if there were any VW vans in America without at least a few similar decorations. Maybe they were installed at the factory? But she had a more immediate concern. "Do you think there's room for her . . . for the box back there?"

"No problem. I'll just shove a bunch of stuff around—it will be fine. You think it's fragile, don't you?"

"I think we should assume it is," Susan said carefully.

"Yeah, could be a piece of sculpture—Chrissy would like an interesting gift like that. On the other hand, maybe it's a really ugly lamp. She'd hate that, and she's such a sweet girl that she might feel she has to use it. Hey, maybe we should take a peek and if it's something awful, break it so she has an excuse . . ."

"No! Don't do that!" Susan realized she was shouting.

"Hey, don't panic. I was just kidding! I . . . I wouldn't do anything to upset Chrissy."

"Good. So let's just get this thing in your van and forget about it until . . . until after the wedding. There'll be lots of time to open wedding presents later."

"What if the person who sent the gift is at the reception?"

Susan wondered if he was some sort of obsessive-compulsive personality. "So what if he—or she—is?"

"My mother was a big believer in thanking people immediately," Tom explained, almost apologetic.

"Weddings are a little different from birthdays or Christmas," Susan explained patiently. "The bride has a year to write her thank-yous—according to most etiquette books," she added, wondering if she had gone crazy—here she was loading an unidentified, and murdered, body into the van of someone she barely knew while discussing the finer points of wedding etiquette. "I really have to get going," she added. "My mother-in-law is meeting me at a restaurant downtown."

"Oh, hey, I didn't understand. I . . . well, I know how important that relationship can be, Mrs. Henshaw. Why don't you just leave this thing to me? I can take care of it."

"I'm sure you can. But I think I'd better be able to tell Chrissy that I . . . that I saw it safely in place," she finished weakly.

"Okay. Fine by me, Mrs. Henshaw." And so saying, Tom Davidson slid the box into the spot he had cleared in the back of his van and slammed the door shut. "I'll drop it off at your house this evening, okay?"

"What?" Susan asked, confused by his reference to "it."

"The present, of course." He looked at her curiously. "What else would I be talking about?"

"Sorry," Susan muttered. "I was thinking about something else. Sure. Drop it off whenever you get a chance, but . . . but put it in the garage."

"The garage?"

"Yes, otherwise someone might open it by mistake."

"Whatever you say, Mrs. Henshaw. Whatever you say."

Susan would have felt less certain of his acquiescence if she had seen the unhappy expression on Tom Davidson's face.

NINE

Susan DROVE UP AND DOWN THE BLOCK WHERE THE TEA-room was located five times before realizing that Tea for Two had become Smoke 'Em Here. Wondering precisely what the patrons were being encouraged to smoke, she found a parking spot, hopped out of her car and hurried through the green enameled door, trying to think up an explanation for her lateness that her mother-in-law would accept.

If she could find her mother-in-law.

Her first instinct, upon entering the room, was to dash back into the street screaming, *"Fire!"* as loudly as she could. But the young woman who appeared through the smoke seemed rather too calm for the building to be ablaze.

"Would you like a seat at the bar?"

Realizing she looked like someone in need of a drink (and only she knew exactly how true that was), Susan restrained herself and declined the offer. "Actually, I'm supposed to be meeting someone here. At this address, at least," she added, peering into the dark and smoky room. What had happened to the charming faux-English tea shop interior? Crisp lace curtains had been replaced by dusty mahogany shutters. The etched clear glass globes that hung over brass lamps on the walls and from the ceiling were now amber and opaque. Starched linen tablecloths had been whisked off tables. The charming bouquets that had been centered on the tables equipped with bowls of rock sugar, tiny pitchers of cream and milk, and dainty crystal dishes of sliced lemons had been replaced with heavy brass ashtrays—which needed polishing just as soon as someone got around to empty-ing them.

The room was mobbed with young people, talking, smoking, and playing various board games (backgammon and chess, not

Monopoly). Susan wondered what Claire had thought about the place—before she discovered the subject of that question sitting near the bar, with what looked like a martini in one hand and what could only be a cigar in the other.

"Claire?"

"Susan! What a wonderful place to choose to meet. I was expecting one of those cliché suburban spots you usually prefer. You know, one of those prissy women's places. But this is absolutely fabulous. What do you think?" She waved her cigar in the air.

Susan correctly guessed that Claire was interested in a compliment. "Very sophisticated," she muttered. Claire, in fact, looked adorable. Her violet silk shirt was open at the neck; her hair was arranged to look casual and chic; the cigar was held in a hand that had been carefully manicured. All she needed was a beret to look like an advertisement for French vermouth. Susan wondered if her daughter would be spared a lifetime of jealousy by the person who had murdered her future mother-in-law.

Claire's next words reminded her that she didn't actually know the identity of the victim.

"Did you run into Stephen's mother?" She knocked ash into the tray provided.

"I . . . she . . . what do you mean?"

"You do know that she called your house more than once. I think Jed gave her your cell phone number, in fact."

"I didn't know that."

"What is that woman's name, anyway?" Claire continued, always inclined to get involved in her own thoughts. "Something musical."

"Barbara Canfield . . ."

"But she doesn't call herself Barbara or Barb or something normal, does she?"

"I don't know," Susan admitted.

"I thought it was such an interesting name. So very California, if you know what I mean," Claire mused.

"I guess. My phone may have been turned off. She'll probably call back if . . . if she can," Susan said, wanting this conversation to end. "Why did you want to see me, Claire? You said something about a wedding present?"

"Yes. The wedding present. Well, I'm not so sure about that now."

"You certainly don't have to give them a present."

"Oh, I would never think of not giving Chrissy a gift. She's my favorite granddaughter. And we've always been so close." Claire smiled. "I'll always remember how she used to call me when she was in high school and complain that you didn't understand her. . . . Well, you know how adolescents are."

Susan nodded. She did. And she had paid her dues, lived through that time with two different children. And she wasn't going to think about it anymore—even if she hadn't realized that her daughter had been calling Claire and complaining about her mother during those difficult years. "What does this have to do with a wedding gift?"

"It's just that I wanted to get her something special. I shopped and I shopped. I even thought about just writing them a generous check. And then the answer came to me. Do you remember the land I own on the lake?"

Susan did. Jed had bored her with tales of his camping trips in the rolling hills of Bucks County, Pennsylvania, more times than she could count. "Yes, of course. The Boy Scouts use the land now, don't they?" she asked politely. She knew damn well that they did; many times she had thanked her lucky stars that the land was rented to that organization and she hadn't been forced to endure her own wilderness experiences with her family. (Jed's frequent descriptions of the night he had feasted on almost-raw chicken and the ensuing twenty-four hours without indoor plumbing had done nothing to pique her interest in the experience.)

"They had a twenty-year lease on the land."

"Oh, does that mean the lease is up soon?" She had a definite feeling of foreboding.

"It was up last December. And they're not interested in renewing it. The suburbs have expanded, and the area is more suburb than wilderness. A bunch of Cub Scouts got fed up with the food their counselors had provided and hiked to the local McDonald's last fall."

"Smart kids." (No one had ever undercooked a Chicken McNugget.) "So what does this have to do with . . . Claire, you're not going to!"

"Yes. I thought it would make a nice gift for Chrissy and Stephen."

"But—"

"I know what you're going to say. Owning property is a big responsibility. I've thought of that. I've paid the taxes for the next ten years."

"But—"

"And I'd make sure I covered any expenses or . . . or those things they're always adding to the taxes for water or curbs or sidewalks and things."

"But—"

"The only problem, as I see it, is whether to put the land in Chrissy's name or in her name and Stephen's—with the right of survivorship, of course. Or whether I should put it in Chrissy's name with the intention that the land go to Chad if Chrissy dies before she has any children. Who knows where they're going to end up living. If it's California, community property laws would make all this insignificant—but if they end up living in a state without laws like that, and I give it to Chrissy outright, she'll be able to decide when she makes out her own will—unless I make the decision for her. What do you think?"

"Well, I think—"

"I don't want to offend Stephen—don't you wonder why he has such a straight name, when his parents have such interesting ones? What is it that his father calls himself again?"

"I'm not sure. . . ." Susan was beginning to wonder why everyone kept asking her the same question. What *did* these people call themselves anyway?

"Well, it doesn't matter. What matters is what should be written on the deed to this land. Now, I thought I would be sneaky and find out what Stephen thought without actually asking him outright. You know?"

She had Susan's complete attention. "No, I don't know. What did you do?" She glanced down at the martini a waitress had just placed on the table in front of Claire. "I'd like one of those, too," she said. "So what did you do?" she asked, as the waitress slouched off to fill her order.

"Well, I asked him what he thought—as a future student at one of the best business schools in the country—about inheritance laws. And after he had bored me about that for at least fifteen minutes, I sort of snuck in a question or two concerning families and inheritance." She frowned.

"What's wrong?"

"Well, I don't want to disturb you, dear, but I didn't get the impression that the young man is . . . what should I say? That he is overwhelmingly generous."

Susan was instantly alert. "You don't like him. You don't think he's good enough for Chrissy."

"How could we possibly know that now? I remember when Jed brought you home to meet us. You were wearing this tacky polyester minidress with apples printed all over it and I thought . . ." She seemed to realize the expression on Susan's face had changed. "Well, what I thought doesn't matter. Chrissy has decided to marry Stephen Canfield and we certainly have to respect her decision. I merely think he might have answered my question differently if he had known it was Chrissy's money we were discussing rather than his."

"So he thinks money should go only to blood relatives," Susan concluded, accepting the martini the waitress brought without a smile, lifting it immediately to her lips, and forcing herself to sip rather than gulp.

"Well, he made it easy for me to decide to have the deed made out to Chrissy." Claire drained her glass. "I'm glad you approve, dear."

But did she? And did it matter, really, what she thought? Claire's offer was very generous. Chrissy, she knew, would be thrilled. And Stephen? Well, he'd cooked his own goose, Susan decided. She followed Claire's example and downed the rest of her drink. "What sort of impression did Stephen give you?" she asked.

"Susan, I've only had one short conversation with him," Claire equivocated. "About all I can tell you is what you told me. He must be smart. Wharton doesn't accept dummies. And he's certainly good-looking. What do you think?"

"I think he's . . . actually, I don't know what I think." She paused. "He's not much like the man I thought Chrissy would marry. He's not even very much like the boys and men she's dated over the years. I was surprised when she brought him home—but apparently you felt the same way about me."

"True," Claire admitted.

"I'm a little surprised," Susan said, when Claire didn't continue. "I thought . . . well, actually, I thought you were crazy about me."

"Well, of course, we wanted you to think that. You were so . . . so young and . . . and you obviously loved Jed. In the long run that's really all that matters."

Susan smiled. She had an image of herself in that dress Claire had found so tacky. She'd been young, thin, astounded to find herself in love with a man heading for a career in business rather than the English and philosophy majors she'd been dating throughout college. And here they were twenty-five years later, still in love and marrying off their daughter. She might have had another martini and mused about this for a while longer if her purse hadn't rung. She found her phone and answered on the third ring—a record. Maybe she was really moving into the twenty-first century.

Kathleen was on the other end of the line. "Susan, how many of Stephen's relatives are you expecting to come to the rehearsal dinner?"

"Ah . . . let me check my list. Seven, I think." Luckily her notebook had made it to the top of the pile. "Yes, seven. Stephen, of course, his parents and his father's mother, his father's sister and her husband, and the minister who is sharing the service with our minister. That's seven, isn't it?"

"That is. But there are eleven people in your living room right now, and Rhythm just said something about six more on the way. I think you'd better get home right now."

Kathleen hung up before Susan could ask any more questions, which might have been fortunate. She had no idea exactly what question she would have asked first. Who were the eleven people? What were they doing in her living room half an hour before they were invited for cocktails? Had Kathleen bought enough food? Who or what was Rhythm?

And then there were the questions Claire, cigar smoke streaming from her lips, was asking.

"Susan, what exactly do you know about Stephen's parents? What do they do out there in California? What is it that they call themselves?"

All good questions. Almost as good as whether Stephen's mother was dead or alive.

TEN

Susan was so upset that she was halfway to her car before realizing it had started to drizzle. Luckily, she had stocked up on little Kleenex purse packs, and she drove home with one hand on the steering wheel, leaving the other free to gently dab the moisture from her face and hair.

As Kathleen had reported, her company had arrived. The driveway and the street in front of her house were filled with cars. And the drizzle had become a deluge. By the time she had dashed from her parking spot in the next-door neighbor's driveway into her home, she was soaked. Maybe she could sneak past the living room without attracting any attention and spend a few minutes upstairs with her hair dryer before greeting her guests.

If you're going to make an unobtrusive entrance, it's a good idea not to knock a pile of beautifully wrapped boxes against a large crystal vase of yellow roses. There were at least two dozen people crowded into her living room. And they all were watching as Susan walked by the door.

"Susan! Come on in and say hello. We were just talking about where you might be." Jed's voice, uncharacteristically hearty, alerted her to his discomfort.

"Hi, Jed. Hi, Kathleen," she greeted the only two people she knew in the crowd. "I spilled some flowers in the hall." Susan ran her fingers through her wet hair, a polite smile on her face.

"I'll clean it up," Kathleen volunteered, hurrying off to do just that. "And I'll take care of that other thing right away," she added mysteriously to Jed, as she left the room.

Jed, carefully setting the champagne bottle he was holding on the mantel, moved to his wife's side without answering. "Good to see you, Susan," he said, kissing her on the cheek. "Our guests have been here for quite a while."

"But we all know how very busy you must be less than twenty-four hours before your lovely daughter is to be wed."

Susan smiled uncertainly at the speaker, a tall, lean man with an extraordinarily long gray ponytail, dressed entirely in black. She assumed from his stilted speech that he was the Canfields' family minister. How he would get along with the straightforward man who led the congregation at the Henshaws' church was something that Susan decided didn't concern her. "I . . . I know . . . you know I want to meet you all, but I was . . . uh, outside—"

"Either that or the local swim club," suggested an elegant woman, with not a hair out of place, sitting in the window seat at the far side of the room. There was a slight smirk on her immaculately made-up face and Susan wondered, a mite spitefully, how the woman would feel when she stood up and realized that her elegant black-silk-encased derriere was covered with Clue's golden hair. "I got caught in the rain," Susan said.

"We can see that, hon," Jed said. "Why doesn't everyone introduce themselves and then you can run upstairs and change? I can take care of things down here for a while longer."

Susan picked up the cue immediately. Jed either hadn't caught or had forgotten the names of their guests. "What a good idea! You all know who I am," she began, feeling more than a little like an overly enthusiastic camp counselor assigned a group of young children.

But she immediately realized why Jed was so confused. Was everyone in the groom's family named after something—as opposed to someone? Not the men so much as the women, she realized, when they had gone about halfway around the room and she was trying not to be surprised to find a woman named "Rivermist" sitting between a man called "Freedom" and another woman who referred to herself as "Moonbeam." But the entire group was certainly good-natured, she had to admit. By the time everyone had introduced themselves, all her guests were smiling and a few were laughing. A tall, good-looking man stood up as they finished and walked to Susan's side.

"I'm Stephen's father and you both must be terribly confused." He included Jed in the statement.

"Definitely." Jed smiled back. "I've been sitting here wondering how to admit I caught only a couple of your names—and yours wasn't among them."

"My name is Robert. Of course, you know that. It was on the wedding invitation you and your wife sent out. But what you don't know is that everyone has called me Rhythm for the past twenty years or so."

"Everyone except his son, of course." A woman, who combined bleached hair with such a dark tan that she looked almost like the negative of a photograph, jumped up beside Robert Canfield and took his arm in hers. "My real name is Jennifer, but everyone . . . everyone here, that is," she added, looking around the room, "calls me Rivermist. But what we all want to tell you is how . . . how enchanted we are with your daughter. Chrissy is one of the loveliest young ladies we've ever met. And we've all been looking forward to this wedding so much! It's almost a reunion for the group. We're so happy, we just can't tell you!" And, much to Susan's surprise, she found herself being warmly embraced.

"Now, Rivermist, thrilled as we all are that you haven't lost your enthusiasm for life, this poor woman must be desperate to go dry her hair. Why don't we just have another glass of this delicious champagne and then we'll be ready to toast the young couple when she returns." Robert—Rhythm—Canfield had a warm smile on his face.

"An excellent idea!" Jed agreed, grabbing the bottle from its resting place and filling the flutes of the two men nearest him. "I'll just go get more champagne."

"I thought Kathleen . . ." Susan began. But Jed swept by her on his way, and grabbing her elbow, carried her in his wake before she could finish her sentence.

"I need to talk to you. Where's the Mumm's we were given last Christmas?"

"We drank it on Valentine's Day."

"What about the leftovers from our New Year's Eve party?"

"I think you and I finished those up early on January first. . . ."

"But—"

"And there wasn't a single bottle left from the three cases we ordered for Chrissy's engagement party," Susan answered the question he hadn't yet asked. "Jed, don't tell me we're running out of champagne already. How long have these people been here?"

"Less than an hour. And we don't have very many bottles left.

Kathleen was going to call Jerry and see if he could bring some over. . . ."

"Kathleen did that and also called the liquor store. Don't worry. Supplies are on the way." Kathleen appeared in the hallway, three bottles of Dom Pérignon in her arms and a smile on her face. "I also talked the Hancock Gourmet into dashing right over with two platters of vegetarian munchies."

Susan gasped. "Some of them are vegetarians? What are they going to do at the reception tomorrow? There are a few vegetarian dishes because some of Chrissy's friends don't eat meat, but it never occurred to me that some of the adults would eat like that, too. Not that Chrissy's friends aren't pretty grown-up . . . but I should have known that with so many people coming from California . . . But they do seem nice, don't they, Jed? I mean, they have some pretty strange names, but—"

"They're commune family names," Kathleen muttered.

"They're what?"

"They were all in a commune together in the mid-Sixties and they still seem to consider themselves a family group of some sort," Jed explained. "I'll fill you in later." He glanced down at his watch. "You'd better get moving if we're going to get to the church on time."

"I . . ."

Kathleen thrust the bottles at Jed. "You go serve your guests and I'll go upstairs with Susan and fill her in until either Jerry or a delivery truck arrives—I can see the street from your bedroom windows."

"I . . ."

"We're supposed to meet the wedding party in the narthex in less than a hour," Jed said, putting a smile on his face and turning back to the room where their guests waited.

Susan and Kathleen trotted up the carpeted stairway.

"Is she here?" Susan whispered the question she had been wondering about since she walked into her living room.

"If you mean Mrs. Canfield, I have no idea. Rhythm—that's what Robert Canfield calls himself—has had a woman hanging on either arm ever since he arrived. I couldn't tell you which one is his wife—if one of them actually is his wife. Maybe Jed managed to sort out who everyone is better than I did."

"Not a chance." Susan hurried into the bedroom she shared

with Jed, removing damp clothing and tossing it on the bed as she went.

"So you still don't know the identity of the murdered woman in the ladies' room."

"No, but she's not in the ladies' room anymore. She's in the back of Tom Davidson's van."

"Tom Davidson? The young man who reports for the cable news station?"

"Yup. But he's freelancing as a photographer and taking photographs of the church for Erika tonight."

"Why did he want a dead body in the back of his van?" Kathleen looked suspiciously at Susan. "You didn't just slip her in and not mention it to him?"

"Of course not! He put her in himself. Although he thinks she's a rather unwieldy wedding gift." Susan, opening the drawer where she kept her underwear, frowned. "You know, I think he has a sort of crush on Chrissy."

"You must be the last person in town to notice. He's been in love with her from . . . from the first time he met her," Kathleen said, peering out the window.

"Really?" Susan stopped ripping into the cellophane that covered her stockings and stared at Kathleen. "Does Chrissy know?"

Kathleen shrugged. "I have no idea. Did he ever ask her out? "Oh, wait! That's Jerry's car. There's no way he's going to make it into the driveway," Kathleen added, not allowing Susan time to answer her. "I'd better run out and help him."

"Carry everything in through the kitchen," Susan said. "I don't want my guests to realize we weren't expecting them. Or so many of them," she muttered to herself, snagging the stockings on a torn fingernail as she pulled them from their packaging. "Damn!" Luckily, she had planned for this particular emergency; there were three more pairs waiting in her dresser.

She wasn't congratulating herself quite so enthusiastically when she got down to the last pair in the pile. A voice from an old *Seventeen* article read in her teens seemed to whisper in her ear: "Always wear gloves when putting on stockings." Unfortunately, the only gloves available were a pair of ski gloves she had been meaning to put up with the winter things in the attic for the past few months. But they worked! She stood up, dressed and ready to face her hair in the bathroom mirror.

"Are you planning to strangle someone?"

Susan, startled, looked up at her son standing in the open doorway. "What do you mean? There aren't any dead bodies around here."

"Mom! For Pete's sake. I was just kidding you. You have to admit it's a little strange to see a person wearing those things in Connecticut in the middle of June." He glanced down at the bulky, neon-colored nylon covering her hands. "Oh, by the way, Dad is wondering what the hell is taking you so long—I'm just quoting him," he insisted quickly, before she could comment on his choice of language.

"He didn't say that in front of our guests!"

"Not really. He was in the hallway, but he was sort of loud. I think most of them were probably able to hear him. Oh, by the way, I helped the deliverymen from the gourmet store carry two large platters of food into the kitchen."

"Oh, thanks, honey. Could you go tell Kathleen they're there? They should be brought out to our guests as soon as possible."

Chad sprinted off before she could be sure he was going to do as asked. Susan decided she had accomplished as much as possible and went into the bathroom.

It was worse than she thought. Her hair was pinned up in the back and falling down on the sides. And the top . . . She sighed. There was nothing to be done but start from scratch. She began to take off the clothing she'd just put on. It surely wouldn't take more than fifteen minutes to wash and blow-dry her hair. And put on fresh makeup. And make a few phone calls to see if anyone at the Hancock Inn knew if Mrs. Canfield had left the place in the company of the man who called himself Rhythm.

ELEVEN

WELL, TO JUDGE BY THE NOISE LEVEL IN THE ROOM, HER guests were certainly starting the wedding weekend off with a bang. In the hallway, Kathleen had cleaned up the flowers and glass and neatly piled the presents on the table where the flowers had been.

Claire walked out of the living room as Susan was about to enter. There was a glass of champagne in her hand. "Susan, what a wonderful family Stephen has!" she cried. "I don't think we have to worry about anything!"

"Is that Susan?"

Susan recognized the less enthusiastic tones of her mother's voice floating out the door. "Yes, it is, Mother. Is there anything I can get—"

"Susan, I need a moment of your time. Just a moment."

"Mother, I . . ." But she had no choice. Her mother grabbed her arm and tugged her out into the hallway.

"Susan, did you know your daughter is marrying into a family of flakes? And what have you done to your hair?"

Trust her mother to get right to the essentials. "I was caught in the rain. And what do you mean 'flakes'? Is there something wrong with Stephen's family?" Other than the fact that one of them might have been murdered recently, she added silently.

"Well, probably nothing *you* would think wrong, but they belonged to a commune in the Sixties—and they still keep up with those people."

"What people?"

"Their commune-mates or whatever you call them."

"But—"

"And you know what they did in those communes . . ." The frown on Susan's mother's face deepened.

"What?"

"Communal sex!"

"I don't think—"

"Susan, it was in *Time* and *Newsweek*. I remember reading the articles and being so thankful that you and Jed were such a serious young couple."

"Mother, I visited communes and I don't think . . ." Her mother gave her a piercing glance, and Susan changed her tactics. This was going to get her nowhere. She started over. "Mother, what people do when they're young . . ." The look on her mother's face convinced her she was still on dangerous ground. She tried a completely different tactic. "Mother, I need your help."

"Susan! Why didn't you say something right away? What do you need?"

Nothing like her mother—the woman drove her crazy, but she could be depended on in a crisis. "I don't know who Stephen's mother is."

Susan's mother nodded seriously. "That's exactly what I was talking about—indiscriminate sex . . ."

"No, I don't mean he's illegitimate or anything. I just don't know which woman is his mother—or Rhythm's wife," she added, hoping they were one and the same.

"I think I met her. She must have one of those strange names. I don't quite remember. But I'll find out and give you a sign."

"Mo-omm . . ." Susan was amazed to hear the tone of her own voice. First she sounded like her mother. Now she was sounding like her daughter. And it wasn't yet dinnertime. . . . Dinner! She had to call the Inn and make sure there were vegetarian entrées available. . . .

"Susan, where are you going?" her husband demanded, joining her in the hallway. "Those people are going to think there's something seriously wrong if you keep disappearing."

Well, she certainly didn't want anyone to think that! She spun around and, putting a smile on her face, entered her living room.

"Ah! Here she is. The lovely mother of the bride."

Happily, the man who spoke was Stephen's father. Susan turned up the wattage of her smile and headed across the room to him, scooping up a glass of champagne as she passed the coffee table. "I can't tell you how glad I am to meet you. I've been following you around all afternoon."

"Ah! What would Blues say about that, I wonder?"

"Who?"

"My wife. Blues. You know, Rhythm and Blues. R and B. Robbie and Barbie. Robert and Barbara."

"Oh! How clever!" Susan looked around the room, wishing there were some sort of name tag tradition for wedding guests.

"But we need to talk immediately," Rhythm insisted. "About the present we're giving the kids."

"A box did arrive the other day," Susan said vaguely.

"Oh, good. Excellent. But that's not the present. That's more the wrapping for the present."

"Well, we didn't know what . . ." Susan began to explain the lost packages, but he interrupted her.

"Exactly. What to give the kids—that was the question we grappled with as well. We thought and we thought and we thought. We wanted something that would look toward the future, while at the same time being a tribute to their lives and their love in the present."

Susan found herself wondering if the check she and Jed were going to present Stephen and Chrissy with this evening qualified on either score. But her future relative was continuing.

"We got nowhere on our own, so we consulted our spiritual advisor, our astrologer, and our guru."

Susan didn't have any idea how to respond. She realized most of the eyes in the room were on Rhythm—and the rest were on her. She sipped her drink and tried to look intelligent.

"We were desperate. Blues was writing down her dreams each morning looking for a clue. She'd found her old tarot cards and was playing and replaying her future. I had plans to go on a spiritual retreat and think of nothing, absolutely nothing else, and then the answer walked right into our front yard." He paused and looked around the room at his friends, who were looking back, expectant expressions on their faces.

"What walked into your yard?" Jed asked.

"The answer to our dilemma. The perfect present for the kids."

"Which is . . ." Susan prompted, finishing off her drink, hoping for something to dull the shock of whatever was coming.

"The obvious. Something for them to grow together in their care. Something that will teach them responsibility and discipline, yet will provide continuous love. . . ."

Susan tried not to giggle. It almost sounded like he was talking about buying a dog for a young child. . . .

And then she couldn't believe her ears—he was talking about a dog! Or, more correctly, a pair of dogs.

"Potential show dogs, naturally, so if the kids decide that they want to go in that direction . . ." Rhythm continued, apparently unaware of the surprised expressions on Jed's and Susan's faces.

But Stephen and Chrissy were going to start their married life in a small apartment in Philadelphia! Where would they put two dogs? Who would housebreak them? Train them? Walk them? Susan was still asking herself these questions when she realized everyone in the room was looking at her expectantly. "What a . . . What an interesting, creative wedding gift!" she said, as enthusiastically as she could manage.

"Yes. Definitely."

Well, apparently Jed wasn't going to be much help here.

"We love dogs, of course, and I'm sure Chrissy will be thrilled . . ."

"That's what we all thought!" A woman came across the room and put her arm through Rhythm's. Thank heavens! This must be Stephen's mother. The dead woman was a stranger. . . . Susan spoke her first thought aloud, only to be disappointed.

"No, I'm his aunt. His real aunt, not his commune aunt," came the reply.

"I guess we should explain that all of us in the commune felt that we were related. And the children were raised to use familial terms when they spoke with us." This from the man Susan had assumed was the Canfields' minister.

"But the dogs. The important thing here is the dogs!" A red-headed woman (surely too young to be Stephen's mother) got them all back on track. "The dogs are here. I have them. They're in my car. And they should come out," she added, when neither Susan nor Jed responded immediately.

"Oh, yes! Of course!" Susan jumped. "But where will we put them?" She noticed that no one had yet identified the breed of dog. But all puppies were small, weren't they?

"I thought your daughter's room would be the choice. Then she can get to know them. Brides never get much sleep the night before the wedding now, do they?" the dog-keeper continued.

"No, but . . ." Susan didn't know what to say, but she certainly didn't think much of that idea.

"Why don't I help you get them from your car, and they can

stay in Clue's run for the time being," Jed suggested. "That way they can get used to a new place without being . . . uh, without being overwhelmed by too many strangers," he ended tactfully.

"Clue? I assume that's a dog's name."

"Actually, her full name is Susan Hasn't Got . . ." her husband started to explain.

"She's a golden retriever. She's very sweet and friendly. I'm sure they'll all get along," Susan interrupted. There was little need to share this particular family joke now, as far as she was concerned.

"We'd better get them out right away," Jed insisted. "Then we've all got time for one more drink—if anybody wants one— before we go to the church. Wouldn't want the bridal party to think we'd deserted them." He left with the puppies' caretaker and Rhythm.

"No more champagne for me . . . Maybe some bottled water."

"Yes, I'm thirsty, too . . ."

"You know, water will help with the jet lag and . . ."

Susan and Kathleen exchanged looks across the room, then they both headed out to the kitchen.

"How many glasses? I haven't had time to count heads," Susan said, pushing the door open. "Oh, my goodness!" The kitchen was a disaster area. Cardboard boxes lay open on all the countertops. Empty champagne bottles filled the sink. The table was covered with an even larger pile of wedding presents than the one in the front hall.

"It's a mess, but don't worry. No one is going to look in here . . ."

"What about breakfast tomorrow?" Susan asked, deciding, first things first, and emptying the cupboard where her glasses were stored onto a large tray.

"You think you'll have time to eat?" Kathleen asked, her head in the refrigerator.

"I invited both mothers and a few of Jed's and my family members here for breakfast."

"Boy, you really do know how to fill a weekend, don't you?"

"Everything worked out on paper. Of course, I didn't plan on extra relatives, two puppies, or a dead body . . ."

"Who's dead?"

The women turned around and discovered Jed standing in the back doorway. They exchanged glances, but didn't answer him.

"Everyone is thirsty, but they seem to want seltzer, not more champagne," Susan said.

"Amazing how many people brought wedding gifts with them instead of mailing them," Kathleen said, walking over to the pile on the table. "Wonder how all these things got through security at the airport."

"You mentioned a dead body." Jed insisted on sticking to the point.

Susan frowned. "Believe me, Jed, you don't want to know about it. You see—"

"That dog . . . your dog . . . Your dog is attacking the puppies!"

Later, Susan realized it was as effective a way to clear the house as yelling, "Fire!"

Fortunately the rain had stopped or everyone would have looked as casual as Susan. But one end of the dog run was a bowl of mud. And, naturally enough, that was the end in which the animals had chosen to cavort. The puppies were not, of course, being attacked by Clue. The golden retriever (now more chocolate brown than golden) was doing her best to make the little fellows feel at home, rolling around on the ground to the yipping delight of the youngsters.

Susan realized everyone was smiling at the sight. Except for Jed. He was motioning for Susan to head back to the house with him.

"I think your husband wants you," Rhythm said.

"And I think we should leave you two alone and head on over to the church. We have these wonderful directions and I'm sure we'll make it." The woman who had taken care of the puppies made the suggestion.

"Why don't you all just follow my car?" Kathleen suggested.

"Good idea," she agreed.

"We'll leave you two alone for now—but you'll be at the church . . ." Rhythm said.

"We'll be right behind you," Susan said. "Don't worry."

Jed waited until everyone had decided who was going to ride with whom and the last car was backing out of the driveway before turning to his wife.

Susan was staring at the animals in the pen. "What sort of puppies do they look like to you, Jed? They seem awfully large—"

"Susan, this is no time to worry about unimportant things. Who is dead? And who do you think the murderer is?"

TWELVE

"... AND I DON'T, OF COURSE, HAVE ANY IDEA WHO THE murderer is." Susan ended her explanation as Jed steered his Mercedes into the parking lot beside the Hancock Presbyterian Church.

"No, I guess it's difficult to figure that out when you don't even know the identity of the victim," Jed said, turning off the motor, leaning back in his seat, and closing his eyes.

Susan bit her lip, wondering what he was thinking about all this. If he was going to insist on calling the police. How she would convince him that was unnecessary . . .

"I don't suppose it will be possible to discover the identity of the murderer before the wedding," Jed mused, a stern expression on his face.

"Well, the police—"

Jed opened his eyes, turned, and looked directly at his wife. "I got the impression you weren't going to call Brett about this—otherwise you wouldn't have worked so hard to keep the body hidden."

"True." Susan realized what he was—or wasn't—saying. "Do you think I should try to solve this myself? That I don't need to notify the police?"

"I think—even though Brett is as tactful a person as you could want—I think it will destroy Chrissy's wedding if this becomes known right now," he said solemnly.

"That's what I thought!" Susan cried.

"Which is not to say that I think you're doing the right thing. Hiding the body is illegal—and you're putting that nice Tom Davidson in jeopardy, too. But you had no choice. To do anything else would ruin the most important day in Chrissy's life."

Susan could hardly believe her ears. "So you think I'm right.

And you'll help me investigate . . ." She saw images of Mr. and Mrs. North, and a smile began to play around her lips.

"Susan, I don't think we—or you—should investigate. I think we should move the body to someplace safer and hope no one finds it until after the wedding. Whoever the woman is, everyone will assume she's just missing, not dead . . . not murdered. Then, tomorrow night, we can take Brett aside, show him the body, tell him the entire story, and throw ourselves on his mercy. And if he doesn't throw us both in jail, I'll be very surprised."

"Then . . ."

"Of course, some of this is going to depend on who the dead woman is . . ."

"Do you want to see her?"

"Ah . . ."

"I think that's Tom's van—parked over near the handicapped ramp." Susan pointed. "She's in the back. But . . . Oh, no. That's the best man," she added as a good-looking young man walked out the back door of the church. "Do you think he's looking for us?"

Jed glanced at his watch. "I don't know. But we're almost fifteen minutes late."

"I need to talk to him—just for a moment—he delivered the dress to the Yacht Club, Jed. I have some questions to ask him—"

"You seem to have missed your chance to talk with him in private," Jed said, motioning to a young woman with flaming red hair who had just joined the best man. "I think we'd better get inside and see Reverend Price—and Chrissy."

"And Chrissy! Yes. And maybe I can find out where her gown is." Susan remembered the other problem that had been worrying her, and she leapt out of the car and trotted toward the church. Jed glanced at the best man, who now seemed to be throwing up in some bushes by the parking lot; the young woman, with a concerned look on her face, was standing by his side. Jed, deciding that the best man didn't seem to need his care, hurried after his wife.

The decorating seemed to be finished, and Erika and Tom Davidson were busy setting up lights at the back of the sanctuary. Chrissy, Stephen, and the rest of the wedding party (minus the best man) were standing around the chancel laughing at something Reverend Richard Price had just said. Susan stopped for a moment and admired her daughter. Chrissy, tall and thin, wearing a navy miniskirt, white silk shell, and high-heeled white sandals, her long blond hair pulled off her face with a scarlet silk scarf, looked excited and happy—the very picture of a young woman on the eve of her wedding. The minister waved and Susan hurried up the green carpeted aisle.

"Ah, here comes the mother of the bride now. Good evening, Susan."

"Hi, Dick." The Henshaws had been friends of their minister for years. "Sorry to be so late."

"You're not late." He glanced down at his watch. "In fact, you're a little early. We plan on at least a twenty-minute delay in the schedule the day before the wedding. Tomorrow is another story. You would not believe how late some people are for their own weddings. Not that we would expect that sort of behavior from Chrissy," he added, beaming at the young woman.

"Chrissy's never late," Stephen asserted, apparently believing he was standing up for his betrothed.

Susan wondered if he was marrying another Chrissy than her daughter. Her Chrissy had made lateness something of an art form. On her sixteenth birthday she had not only been the last person to arrive at a party given in her honor, but she had arrived at the wrong restaurant. And while being late to meet her parents for her graduation ceremony from college, she had discovered, and adopted, and then found good homes for three tiny calico kittens abandoned in a field near the campus. Susan glanced at her daughter to see how she felt about her future husband's assertion. Chrissy, however, was staring intently at something—or someone—at the back of the church.

Susan turned around and spied Erika high up on a tall ladder, attaching a light to the bottom of the balcony. She frowned as Erika swayed slightly, then was relieved to notice that Tom Davidson shared her concern and had dashed across the room to stabilize the ladder. Thank goodness; all they needed was for Erika to fall and break her neck the night before Chrissy's wedding.

"Mother, you didn't hear a word of what Stephen just said to you, did you?"

Susan, realizing how self-centered she had become, returned to the present. "I'm sorry, Stephen. It's just that I have so much on my mind these days. . . ."

"Stay in the present. Don't fret about the past. Don't worry about the future. The way to enlightenment is here. Now."

"I wonder if you've met my mother, Reverend Price," Stephen said dryly.

"Mom! I was wondering where you were. How was your flight?" Chrissy asked, walking down the steps to greet the large woman with flowing gray hair who had walked down the aisle to stand beside Susan.

Susan watched awkwardly as her daughter and Blues Canfield threw their arms around each other. She had noticed this woman at her own home earlier, but hadn't caught her name. So Stephen's mother wasn't dead. She was relieved, of course. But then who the hell was the dead woman? How could she find a murderer in less than twenty-four hours when she didn't even know who, exactly, had been murdered?

"My mother," Stephen was explaining to Dick Price, "is something of a free spirit. She's probably spent the last few hours alone in her hotel room meditating—"

"My son is trying to convince you I'm a flake, Reverend," Blues said, holding out her hand to greet the minister before she turned to her son. "I have not been meditating. I've actually spent the afternoon since we arrived in this beautiful town very productively. And, in fact, we've been at your future in-laws' home drinking champagne for the past hour or so. Lovely home. And lovely people."

Blues smiled so sincerely at Susan that she couldn't resist smiling back. "We enjoyed having you all," she said sincerely.

"You all? Mother, you didn't take the entire crowd over to the Henshaws?"

"We enjoyed it," Susan insisted. "Such interesting people . . ."

"Mother . . ."

"You heard what your future mother-in-law said, Stephen," his mother interrupted sweetly. "Isn't it time we got this show on the road, Reverend Price?"

The minister, recognizing his role as a man of peace, picked up the hint. "Excellent idea. Now, Chrissy, are you going to rehearse or is someone going to stand in for you?"

"I'm not superstitious," Chrissy claimed. "But . . ."

"It's tradition," Stephen stated flatly. "Brides don't rehearse for their weddings."

Chrissy looked up at her fiancé. The expression on her face was closer to that of Nancy Reagan when her husband was president than Susan liked to think about. "You're right, Stephen. I'll just sit in the first pew and watch."

"Fine. Now, I understand the person who is going to help me marry this young couple isn't here?"

"No, the Archangel has been held up," Stephen said.

"Well, that's no problem. I'll just go on and we'll get together when the other minister arrives. The first thing I do on these occasions is talk to all the ushers. We want to make sure people are seated evenly throughout the congregation, which is sometimes a more difficult task than it might appear to be. So, if you don't mind, ushers to the front of the room, everyone else to the rear. Bridesmaids should figure out what order they want to be in to proceed down the aisle. . . ."

"Oh, I have a list," Susan said, putting her hand in her purse.

"Are we going to have a flower girl or a ring . . . Oh, there we are." Reverend Price looked over his wire-rimmed glasses at Kathleen's children Alex and Alice Gordon, sitting in the second row of pews. "Alex and Alice. You were so quiet and good that I didn't even know you were here."

Three-year-old Alice smiled complacently, but her seven-year-old brother spoke up loudly. "My mother told me to take care of her."

"You've obviously done an excellent job."

"I told her if she didn't shut up, I'd put a snake in her bed tonight," Alex announced proudly.

Alice's mouth started to curve downward, and Susan saw it was time to act.

"You two come with me to the back of the room. Ms. Eden has a beautiful basket of petals for you to practice with, Alice. It's covered with such pretty ribbons," Susan announced, knowing that would appeal to the decidedly feminine child.

"No ribbons for me, right?" Alex asked for reassurance, as he followed them down the aisle.

"None like your sister is going to carry," Susan answered. Actually, the pillow on which the ring was to be carried was made from silk ribbons woven together. But she was hoping the young man wouldn't find them too threatening to his immature masculinity.

"You know, it would be interesting to drive the ring down here in a remote-control car," Alex remarked thoughtfully, smacking the end of each pew they passed.

"But you wouldn't want anyone to walk out into the aisle and step on it." Susan had raised a son of her own; she knew it was easier to distract a child than to try to win an argument with one.

"Yeah. It's amazing how not-careful some people are," he said, giving the pew they were passing a kick for good measure.

"Mom! What do you think? Aren't they interesting people?" Chrissy had run up behind them. "Don't you just love Stephen's parents?"

"They certainly are different from what I expected—from knowing Stephen, that is . . ." Susan stumbled around for the correct words. "But completely charming. So California . . ."

"And don't you just love the fact that Stephen spent his first ten years living in a commune?" Chrissy continued, apparently satisfied with Susan's answer.

"Who would have thought?" Susan answered sincerely.

"I think that's why he's such a sensitive person. You know, underneath it all."

"Probably so . . ." Susan decided it was time to change the subject. "Chrissy, where is your wedding gown? I haven't even seen it! I looked in your room and . . ."

"It's there—it's in my room! I took it over to show Stephen's mother and she promised she would bring it to the house and put it in my room when she came over for cocktails. She always does what she says she's going to. Ask Stephen."

"But, Chrissy, it's not in your room!" Susan insisted, coming to a standstill at the end of the aisle.

"Mom, of course it is. Mom promised she would take it there and I'm sure she did. . . ." She paused, a slight flush rising to her cheeks. "Mom . . . You don't mind that I call Mrs. Canfield 'Mom,' do you?"

What could she say? "Well, it's going to be a little confusing, but we'll get everything figured out eventually. I'm just glad you like his family so much," she ended, realizing it was the truth. Chrissy's ebullient nature would have been damaged if she had in-laws she couldn't relate to. But it was time to get back to her original question. "When did you show Blues your gown?"

"Right before I went out with Rhythm—we went to this art gallery a friend of his owns in Greenwich, and guess what?"

"What?"

"I think it's possible I'm going to be offered a job at a gallery in Philadelphia—on Rittenhouse Square, actually."

"How wonderful!" This was just what Chrissy had wanted to do, and Susan knew how difficult these jobs were to come by. "How did that happen?"

"Well, this gallery owner Rhythm and Blues know is the silent partner of this other gallery, and Rhythm showed him some of my work—and he thought I had a lot of promise as an artist. And he's always looking for artists who get along with other people to work in his gallery. He thinks it establishes the right tone. . . . Oh, Reverend Price is getting ready to begin."

"Okay, now the last person to be seated is the mother of the bride. Chad should be the one to seat her. . . . Susan! Mother of the bride. Where is our mother of the bride?"

"I'm right here, Dick!" Susan called back.

"Mom, if I'm going to walk you down the aisle, I'd better be able to find you tomorrow." Chad appeared next to her, a "you're going to embarrass me in front of my friends, aren't you?" expression on his face.

"You offer me your arm. . . ."

"I know how to do this." And he showed her that he did.

Susan, walking slowly, remembering her dream of that afternoon, smiled. Maybe the body had nothing to do with the wedding. Maybe it would stay hidden until tomorrow evening. Maybe nothing would go wrong. . . .

A bloodcurdling scream from the back of the church stopped her wishes.

THIRTEEN

"LEAVE IT TO THE FLOWER GIRL TO STEAL THE SHOW." DICK Price peered down at his small—and startled—congregation. "Are you all right, honey?" he called to the back of the church.

Alice peered up from her mother's arms with tear-filled eyes. "Did I ruin Chrissy's wedding?" she asked, sniffling. "I just got scared when something fell on my head. I didn't mean to ruin the wedding."

"Of course you didn't. This is only the rehearsal—and anyone else would have yelled just as loudly if that branch of fluffy flowers had fallen on them. You didn't ruin—or even hurt—anything." Chrissy had run back to the rear of the room to reassure the child. "You just woke everyone up—and we all needed it. Now, are you sure you're all right? The flowers didn't scratch you or anything?"

Alice climbed down from Kathleen's arms, smoothed out the front of her dress with chubby fingers, and straightened her shoulders. "I was scared. But now I'm all right. It was just that flower." She looked down at the white lilacs lying on the rug. "It hit me."

"And that was my fault," Erika insisted, leaning over the balcony to talk to the people on the floor. "I thought these were firmly attached, but . . . but this branch must have come loose somehow. I'll check out all the ties myself before I go home tonight. No one has to worry about this during the service tomorrow. It will not happen again."

"I'm glad it won't. We don't want anyone else beaned while walking down the aisle," Dick Price said. "Now, if we're all settled again, I think you'd better show your mother to her seat, Chad. Let's get this rehearsal going. I don't know about everyone else, but I'm getting hungry. Now, where is the best man?"

"He's not feeling well." The young redheaded woman who had

been outside appeared in the doorway. "He said you should go on without him. He'll be better soon—and he's been in lots of weddings. He'll know what to do tomorrow afternoon."

Susan, remembering what Jed had told her about the young man throwing up in the parking lot earlier, made a note to ask what was going to happen if they found themselves short one member of the wedding party tomorrow. She was just wondering if there was some sort of protocol here—if the best man didn't show up, did one of the ushers move up into his place? If that were so, what happened to the extra bridesmaid? Could she walk down the aisle unescorted? Could one usher escort a girl on each arm? She was just deciding that was the only answer when the best man appeared, dashing up the aisle with a slightly foolish expression on his face.

"Sorry to be late. I . . . I guess it was something I ate for lunch," he apologized to everyone.

"More likely something he drank at lunch," one of the bridesmaids muttered under her breath.

"Yeah, I thought he was cute, but who needs a date who's going to throw up on you?" another bridesmaid answered.

"I heard a story about him at another fraternity brother's wedding. . . ." Chrissy's college roommate giggled. But the young women suddenly realized that Susan could hear them and lowered their voices.

"I'm waiting." Chad was at her side, offering his arm. Remembering her dream, she glanced down at his feet. Birkenstocks—well, it was better than red Converse sneakers. And this was only the rehearsal, after all.

Susan took his arm and again started down the aisle at his side. "What's happening with the best man?"

"Dave? What do you mean? Dave's great!" Chad protested, moving a little too quickly.

"Chad, slow down! There's no reason to rush down the aisle! And what do you mean, Dave's great? How do you know him?"

"Hey, I've been hanging with the ushers for the past few days. Dave's great . . ."

"You said that already."

"Well, he's Stephen's best friend. They grew up together. Dave's been telling us stories about the good times they had when they were kids.'"

"In the commune?" Susan whispered.

"Yeah. Neat, isn't it? I've never known anyone who grew up in a commune before. You should hear the stories that guy tells . . ."

"But does he drink? Take drugs?"

"Nah! Why do you think that?"

"Just something one of the bridesmaids said—"

"It's the commune thing," Chad interrupted. "But this commune wasn't like that—it was based on spiritual principles. Hasn't Chrissy told you about all this?"

"Not a word. I hadn't even known about the commune until Stephen's extended family appeared at the house this afternoon." She frowned.

"Well, you know how busy Chrissy's been since she got engaged."

Susan smiled up at her son, thinking for the hundredth time that she would never stop being amazed by the fact that she was shorter than the child she once had to stoop down to when she wanted to hold his hand. And now he was taking care of her. How nice . . .

"Okay, now let's go through the beginning of the service. Jed, you're supposed to speak up when I ask who gives this woman to be wed, but don't worry about your guests hearing it. They know how the service goes as well as the next guy. Just don't trip as you head back to join Susan in her pew. Now . . ."

The rehearsal continued on its accustomed path with no more— or fewer—than the normal hitches. When Jed joined Susan he said that the Canfields' minister had called and was stuck between flights at O'Hare. There was a small panic when it turned out that not only did no one have the ring, but no one could remember who picked it up from the table at the restaurant where much of the wedding party had apparently eaten lunch. That particular crisis was solved when the best man discovered the ring in his shirt pocket. When he claimed not to know how it got there, Susan decided the bridesmaid had been correct and made a mental note to ask Jed to check the whereabouts of the ring in the morning.

She wasn't, in fact, all that interested in what was going on in front of her—and neither was Chrissy. Susan, remembering her own discomfort at her wedding rehearsal, had glanced to the back of the room to check out her daughter's reaction to watching her own wedding. And discovered that Chrissy wasn't watching at all. Her daughter had her gaze on something happening in the balcony. Susan glanced up there; Tom Davidson seemed to be helping Erika check out whatever was keeping the flowers up. She frowned, wondering why her daughter found this such an interesting sight. And then her attention was drawn back to the wedding party. Still standing before the minister, Stephen Canfield seemed to be as interested in his fiancée's lack of attention as she was in the goings-on above her head.

"What are you looking at?" Jed whispered.

"Nothing."

"Then why do you keep twisting your head around like that?"

"Shh . . ."

"What's wrong?"

"Jed, there's no reason for you to be looking back there. The Canfields are going to think we're a little strange."

"The Canfields seem to be a little strange themselves," he whispered back.

"Shh . . . How can you say that?" Susan whispered back.

"Well, not many adults are still known by nicknames . . ."

"What about Skip down at the club? And that man from your firm that we had dinner with in the city a few months ago? He was called Bones, wasn't he? And your boss's wife couldn't possibly actually have been named Panama at birth. And what about . . . ?"

"So let's all go eat!" Dick Price announced, raising his voice and staring straight at the Henshaws.

Susan put a grin on her face. "Yes, let's!" she agreed loudly. "Now, why don't we split up," she suggested to Jed. "You drive Mrs . . . Blues to the Inn and I'll go with Rhythm." Since she and Jed had discussed this idea just that morning, she wasn't terribly surprised when he agreed.

The Henshaws had thought it would not only be more hospitable to spend some time with each of the Canfields, but possibly a good way to get to know them individually. Susan suspected she had read this idea in one of the dozens of bridal magazines she'd studied in the past few months, but she had claimed it as her own.

"Fabulous thought!" Rhythm boomed heartily. "There's nothing I like better than spending time with another man's wife—especially one as good-looking as Susan."

Susan smiled, wondering what her mother was thinking about all this. She knew Rhythm was just kidding, but considering her mother's idea of what went on in communes . . .

She was still thinking about this when Rhythm put his hand on her knee as they drove out of the church parking lot.

"Susan, we like your daughter so much. It's a positive joy to welcome her to the family."

Susan was relieved when the tricky turn out of the parking lot made it necessary for him to put two hands on the steering wheel. "Well, of course, we're thrilled about Stephen," she reciprocated, hoping he didn't notice any lack of enthusiasm. It wasn't as though she didn't like Stephen, she reminded herself, it's just that he was . . . well, so stuffy. Listening to Stephen's father, she began to suspect she wasn't the only person to think so.

"Blues and I think Chrissy will be so good for Stephen. She's already brightened him up. He's sort of . . ." Susan was surprised when the usually loquacious Rhythm seemed at a loss for the correct word. "Old," he concluded. "Not like his parents, huh? Blues and I are always saying we're just a couple of kids."

Susan, who wasn't sure she found the idea of a couple of "kids" in their fifties all that appealing, just smiled and offered directions to the Inn.

But Rhythm wasn't so easily stopped in his enthusiasms. "And we love Chad and you guys, too, of course. And we'll all be getting to know one another a whole lot better—spending holidays and vacations together. Blues and I have been thinking about renting a place up on Cape Cod for the month of August. And we'll be expecting you and Jed for as much time as possible."

"We . . ." Susan wondered if it was possible to make a nonrefundable deposit on an expensive cruise at this late date. And she didn't want to mention the possibility that they'd be in Maine for fear this man would invite himself and his wife along for a long visit.

"Chad's already told us he'd love to come."

He had? "Well, then . . ."

"And we don't want to leave without doing some serious thinking about the holidays. The kids will begin developing their own traditions this year and we don't want us oldsters to be left out."

Chrissy wasn't going to be home for Christmas! The thought caused Susan more than a slight pang. "But maybe . . ."

"Chrissy tells me that you guys really get into this Christmas-in-Connecticut thing, but what Blues and I think is, maybe a change would do the entire family good. You could all come to California for the holidays—or maybe we could talk the kids into joining us on a trek down through Baja. I know Stephen has always wanted to try the snorkeling down there. What do you think?"

Susan took a deep breath and tried to finish a sentence. "I think we should leave that up to Chrissy and Stephen to worry about. We have this wedding to get through . . ."

"Yes, we do. I can see you're a woman who likes to stay focused on the present. You know what I say—one day at a time." He chuckled. "I let Alcoholics Anonymous use the slogan for a small fee."

"I . . ."

"Just kidding. Just kidding. Now, what are we going to do about the Archangel?"

"I . . . What? What are you talking about?"

"The Archangel—that's the name we gave our spiritual advisor at the commune."

"That's the minister who is stuck at the airport?" Susan asked, hoping she hadn't missed something here.

"Yup. Probably started a theological-slash-philosophical discussion with someone and forgot to get on the plane. The Archangel has always been like that."

Susan had a vision of a tall, emaciated man dressed entirely in black, sitting on a purple or orange polystyrene chair, a Bible held in his lap, chatting about Kant with a harried businessman. . . . She had to admit, her imagination boggled at the thought. "How do you know where—?"

"We got a message at the Inn. The Archangel had missed the plane and would be arriving at LaGuardia at nine-thirty tonight."

That was a relief, because Susan was beginning to realize this wedding was going to need all the help—spiritual or otherwise—it could get.

FOURTEEN

"CHARLES, YOU ARE A GENIUS!" SUSAN STARED AT THE room filled with more tables than she had even considered ordering. Glasses gleamed. Flowers perfumed the air. Candles flickered. Everything was beautiful. She was so relieved, she thought for a moment she might cry. "How did you accomplish so much so quickly? We had no idea this many people were going to show up for the dinner tonight . . ."

"I was prepared for Jed's call. Everyone at the Inn is well aware of the fact that your wedding party is . . . uh . . . slightly larger than you were expecting it to be."

"They're pretty hard to miss, aren't they?"

"Let's just say they're all very energetic—old and young alike," he added, as a male voice called out for more champagne from the bar.

Susan wondered if her daughter was joining a family of problem drinkers—not that they seemed to be having any problem drinking, she thought, remembering the old joke and starting to giggle.

"Susan?" Charles leaned toward her, a concerned look on his face.

"Sorry. I was just remembering a . . . a stupid joke."

He nodded. "No one realizes just how much strain the bride's mother is under."

"Well, you've made everything much easier. Did you manage to come up with anything to feed all these vegetarians?"

"Naturally. Wild mushroom bisque or asparagus torte for a first course. Then the mâche, pomegranate, walnut salad with champagne dressing like the rest of the guests. For the main course there's a choice of herbed risotto, gorgonzola gnocchi, or a French spring vegetable stew. And the same selection of desserts as the rest of the guests."

Susan remembered the honey Bavarian with fresh raspberries she had been looking forward to all week. "I'm sure everything will be wonderful." She looked up at Charles. He had a serious expression on his face. "There is something else, isn't there?"

"I don't want to worry you, but . . ."

"Go ahead. Better the problem I'm prepared for than something coming at me out of the blue. What's up?"

"We've been getting some slightly strange phone calls."

Susan gasped. "About the murder?"

Now it was Charles's turn to look confused. "The one at the Women's Club?" he asked, referring to a murder that had taken place at election time a few years ago.

"Ah . . . sort of," Susan answered awkwardly. She'd better watch what she said. "What are the calls about?" She asked the question she wished she had asked before.

"Well, most of them seem to be referring to a missing minister, but the others . . ."

"The Archangel," Susan said, realizing just how strange she sounded.

Charles seemed startled.

"The missing minister is known as the Archangel."

"Oh, that's a person's nickname. . . . That explains a lot. The girl at the reception desk thought maybe someone was putting a curse on Chrissy's wedding." He chuckled. "It's funny, when you think about it. The poor girl really panicked. Apparently someone called up and announced that the Archangel would be there for Chrissy's wedding rehearsal. You can see why she thought it was rather creepy."

"Especially since the Archangel is stuck between planes in Chicago," Susan explained, and then grinned. "That really does sound strange, doesn't it?"

Charles was looking over her shoulder. "It does. . . . You're going to have to excuse me. I think I'm needed in the kitchen."

"And I'm sure my guests are wondering where I am," Susan said. Whatever the kitchen crisis, she knew she could leave everything up to Charles. And Jed was trying to attract her attention, she realized—either that, or he had developed some sort of strange twitch in his left hand, which was waving strangely behind his back.

She hurried over to her husband's side with what she hoped was a bright smile on her face.

"Cat got your tongue?" Blues asked.

Susan just stared at Blues. "Excuse me?"

"You know, it's just an expression. You looked like you had something on your mind. A secret."

"Oh, not really . . ."

"Don't worry. Your secret is safe with me. I'm certainly not psychic. Now, when the Archangel is here, things will be different."

"How?"

"Oh, she's psychic. She can read minds."

"The Archangel . . . your minister . . . is a woman . . ."

"Yes. Don't tell me things are so conservative in this part of the world that you've never heard of a female minister."

"No, or course not. I just wasn't thinking of her that way . . ." Susan's voice drifted off.

"What way?"

"As a . . . a missing woman." Susan realized she was sounding more than a little idiotic. "Sorry, I was thinking about other things, I guess."

"Of course, you must have so much on your mind—or did you hire someone to do all this? One of those wedding consultants I've read so much about?"

"No, I thought it would be much more meaningful if I planned everything myself," Susan said, feeling slightly insulted that Blues had thought such a thing. On the other hand, maybe Blues thought that a woman who would take on a task like creating a wedding for four hundred and fifty people without professional help was insane. And perhaps, if she thought that, Blues was right.

Then Susan had another idea. "What does the Archangel look like? I mean, it's such an interesting name—and I want to recognize her when she appears," she added.

Blues thought for a moment before she answered. "Well, I have only seen her once in the past ten years, and she had dyed her hair orange then."

"That sounds interesting." But Susan had noticed movement toward the tables. "Why don't we find our seats and you can tell me more about her—I thought you all were very close."

"You mean our commune family?" Blues allowed Susan to guide her to a seat near the large bay window which looked out over the rear gardens of the Inn. The outdoor lights had been skillfully placed, and pockets of flowers glowed in the darkness.

"Yes. You call yourself a family. . . . Do you have regular reunions?"

"Oh, we don't get together regularly at all. In fact, this is the first time everyone in the commune has been together since it broke up."

"You don't live near each other?" The women were seated across the table from each other as the rest of the guests milled around looking at place cards and finding their seats.

"Heavens, no! We made a pact, see, when the commune dissolved. That's why we're all here."

"A pact?"

"Yes, we promised to rejoin for any and all life-changing events in the lives of our members."

"Like weddings," Susan said.

"And funerals, yes. But when it comes right down to it, people in the family don't seem to get married very often . . ."

"And we didn't agree to celebrate the divorces," the red-haired man sitting next to Blues added, a grin on his face.

Susan wracked her brain for his name—certainly a close relative to be seated at the head table . . . ?

"Well, a lot of us haven't even bothered to get divorced—you know how couples can just drift apart over the years," Blues said.

"And we shouldn't complain about not seeing each other, after all," Rhythm said, sitting down next to Susan. "We do seem to be living a nice long time—no funerals so far. I guess we all are lucky enough to have good healthy genes."

"Probably all those bean sprouts we ate back at the commune."

"Certainly the lack of chemicals in our diet . . ."

"Don't let's get started on that."

"You know the additives in our foods are killing us all!"

"The additives in our foods are keeping us all from severe cases of food poisoning . . ."

Susan glanced down the table at her parents. Her father seemed amused by the energetic conversation her question had engendered; her mother's expression was less enthusiastic. But waiters were circling the table with bottles of pinot blanc and merlot—perhaps that would help.

"Organic versus inorganic—it's an old argument," Rhythm said, leaning uncomfortably close to Susan's ear.

"One of the reasons the commune broke up . . . at least that's what we all thought at the time, wasn't it?" Blues said, interrupting herself to ascertain that the merlot was indeed from California before allowing it to be poured into her glass.

"Well, that's all ancient history, isn't it?" Rhythm said, nodding his acceptance of his wife's choice of wine. "But you were asking about our Archangel, weren't you?"

"It's just that it's such an unusual name . . ." Susan said. Actually, she had been wondering if the unknown woman's death was going to occasion the first funeral the group attended.

"Of course. And the Archangel is an unusual person. She was training to become a nun when she—as she puts it—saw the light and decided traditional religion was too sexist, too elitist, and too bound by traditions to be relevant in modern life. So she traveled and studied and experimented with differing views and beliefs until she came up with something she felt she could live with and preach. She was looking for a congregation when she came across our group. We were in need of a spiritual leader—at least some of us were—and she fit right in."

"You know, I've always wondered exactly how communes get started. Does a group of people get together and form one, agree on rules, find a place to live, accept new members . . ." Susan stopped talking. It suddenly seemed like an incredibly difficult task.

"It was pretty easy for us," he said.

"We had a place to live, which helped," Blues explained.

"You owned a farm?"

Both Canfields chuckled.

"Many communes aren't land-based," Rhythm explained.

"But they all need a place to live," his wife added.

"We lived in a hotel in the middle of San Francisco," her husband continued, accepting a large plate of wild mushroom risotto from the waiter.

Susan saw that meditation might be more appealing if it was accompanied by room service.

"It wasn't a hotel when we were living there," Blues continued, destroying the image Susan was busy creating. "We just used it as a place to live—like an apartment house. It was owned by Wind Song." She interrupted herself and pointed to the end of the table where a large, brassy woman with bright red hair was tucking into a pile of sautéed bay scallops. The woman wore a remarkable (and large) collection of silver and turquoise jewelry. Much of it was in need of a thorough polishing.

"Wind Song inherited the hotel from her grandparents. They had built it the year after the Great Quake. She and her husband contributed it to the commune. In fact, I always thought he talked her into the contribution."

"That's all water under the bridge, Blues," her husband insisted.

"Who is she married to?" Susan asked, hoping to prevent an argument.

"High Hopes is what we called him then. That's him, sitting on her right," Blues continued.

The man on Wind Song's right was as unlike his name as possible: middle-aged and portly. Thick horn-rimmed glasses kept sliding down a large ruddy nose, and the only indication of an allegiance to the counterculture was the Jerry Garcia tie around his neck.

"They had a wonderful wedding," Blues said nostalgically. "Nothing at all like this, of course. We got up at sunrise and fasted and meditated all day long, writing down wishes and messages for the couple's future. Then we had the service." She paused and a frown appeared on her face. "It was held outdoors, but we couldn't find a stream so instead of sending all our good wishes out into the water, we burned them in a campfire there. Air instead of water, you know, completely different symbols—I remember the Archangel commenting on it at the time. The practice of burning symbols for luck is quite common in China, she said." Then Blues smiled, the next memory being even more pleasant, apparently. "Then we all ate a huge meal and got completely drunk on cheap champagne. It was the best wedding I've ever been to—except for this one, of course," she added quickly, returning to the present.

"Yes, why are we sitting here talking about the past, when it's the present that should interest us now?" Rhythm spoke up. "I'd like to propose a toast," he said, standing up and lifting his wine glass. "To our new friends and new family—to Susan and Jed Henshaw!"

Jed, smiling, raised his glass to salute the Canfields. Susan, however, was busy wondering why Kathleen was standing in the doorway, waving to get her attention.

FIFTEEN

"LADIES' ROOM," KATHLEEN WHISPERED IN SUSAN'S EAR, AS she passed behind her chair.

"If you'll excuse me for a moment," Susan murmured, looking regretfully at the full plate a waiter had just placed before her. But she knew from the expression on Kathleen's face that something had happened. She hurried up the stairs to the second-floor ladies' room, wondering what was up—and why they were always rushing off to the ladies' room together.

"There isn't another dead woman in here, is there?" she joked—and then realized she and Kathleen weren't alone. One of the bridesmaids (Susan couldn't remember the girl's name) was standing at the mirror, swabbing her eyelashes with mascara. She looked more than a little startled by Susan's question.

"Oh, that's right, Chrissy said you sometimes got mixed up in murders—like that woman on TV—Miss Marple."

Susan, who enjoyed the mysteries on PBS as much as anyone (and much more than her husband), wondered what the world was coming to when the younger generation seemed to think Agatha Christie was a scriptwriter rather than a novelist. But she had no time to lecture now. "I have done some investigating," she explained modestly to the bridesmaid.

The young woman looked as though she didn't believe it but, her makeup apparently perfect, she piled her equipment back in her purse and fled from the room.

"I guess I have to be more careful about what I say."

"The younger generation isn't as tough as we are," Kathleen said. "Now, tell me who you think the dead woman is."

"I was wondering about—heavens, I don't know her name—about the minister everyone calls the Archangel. But she's supposed to be held up at O'Hare. Why? Did someone say something significant?"

"Actually, you just did. At the end of the table I'm at, there are two discussions going on. One, led by your mother, is whether or not you should have gotten your hair done today. . . . Don't say it! I know perfectly well what happened, but when I tried to explain, she insisted on telling everyone how you would never carry an umbrella when you were in grade school, either."

"I have an umbrella," Susan started to protest, and then got back to the point. "That's not why you called me in here, is it?"

"No, and I think you're right. I think the Archangel is the woman in the restroom at the Yacht Club."

"You mean, in the back of Tom Davidson's van."

"Oh, that's right."

"But why are you so sure it's her?"

"Because the story that she's in Chicago is just that—a story!"

"How do you know?"

"Well, apparently she's flying here from D.C."

"Washington, D.C.?"

"Yup. And I don't think they route flights from D.C. to New York City through Chicago."

"It doesn't seem likely. But maybe she had something to do in Chicago?"

"The man sitting next to me claims to be Stephen's closest relative—an uncle. Does he have any grandparents?"

"No. They all died either before he was born or when he was young. I gather, from what Chrissy says, they were both part of the San Francisco old money scene."

"Then they probably died of embarrassment from their children's antics."

Susan quickly lost interest in the murdered woman and focused on her future in-laws. "Why? What do you know about Blues and Rhythm?"

"You know the reason for the commune, don't you?"

"Not sex, drugs, and rock and roll?"

"Art and politics. Or, to be more specific, guerrilla theater . . . street theater."

Susan frowned.

"You know. People dressed up in army fatigues bleeding

catsup and Karo syrup on the steps in front of the offices of the draft board."

"Rhythm and Blues did things like that?"

"Oh boy, did they. This group is big on reminiscing. So far I've heard about the time they held a funeral service over the bodies of slaughtered baby piglets in front of the Marine recruitment center—or maybe it was the wedding of Satan and Uncle Sam they held there, and the funeral service was at City Hall." Kathleen pushed her gorgeous blond hair back over her shoulder and yawned. "Frankly, I've heard so many strange stories in the past ten minutes that I'm completely confused. It's an unusual thing for an ex-police officer to hear—being arrested was apparently the high point of these people's lives at that time."

"You mean they have police records, they're—what do you call them? Habitual offenders?"

"Yeah, but the charges were minor. Disorderly conduct. Unlawful assembly. Demonstrating without the necessary permit. Indecent exposure. Urinating in a public place—you don't want to know about that one," Kathleen insisted, seeing that Susan was about to ask. "Anyway, I think you could chalk most of this up to overenthusiastic youthful high jinks."

"What does it all have to do with the Archangel and where she is now?"

"She apparently didn't give this up when the commune split up—didn't settle down and buy a house in a suburb, or a town house on Nob Hill either. She's been politically active ever since; that's why she was in Washington. She was addressing some sort of congressional committee yesterday."

"Sounds like she's involved in more legit activities these days . . ."

"Definitely."

"So you think the Archangel is the murdered woman because she was in D.C. and someone claimed to have gotten a call from her from Chicago." Susan frowned. "Pretty flimsy evidence for an ex-cop."

"No. Because she's here—and someone wants us to think she isn't."

"I don't get it. We're not absolutely sure she's dead . . ."

"No, but she is here. Apparently some of the commune members had brunch with her right here at the Inn. At least, that's what one of the men—I can't remember his name, but he's the best man's father—told me."

"Really?" Susan realized she couldn't identify him either.

"I suppose he could be lying, but we could just ask some of the waitresses and find out about that quickly enough."

"True."

"And she was supposed to be driving over to your house with Rhythm and Blues."

"And she didn't show up?"

Kathleen nodded seriously. "And she didn't show up."

"Maybe she's been detained . . ."

"I considered that. So I asked some questions, like what does she look like . . ."

"I asked that, too—all I could find out was that her hair was green—or orange—or some other strange color at least once in the past ten years," Susan explained. "What did you find out? Does she look like the murdered woman?"

Kathleen grimaced. "Men! He couldn't even describe what the woman he ate a meal with just this morning had worn! Not even the color of her dress. And I thought Jerry was bad."

Susan nodded. She remembered the time she had asked Jed why he hadn't commented on her new dress, and he had answered that he had been afraid to say anything since he was never absolutely sure if he had seen it before. "I know what you mean. And she might have changed, of course. Did you ask about anything else, like hair color?"

"Actually, I did, because he mentioned the fact that the Archangel had been the first person he'd known to dye her hair purple. So it was easy to ask about her hair now."

"And what did he say?"

"Sort of light blond—or maybe brunette, was his accurate description!"

Susan thought about the woman in the box. "I suppose you could call her a dirty blonde."

"Maybe."

"No one seems particularly worried about the Archangel."

"Why should we be worried about her?"

Susan and Kathleen turned around and discovered they had been joined by Blues.

"We were just wondering why she didn't show up at the rehearsal . . ." Susan said.

"If something might have happened to her," Kathleen added.

"You know, we were hoping nothing had happened to her—not that there's any reason to think anything is wrong—"

"She probably just got lost," Kathleen said very quickly.

But Blues had a serious expression on her face. "I'm worried about her, too."

Susan and Kathleen exchanged looks. "Why?" Susan asked gently.

"She's the type of person everyone worries about. The Archangel just won't grow up!"

Well, it was one of the strangest statements Susan had ever heard.

"Here the rest of us have gone on with our lives, gotten married, gotten divorced, had children, built careers. All the normal things. And she's still planning demonstrations, organizing petitions, worrying about politicians—she still acts like she's living in the Sixties, for heaven's sakes!"

"But . . ."

"I know. I know. She's dedicated. Hardworking. Caring. An inspiration to us all. And she is—but she makes such a big deal of it. I mean, I take care of my inner self. I do yoga. I meditate. But I don't brag about it. The Archangel is always telling stories about how she meditates so much that she no longer needs to sleep. . . . Silliness, sheer silliness. Bragging about having insomnia—"

They were interrupted by the entrance of three of Chrissy's bridesmaids—all giggling.

"I couldn't believe . . . Talk about a rude pass."

"Did you hear what he said about—"

"Hi, Mrs. Henshaw! Hey, Mrs. Henshaw is here." It was said in the nature of a warning, and they all shut up immediately.

"Oh, your husband was wondering what had happened to you, Mrs. Henshaw."

Susan assumed the young woman's helpfulness was at least partially the result of a desire to talk without being overheard by an adult. "Thanks. I was just getting ready to go back to the table." Actually, she was getting hungry, she realized.

Blues hurried into an available stall. "Yes, we don't want to be late for the main course. The appetizer was so wonderful. And the salad was as good as what we get out in California. Such lovely fresh greens."

Not hungry, starving. Susan left the room and hurried back to her place at the table.

"Susan? I was wondering where you'd gone. Are you feeling well? Is there a problem . . . with the meal or anything?" Jed asked brightly.

Susan knew he was worried about the body. "Everything's fine. Kathleen and I got to talking in the ladies' room—about her kids. Alex and Alice are Kathleen Gordon's children—they're very excited about being members of the wedding party."

"Charming children," Rhythm boomed. "The little boy reminds me of Stephen when he was that age. He was a real spunky little kid—always up to some sort of devilment."

"Stephen?" Susan looked around for any sign of her appetizer or salad, but apparently both had been cleared away. She reached out for the basket of hot rolls in front of her. The Inn was known for its breads, going so far as to suggest to diners which dishes went with which grains and flavors, and its baskets were piled high with a generous selection. She flipped back the Irish linen napkin and found a small mixed-seed dinner roll lying next to half a square of cornbread with red peppers. She chose the cornbread and buttered it, as Rhythm told stories from Stephen's childhood.

". . . home schooling was the only answer after he was suspended for the third time, I'm afraid . . ." he was saying, as a fresh basket of rolls appeared.

"How interesting . . ." Then she realized what she had just heard. "Stephen was expelled from elementary school? Your son, Stephen? The one who is marrying my daughter tomorrow afternoon?" she asked, so surprised she forgot her hunger. "What did he do?"

"What didn't he do? He refused to salute the flag and then, when he was asked why, he told his second-grade teacher that the United States was soft on fascism. And that was the same year the gym teacher—a failed junior high football coach—decided that the kids must live up to physical standards. You know, the fifty-sit-ups, fifty-push-ups type of guy. Stephen threatened to stage a sit-in protesting the conformity of the educational system."

Susan glanced at Stephen. Twenty years seemed to have made

a huge difference in his life. From his rep tie to his cordovan loafers, Stephen was the image of a young man trying to conform to the most conservative of standards.

"But I think the system could have accepted all that. If it just hadn't been for those dead bodies," Rhythm said.

Across the table, Blues nodded at her husband. "You're right, dear. Public education is simply not ready for corpses."

SIXTEEN

"So I GATHER MY PARENTS HAVE BEEN BRAGGING ABOUT MY misspent youth. Did they tell you about the decapitated Barbie dolls that were part of my third grade civics project?" Stephen leaned over Susan's shoulder as the waiter placed an artistically arranged plate before her.

"They did," she answered, picking up her fork. "They seem very proud of you."

He smiled and managed to include both his mother and father in one affectionate glance. "They have always been proud of the strangest things. When I was younger it bothered me, but now I just accept the way they are." His attention was drawn back to the head of the table. "I think Chrissy's calling me."

"So go to her, young man. Go to her," his father urged.

Stephen gave the impression that he had no intention of doing anything else. He smiled at Susan and headed off.

"Have they discussed the evening's activities, I wonder?" his mother mused, watching her son and his fiancée chatting.

"You mean Chrissy and Stephen? What activities?" Susan asked, grimacing as she realized she might be being indiscreet.

"Stephen's bachelor party," his father answered. "The celebration of his last night of freedom."

"Yeah, man, the bachelor party," a male voice yelled from another table. Susan guessed it was the best man, who, she had noticed, had been getting louder and louder as the evening continued.

"There is not going to be a bachelor party," Stephen said, not even bothering to turn his head and address the speaker.

"Excellent decision," a loud female voice stated to the room at large. "There is nothing more male-chauvinistic than the traditional bachelor party. An archaic custom. Disgraceful. A crime before the goddesses."

"Thank goodness! She's here!"

"Archangel!"

"My dear, we're so glad . . ."

"Where have you been?"

"I can't tell you how . . ."

The Archangel had arrived.

Then who, Susan wondered, was the murdered woman? But her duty as a hostess was obvious. Not even taking a last reluctant glance at her cooling entrée, she hopped up from her seat and headed over to greet her guest.

She was one of many. Almost all the adults rushed to the Archangel as well.

The Archangel, for today at least, was blond. Her hair, in fact, was bright yellow. It was also long, thick, and apparently difficult to control. From where Susan stood, she could count three combs and a tie-dyed silk scrunchie, yet locks flew into the air and were tucked behind both ears. The Archangel was busy embracing her friends, so Susan decided not to interrupt. She stood back and watched, thinking that if the minister had come to the party straight from testifying before a congressional committee, she must have made some impression on that particular assembly. The Archangel was wearing a dress that seemed to have been fashioned from overlapping triangles of vividly colored silk. Beads were draped around her neck, hung from her ears, and wrapped around both wrists. Like her hair, her clothing seemed to be in constant motion, as she greeted one old acquaintance after another, with cries and hugs all around.

Finally Susan felt everyone had been given time enough and moved in to greet her guest. "You must be . . ." she began, and then changed tacks. She simply could not say, "You must be the Archangel" to someone she had just met. "I'm Susan Henshaw, Chrissy's mother. We heard you were stuck in . . ." She didn't know whether to say Washington or Chicago and decided to change tack again. "We're so glad you made it. Let me introduce you around and then find you a seat and a waiter so you can order your meal."

"Susan Henshaw, I have been thinking about you all afternoon. I'm psychic, you know and . . . and there are some things we should get together over. Changes are in the air. . . ." She looked at Susan and seemed to think twice about what she had been about to say. "And, of course, an empty nest can be a devastating thing for a domestic woman. . . . But you don't have to worry about the wedding. This is going to be the most beautiful wedding of two of the most beautiful young people in the world. Now tell me, where is your angelic daughter whom everyone has been talking about? And her lucky fiancé? I don't know if I'll recognize him after all these years."

"I think my hair was a bit longer the last time I saw you," Stephen said, coming up to stand beside his future mother-in-law.

"You're Little Spirit?"

Susan, thrilled at his commune name, got the impression that the Archangel was almost at a loss for words.

"Well, I'm not so little anymore, and these days most people call me Stephen." He had taken both her hands in his and was smiling sincerely, Susan noticed, and the Archangel didn't seem to take offense at this transformation of her old friend.

"Well, you've certainly grown up, Stephen," she admitted, grinning proudly at the young man as though she were somehow responsible for this fact. "I remember when you were just a little thing, always taking off your diaper and running around the halls completely naked. . . . Is this your lovely bride?"

Chrissy admitted the fact and allowed herself to be wrapped in a long embrace.

"If you can spare a moment or two in the next few hours, we should get together. The tales I can tell you about this young man you're going to marry . . ."

"I'll have a place for you set at our table," Chrissy said graciously. "Reverend Price is sitting there and you two should meet."

"Wonderful. The other religious . . . And dinner . . . I don't suppose . . ." She looked at Susan.

"There are three different vegetarian selections," Susan said. She didn't claim to be psychic, but she could guess what concerned the Archangel.

"Lovely. I want to speak to the good reverend to plead for an opportunity to spend some quiet time alone in the sanctuary where the service will be held tomorrow."

"Reverend Price can handle all that."

"And then we can get together about the question of that male-chauvinistic tradition known as the bachelor party, young man, and, of course, then I want to spend a few moments with the young angel you are going to marry tomorrow afternoon." The Archangel put one arm around Stephen's waist and the other around Chrissy's and led them off.

"The woman is absolutely amazing, she hasn't changed one bit," Rhythm said.

"Damn right. She's the same bossy bitch she always was."

Susan turned around quickly enough to discover the identity of the speaker: the best man, who, having said his piece, lurched off in the direction of the bar for, presumably, another drink that he certainly did not need. Susan, more worried about the wedding party than the food cooling on her plate, hurried after him.

"Susan? Is there a problem? Anything I can do?" Charles appeared at her side.

"I . . ." She looked around and then pulled him aside where they wouldn't be overheard by any of the guests. "There's this young man—he's supposed to be the best man tomorrow—and I think he's been drinking . . ." She realized that could be said about everyone else in the room and amended her statement. "Well, drinking more than is good for him. He just headed into the bar."

"Don't worry about a thing," Charles said, turning to leave. "I'll alert the bartender and he'll warn him off—and if that doesn't work, we can always water down anything he orders."

"Thanks."

Susan returned to her guests and was relieved to find the meal still in progress. She sat down, picked up her fork, and then realized someone was proposing a toast. She put her fork back beside her plate and picked up her full wineglass.

". . . and, of course, to the Henshaws, who tomorrow will give their lovely daughter to the first son of our commune family. To Susan and Jed, everyone." The Archangel had missed the original toasts and appeared to have decided to do something about it.

She knew Jed couldn't do anything but reciprocate, but then Blues decided to join in and stood up. And next, Susan, realizing the wine was going to her head faster than usual, stood and tried hard not to mispronounce any words in her short (well, maybe not so short, she realized, noticing the expression on Jed's face) tribute to the young couple.

And it took off from there. The next half hour looked like a scene from a toastmaster's club meeting attended by the Marx Brothers. Person after person popped up from their seats and raised their glasses high. Susan smiled, drank too much wine, watched her food get cold, and tried desperately to put names on faces. Beside Stephen's parents there were (she thought) six other couples who had been members of the commune and they all had unusual names.

The best man's parents were Wind Song and High Hopes. (They both had ponytails and rather horsey faces, and Susan decided she would remember their names, as they seemed more appropriate for racehorses than people.)

Then there was a couple who stood out from the crowd because it was difficult to imagine that either had ever been involved in liberal politics or an alternative life style. Dot and Brad Morris were suburban from their loafers up their chinos, around their Polo shirts and Brooks Brothers blazers, and culminating in almost identical short regulation hairstyles. She heard more than one person call Dot something like Peace, only to be firmly corrected, as Dot insisted that she had given up that name.

In complete contrast to Dot and Brad was the couple sitting with them. Freedom and Hubris were middle-aged gay men who had introduced themselves to Susan as the owners of a summer theater up on Cape Cod. They were apparently still involved in political causes as well. The business card Freedom had passed to Susan bore a sketch of a barnlike structure (presumably the theater) and the slogan THEATER THAT WIDENS THE MIND. Hubris and Chrissy were involved in a conversation about set design throughout much of the dinner while Freedom caught the group up on the activities of the couple since the commune had broken up.

The next pair, sitting on the other side of the room, were the parents of the only bridesmaid from the groom's family. The young woman's name was Wendy, and as the person who had ordered her dress, Susan was intimately familiar with Wendy's measurements and coloring. (The bridesmaids were wearing various shades of spring colors, and Wendy's gown of mignonette silk had been selected to contrast with her coppery hair and pale skin. She was, Susan knew before she met her, thin as that prover-bial rail.) Susan would have had no trouble picking out her par-ents in this crowd. Their daughter's coloring had been come by legitimately: Though her father's hair was almost nonexistent and her mother's almost certainly augmented by Clairol, the three of them had fallen from the same tree—probably a Japanese red maple, Susan decided. She remembered Wendy's parents' names from their earlier meeting: Her father was known as Red Man and her mother as Havana Rose.

Wendy herself spent most of the meal flirting with best man David. But that young man was either too drunk or too hungry to notice. He had returned from the bar with a surprisingly sanguine expression on his face and proceeded to wolf down his dinner, accompanied only by the Pellegrino water an obliging waiter poured into his wineglass.

There were four more people from the commune, but Susan couldn't decide whether they were combined into couples or if they were independent.

Rivermist and Moonbeam were women. The men were called the Magician and, strangely enough in this gathering, Ben.

"Ben was always the most sensible of us all," Blues whispered across the table, when Susan's raised eyebrows convinced her an explanation was necessary. "We tried out lots of names. I remem-ber Flame and Moonglow . . . Oh, there were lots. But he called himself Ben the day he appeared at our door and nothing else seemed to stick."

Susan stopped trying to make up her mind about the relation-ships between Rivermist, Moonbeam, the Magician, and Ben (Ben had embraced Moonbeam warmly but was now sitting with a proprietary arm around Rivermist's shoulders), and asked Blues a question.

"How did you get your names? Did you choose them your-selves or were they given to each person?"

Blues shrugged. "I suppose a little of each—and some other things. We all felt that we were starting over, giving up our old identities and creating new selves, new families. And taking new names seemed to go with that—like Chrissy giving up Henshaw and becoming a Canfield, I suppose."

Susan felt a small twinge. "But you didn't all have the same last name," was her only remark.

"No. We did think about it. Because we wanted to be one big family. But there were too many smaller units within the commune family."

"You mean, like you and Rhythm being married."

Blues nodded. "Exactly. And there were other married couples, too."

"When you think about it, we were a pretty conservative group for a bunch of people experimenting with alternative lifestyles," Rhythm added. "Getting married wasn't all that politically correct back in those days."

"Back in those days no one knew the term 'politically correct,'" someone (Susan thought it was the woman known as Rivermist) called out.

"Back in those days we defined what was politically correct," High Hopes insisted loudly.

"Back in those days we wouldn't have listened to a word we were saying," Rhythm insisted. "In those days what we said was, never trust anyone over thirty—and look which side of that marker we all seem to have landed on."

"To those of us who lived to be over thirty!" Blues toasted, holding up her glass.

"To those of us who lived to be over forty!" Freedom called out to the cheers of the group.

"To those of us who have made it over fifty!" came the next toast from across the room.

There was much laughter and giggling.

"And to those of us who didn't."

Susan looked at the speaker. The Archangel had made the final toast, and there was a solemn expression on her face.

SEVENTEEN

THE HENSHAWS AND THE CANFIELDS WERE STANDING IN THE doorway of the Hancock Inn's restaurant, saying good-bye to their guests.

"Lovely, lovely party. Can't tell you how we're looking forward to the wedding tomorrow." Dot and Brad Morris were among the last guests to leave the rehearsal dinner.

The young people had left early. Susan had overheard continued rumblings about a bachelor party, but Chrissy and Stephen had been firmly led off by the Archangel, so apparently any party would be taking place without the groom in attendance.

"You look like you could use a good night's sleep," Dot said.

"Probably just jet lag . . ."

"Lots of last-minute details . . ."

Susan and Blues simultaneously offered excuses for their respective appearances.

"This wedding stuff seems to be harder on the parents than I, at least, would have suspected," Jed said diplomatically.

"True. And I think our wives are coming through with flying colors," Rhythm insisted. "Besides, no one is going to be looking at either of these lovely women tomorrow afternoon. Chrissy will be the center of attention—as a lovely young lady like her should be. Now, who would like to come up to our room for a nightcap? We brought a very special bottle of brandy from a small winery in Sonoma."

Susan, wondering how to refuse without sounding impolite or standoffish, was relieved when Jed found the perfect excuse.

"You know, Rhythm, we'd love that, but I forgot to ask Chad to check on the kids' new puppies, and I'm afraid now he's taken off with his girlfriend. So Susan and I should head over and get them adjusted to the house before Chrissy comes home . . ."

"That's a very good idea!" Blues agreed so eagerly that Susan wondered if she hadn't been terribly happy with her husband's offer. "You're not planning on keeping them in Chrissy's room overnight, are you?"

"Well, we thought . . ." Susan began.

"Don't be tactful. It was stupid of us to think the puppies should spend tonight with Chrissy," Blues insisted. "She should get as much sleep as possible tonight—and you know how puppies like going outside."

"Definitely." Susan nodded vigorously, not knowing exactly who was going to be taking the puppies outside tonight, but hoping it would be either her husband or her son.

"Well, it's been a fine day, but we'd better get going," Jed suggested, tugging on his wife's elbow.

"We won't keep you any longer. Wonderful evening. Going to be a wonderful wedding tomorrow, I'm sure of it."

Susan left the Inn wondering if Rhythm was capable of speaking in a normal, moderate tone of voice. She'd seen no evidence of it all day. "Do you think the puppies will need walking? After all, they've been outside all afternoon," she asked, as Jed opened the door of his Mercedes for her.

"Susan, the damn puppies are the last thing on my mind," Jed answered, starting the ignition. "Have you figured out who the dead woman is?"

"Not at all. Every time I think I've identified her, it turns out that the woman I think is dead is alive . . ." She stopped.

"Don't worry. I know exactly what you mean. Did you think she was the Archangel?"

"Yes, did you?"

"Yup. You could have knocked me over with a feather when that woman walked in the door and everyone started greeting her."

"I must admit I was thrilled when I realized Stephen's mother was alive and well," Susan admitted, thinking back to her earlier assumption. Then another thought struck her. "Jed! I still have no idea where Chrissy's gown is!"

"Didn't you ask her?"

"I started to, but then I stopped . . . I didn't want to say anything about the box the dress was shipped here in . . ."

"Susan? What's wrong?"

"I . . . I just realized something. I've been assuming the dress was shipped in that box, but it could have been something else, couldn't it?"

"Something else that was shipped to our daughter a day before her wedding. Shipped from Milan." Jed was silent for a moment. "Well, I guess anything is possible . . ."

"Maybe the girl who made the dress sent something else. You know, as a wedding present. She's a seamstress. She might just have dress boxes around that she uses to ship other things. . . . It is possible, isn't it?"

"But not likely. Did you ask Chrissy when her dress arrived? I didn't see anything that looked like a dress box in the hallway— although it might have been hidden by last-minute gifts. An elephant could have been hidden under the pile that was delivered this afternoon."

"Jed! Don't you think you're exaggerating?"

"Not one bit." He yawned. "You don't really think we're going to have to walk those puppies, do you? As you said, they've been outside all day long."

"Jed, do you think Stephen's family is a little strange?"

"Which family are you talking about? Rhythm and Blues or the entire commune clan?"

"Well, Rhythm and Blues are the ones I was thinking about. I mean, giving them two dogs . . ."

"A pair of potential prize-winning champion bull mastiffs," Jed corrected her.

"Bull what? Jed, those are the great big, ugly, mean dogs . . ."

"They may not be to our taste, but they're not a breed known for their meanness. . . . At least, I don't think they are," Jed said, a little more slowly.

"You mean, you hope not."

"Definitely." He turned the car on to their street. "Did we leave every light in the house on?"

Susan peered through the windshield. "I can't imagine why. It wasn't even dark when we left. The sidewalk lights are on timers, but I don't understand the rest . . ."

Every window in the house was lit up. Light streamed out the windows of the double garage doors as well. A Volkswagen van was parked at the curb—a very familiar-looking van.

"Jed, that's Tom Davidson's car!"

"The one with the body in the back."

"The one with the back door open ..." Susan said, as Jed, apparently reading her mind, stopped his car on the street behind the van. The Henshaws jumped out of either side of the auto and met at the back of the van so they discovered simultaneously that it was empty. Well, not quite empty, Susan amended. There were at least half a dozen crumpled bags of garbage from various fast food restaurants that had been tossed on the floor sometime in the past.

"What do you think?" Jed asked.

"I suggested he put the body—"

"Susan, you told him—"

"Of course not! He didn't know it was a body! What I meant was that I asked him to put the box—I called it a box—in the garage."

"Why?"

"Well, he thinks it's a wedding present. What excuse can you think of to ask someone to carry a wedding present around in his car the day before the wedding? Jed?" She said his name when he didn't seem to be responding.

"Do you hear someone yelling?" her husband answered slowly.

"Yelling what? Oh, no, you don't think he opened the box, do you?" Without waiting for an answer, Susan started to run up the driveway toward the garage.

"Susan, I think the yelling is coming from the backyard ..." Jed began.

"It's coming from my backyard, to be more precise," Dan Hallard, popular ObGyn, and the Henshaws' next-door neighbor, called out from the front porch of his large home. "The young man making the noise said something about Chrissy's wedding presents, leapt over my hedge, fell onto the barbecue, broke at least two pieces of the expensive outdoor furniture my wife just bought, and ran off. Over his shoulder he called out what he apparently thought was an explanation for his strange behavior. He said there was a problem with one of Chrissy's wedding presents."

"Which direction was he going?"

"Toward the Ledbetters'."

"Let me know the amount and we'll pay for all the damage," Jed said, following Susan in running toward the Hallards' backyard.

"Don't worry about it. The damn stuff was ugly and uncomfortable. I'll just tell my wife it wasn't sturdy enough to be left outside and move the old redwood furniture back out on the patio. I was storing it in the garage, just waiting for an excuse. See you at the wedding tomorrow! . . . Unless, of course, you're in the hospital with a broken leg," he added, as a loud crash indicated that Jed had followed Tom Davidson's lead in demolishing the Hallards' outdoor furniture.

"Jed! Jed!" Susan took the long way through the hedge (via a gate) and sprinted after her husband, calling out his name.

They disappeared into the night, following the sounds of someone crashing through the darkness. Fifteen minutes later, panting, filthy, and more than a little annoyed, they had circled the large block and found Tom. He was sitting, head in hands, on their front doorstep.

The Henshaws were both out of breath, so the younger man spoke first. "I'm afraid I've failed Chrissy—and you two, of course." He spoke sadly. "I was waiting for someone to come home when I heard barking out back. I thought it was Clue and went to say hello. She was lying in one corner of the pen and so I thought I'd go in and see her—it was dark back there, you see, and I had no idea she wasn't alone. And then, when I opened the gate this horde of animals dashed by me. I saw the bows around their necks and realized they must be the dogs that Chrissy and . . . and her fiancé were talking about at the rehearsal, and—"

"The puppies! You're worried about the puppies?" Susan realized that she was so relieved, she actually felt slightly faint—or could that be the result of too little food, too much wine, and an impromptu midnight run?

Tom looked even more depressed, but he answered the question. "And Clue . . . I'm worried about Clue. She dashed right out of the gate after them."

Susan spun around. "Clue's missing?" she cried. "Jed, we should call the police right away. She's wearing her collar. Someone will find her, don't you think?" Her heart was pounding. Clue, the dog who shed on her furniture, stole food from the table, and insisted on slowly sniffing her way around the block in the worst weather imaginable, was missing. Alone somewhere. Maybe frightened . . . hit by a car . . . lying by the side of the road . . . Susan was so upset she didn't even notice at first when a bright red Mustang convertible pulled into the driveway.

"Hey, Mom! Look who I found over on Dogwood Lane!" Chad climbed from the car, followed by a very tired golden retriever.

"Clue! Clue. Come here!" Susan knelt down in the manner approved by her teachers in obedience classes. Clue, sighing loudly, wandered slowly into her arms and allowed herself to be petted.

"Gee, Mom, you've got to be more careful. She could have been hit by a car."

"It isn't your mother's fault the dog got out. She escaped from her run while I had the gate open," Tom said, getting up to greet the dog.

"I don't suppose you have any idea where the other two puppies are?" Jed asked his son.

"Other two puppies? You mean the mastiffs escaped as well?" Chad said.

"Did you say mastiffs? Are you sure about that?" Susan asked. She had been hoping it was just a rumor.

"Yeah. Neat gift, huh? You know they're going to grow up to be over a hundred pounds—they'll make Clue look like a wimp!"

"Over a hundred pounds each?" Susan asked. "Chrissy and Stephen are going to keep two hundred pounds of energetic dogs in an apartment in the middle of Philadelphia?"

"Maybe it's better for the kids if they just stay lost," Jed muttered, starting to walk away.

"Jed! Where are you going?"

"To put the car away. It's going to be a long day tomorrow and I'd like to get at least a little sleep."

"Jed! You're not going to bed!"

"Yes, Susan, I'm going to do exactly that. And I suggest you do the same."

"But the puppies . . . And the . . . the lady . . . the wedding present in the garage . . ."

"Oh, are you talking about that box we put in the back of my van, Mrs. Henshaw? Because you don't have to worry about that anymore. That's what I was coming over here to tell you . . ." Tom began.

"What? What were you going to tell my wife?" Jed stopped dead in his tracks.

"Didn't you put it in the garage?" Susan asked.

"Nope. I didn't have to. The groom—what's his name, Stephen?—he took it from me at the Inn. I figured since he was marrying Chrissy, he would know what to do with it."

EIGHTEEN

That's when Susan's purse (strangely silent for the past few hours) began to ring.

"What the . . ." Jed, tired and unaccustomed to his wife's demanding cell phone, was startled.

Susan, busy trying to figure out what Stephen's possession of the body meant, didn't respond immediately. Besides, her purse seemed to have stretched; she couldn't find the bottom.

"Mom! You're supposed to answer your phone!"

Susan, irritated and tired, emptied the entire contents of her bag onto the top step, much to the delight of Clue, who wolfed down a Mars bar, wrapper and all, before anyone realized what was happening. Susan finally found and flipped open her phone. "Hello? Hello?" She smacked the phone against her thigh. "What's wrong with this thing?" she asked no one in particular.

Jed glanced at the numbers flashing in the dark. "Looks to me like it needs charging. Have you been plugging it in at night?"

"Not enough, obviously. Do you think it's Stephen . . . calling about the bo—" she glanced at Tom Davidson "—calling about the wedding present?"

"Possibly. Maybe we should head inside and see if there are any messages on the answering machine."

"Good thought!" Susan flipped her phone shut and grabbed Clue's collar. "Maybe we better give Clue some cookies—" Before she had finished the sentence, the dog had pulled free and bounded through the door Jed had opened into the house. "I guess she's hungry."

"Do you want me to keep looking for the puppies, Mrs. Henshaw?" Tom asked. "I don't mind. I feel sort of responsible for letting them out of the dog run the way I did."

"We'd appreciate it, but why don't you come inside and have a cup of coffee first?" Jed offered. "And we should call the police station. Those puppies are pretty hard to ignore. It's just possible someone found them and called the police already."

"Sure." Tom and Jed entered the house right behind Susan and Clue. Chad remained outside to say good-bye to his driver.

"If you'll feed Clue, I'll check the answering machine," Susan said, heading back to Jed's study without waiting for a response. She wanted to be alone to listen to any messages. The last thing they needed now was for Tom to overhear anything about the body he had delivered into Stephen's hands.

As she had expected, the light on the machine was flashing. Shoving aside the boxes covering the couch, Susan sat down, fumbling in her purse for a pen and something to write on. By the time she'd unearthed a crumpled envelope and her favorite Waterman, the first two messages had played.

"Susan . . . Jed . . . it's Naomi. My sister-in-law appeared in town this morning. She's been dumped by that bastard she took up with after her divorce and she's been crying ever since she walked in the door—except when she's eating. Susan, I know this is an imposition, but could we possibly bring her along to the reception tomorrow? I suppose the wedding will depress her, but I know you're going to have wonderful food. Well, just let me know if it's impossible. Otherwise, have a good night's sleep, and we'll all see you tomorrow."

"Jed. Susan. It's Melissa Ericksen. My stupid husband broke his ankle falling in a gopher hole on the golf course and has to have some sort of surgery—a pin inserted through the bones, the orthopedist says. So he won't be at the reception tomorrow. I thought you might like to know. When our son got married, so many people called asking to bring last-minute guests . . . Well, I just wanted you to know you have one empty seat available."

Not really, Susan thought, writing furiously.

"Susan, this is Erika. I've been thinking, and if you have a few minutes, there's something I should tell you. I'll be going right home after Tom finishes up. You can call me there tonight. Or tomorrow morning, I guess." She announced her phone number before hanging up.

Susan didn't have time to puzzle over that one. The next call was from the rental company that was providing the cars for the wedding party. The time they were confirming to pick up Chrissy and her bridesmaids was wrong—as was the number of cars. Susan starred that note. Transportation was Jed's department.

Then two other calls from guests. Another plan change and a friend of Chrissy's from NYC who had lost her invitation and needed times, locations, and, please, directions.

Then a call from Chrissy. "Mom. Dad. I'm going to be a little late. Don't worry. But be sure I'm up at eight A.M. tomorrow. Even if I plead to stay in bed, don't let me sleep. I need to be up at eight tomorrow."

And then. "Mrs. Henshaw? Susan? Uh . . . Mom . . . I think I need to talk—"

The tape was filled.

"Susan? Hon? Do you want a cup of decaf?"

"Jed! Listen to this!" After some fancy button pressing, she found the spot she was looking for and replayed the final message.

"Well, what do you make of it?" she asked, when her husband didn't respond immediately.

"Is the machine broken?" he asked, leaning over his wife to look more closely.

"No. It's filled. But what do you think?" she repeated.

"Of what? I can't even tell who the message is from," Jed insisted.

"It has to be from Stephen. You heard how he didn't know whether to call me Mrs. Henshaw or Susan or Mom."

"Well, I guess there isn't anyone else who might consider those three particular options," Jed agreed. "But aside from knowing who called, I don't think there's anything to discuss—actually, there isn't anything there at all."

"Do you think he's found out that the wedding present is a dead body?" Susan asked.

"I haven't the foggiest . . ." Jed sat down on the couch and put his hands over his eyes. "But I've been thinking—ever since Tom explained that Stephen has the box—we have to tell Brett about all this—"

"Jed! You promised! You agreed! You—"

"That was before the kids got involved," her husband answered. "Susan, we sure don't want Stephen getting in trouble with the police the night before he's supposed to be marrying our daughter."

"Supposed to be marrying your daughter! And what sort of trouble? Daddy, what are you talking about?"

Their daughter had returned to spend her last night in her parents' house as an unmarried woman.

Susan was the first to recover. "We were just talking about . . . about your wedding gown. It seems to have disappeared."

Chrissy appeared to forget all about her fiancé and any possible problems with the police or otherwise. She screamed and seemed to levitate about two feet into the air. "Disappeared! What do you mean? What happened to it? Where is it?"

"That's exactly what I want to know," Susan said, loudly enough to stop her daughter's frantically rising voice. "I . . . I feel like I've been following it all over town today. Claire said it was here. But first I thought . . . thought it had been delivered to the Yacht Club . . . and then—" Fortunately, her daughter interrupted, because Susan had absolutely no idea how to go on.

"Of course, it was here. I tried it on for Grandmother. Didn't she tell you?"

"She did, and she said it was the most beautiful wedding dress she's ever seen." At this point, Jed discreetly left to get his cup of decaf.

Chrissy seemed to relax slightly. "It is! It's the most beautiful dress in the world. I have to admit, I was worried when Sophie decided on a new design and new material at the last minute. But, Mother, it really is the most gorgeous thing. And it fits perfectly! That's why I took it over to the Inn to show Blues . . ." Suddenly Chrissy's confidence seemed to dissolve. "I guess I should have shown it to you first . . . I . . ."

"Well, no time like the present," Susan said, standing up. "I can't tell you how I've been waiting for this moment . . ." She glanced at her daughter and stopped moving. "What's wrong? Chrissy, what is it? You did bring the dress home with you, didn't you?"

"I . . . um . . . The dress is back at the Inn. Blues brought it back here when she came for cocktails earlier. But then, tonight, the Archangel wanted to . . . asked if she could . . . she's going to sew a . . . a sort of talisman into it."

"A what?"

"A talisman . . . Or a charm. Something for good luck. She didn't explain, she just said it was important to her—and that it is so small it wouldn't be possible to see it. . . . You know, walking down the aisle or dancing at the reception. So I came home and picked it up and brought it back to her at the Inn." Chrissy stopped speaking, twirling her hair around one finger with a gesture Susan hadn't seen her daughter use in years.

"It's lovely of her to want to do that for you," Susan said, a bit tentatively. Actually, she thought the woman had a lot of nerve—especially since Susan had been planning to offer her daughter a sort of good-luck charm of her own. But Chrissy had slumped down on the sofa with a frown on her face.

"Chrissy? Is something wrong?" It was a silly question: obviously something was bothering her daughter. But was it just prewedding jitters or something more serious? Something like a dead body?

"It's Rhythm and Blues," Chrissy answered quietly. "They keep telling me how they're so thrilled they're going to have a daughter. How they've always wanted one. How if they could have chosen a person to be their daughter they would have chosen one just like me. And I'm really crazy about them. You know that I am."

"I do," Susan said, wondering if she should admit to being jealous.

"But they don't seem to realize I'm a grown-up!" Chrissy exploded. "They not only want a daughter. They want a child. They want to control my life."

"Like giving you those dogs," Susan said, nodding seriously.

"The dogs! Oh, no, that's the best wedding present anyone could possibly have given us. Stephen and I are even thinking of breeding bull mastiffs."

Susan, who had never known her lovely, talented daughter to voluntarily pick up after Clue, wondered what the girl was thinking—and then remembered that Chrissy would be a married woman living on her own. "Then what do you mean?"

"Well, like finding me the job in an art gallery. I mean, I was thrilled—I *am* thrilled. And grateful, too, but now I don't know if I could have found one on my own."

Susan, who had known for years exactly how much Chrissy's independence meant to her, had to resist smiling. "Have you told Stephen how you feel?"

"Of course, but it's different for him. He just says to ignore them and go on and do what I want to do with my life. I know he's right about that, but . . . but it's different for him," she repeated.

"He's their son. He knows they will love him, no matter what he does," Susan said quietly.

"Exactly. You know exactly what I mean!"

"You don't have to be so surprised. I got married once, too."

"But Grandmother hasn't ever tried to take over your life. She's such a cool lady!"

Susan wondered if Claire had told Chrissy about her wedding gift before she continued. "You know, these things will work out. The first year of your marriage will involve lots of different decisions. Like where you will spend Christmas," she couldn't resist adding. "And sometimes your in-laws will approve and sometimes they won't."

"They're saying they're going to take us all to Baja for Christmas vacation," Chrissy confided. "But I talked to Stephen and he said, no way. That we have our own lives, and he'll have school and I'll have a job by then and we won't be able to be gallivanting all over the country on long vacations. So, I think we'll just have a few days off. And we'll come here, of course."

For the first time all day, Susan felt like jumping up in the air and shouting hooray. But her joy was short-lived.

"Unless we can afford to go up to Vermont and ski," Chrissy concluded.

"So when are you going to get your dress back?" Susan, having returned to earth, asked.

"She's going to come over first thing tomorrow morning. I invited them to brunch. You don't mind, do you? I know you're having people in—both grandmothers and all. . . ."

"There's going to be plenty of food for everyone. What time are they going to be here?"

"Nine. I could call if that's too early, though."

"No, I told everyone to be here between eight-thirty and nine-thirty, but I'm sure my mother will be early. She can keep them entertained. They can tell her about their life in the commune. She's been asking me questions about that ever since she heard about Stephen's childhood."

"Good. Rhythm loves telling stories about their protests and arrests. What was Daddy talking about when I came in? He said something about Stephen and the police."

Why had she spent the last few minutes trying to give her daughter good advice instead of dreaming up an answer to this question? Susan asked herself, thinking furiously. And why didn't the phone ring? Or someone arrive at the front door? How come there was never a good distraction around when you needed one?

NINETEEN

Just when Susan thought she had no alternative but to tell her daughter the truth, all hell broke loose.

First, (naturally) the phone rang. Susan picked up the receiver attached to the answering machine. "Hello?"

Then the phone in her purse rang. "Don't bother with that. Its battery is too weak to get anything. . . . No, I wasn't talking to you," she said to the still unidentified person on the other end of the receiver.

Then the doorbell rang.

Before anyone could possibly have answered it, two absolutely filthy puppies ran into the room. Tom Davidson followed them.

Jed, the front of his new Armani shirt betraying an incident involving either a coffee cup or a coffeepot, entered then, and announced the presence of the Hancock police department in the Henshaws' backyard.

And then Dan Hallard appeared. How quaint, Susan thought, to have a doctor who sleeps in old-fashioned nightshirts. That's when she realized her caller had hung up and that the strobe lights flashing in her windows did not mean that a rock concert was taking place in the front yard.

Her entire family seemed to be frozen in position. Then . . .

"What the hell is that dog doing?" Jed yelled.

"No! No! Give that back to me!" Chrissy cried, running over to the corner and yanking the leg of an antique English draw-top table from the animal's mouth.

"Susan, I think we have everything under control." Brett Fortesque stood in the doorway.

"Then you're the only person who does," she replied, replacing the receiver and standing up. "What is happening? Why are all those police cars out front?"

"Actually, that's the Hancock fire department," he explained.

"Wha—?" Jed began, heading out of the room.

"Your alarm went off. Apparently someone, or something, broke one of your connections and the silent alarm contacted the firehouse and police department."

Jed turned and looked at his wife.

Susan and her husband didn't agree about this particular aspect of their life. Jed thought he was protecting his family when he had a state-of-the-art burglar and fire alarm installed. Susan thought the constant false alarms and the time spent resetting the system was a complete waste, and the noise more than a little annoying. "I know what you're thinking, Jed. But I only turned off the siren for the weekend—I just thought that with so many people around, the alarm might be triggered and . . . and I didn't want to annoy the neighbors," she finished, glancing out the window toward the mayhem taking place on the street.

"You turned off your alarm?" Brett asked. "Susan, don't you know that burglars have been known to break into houses during weddings and steal the gifts?"

"I know one or two gifts I'd be happy to leave out on the front lawn for them," Jed muttered, glaring at the two puppies Chrissy was holding. One seemed to be on the verge of falling asleep; the other was busy drooling.

"I guess I'd better take these sweet little guys back to the kitchen," Chrissy said.

"Chrissy . . ."

"I'm going to put them in their crates, Mother. Rhythm and Blues also gave us crates for them, you know."

Susan just smiled. So that explained what the box of bolts had been intended for. "I suppose we'd better find out who or what tripped the alarm," she suggested.

"I'll help you check that out," Brett said.

"I could—" Jed began to offer his assistance.

"I actually have a few things I'd like to talk over with Susan," Brett explained, as something crashed in another room. "Anyway, it sounds as though Chrissy might need some help in the kitchen. That is her voice, isn't it?"

"Sure sounds like it. Well, I'd better go. She won't be calling me for help after tomorrow afternoon."

Susan looked affectionately at her husband's departing back.

"He's going to miss Chrissy. Not that she's been around much these last few years—"

"She's only moving a couple of hundred miles away," Brett said. "And she seems to be marrying a very nice young man. I think you'll be seeing quite a bit of her."

"I hope so."

"Something bothering you?" Brett asked.

God, the last person in the world who she wanted to think something was wrong. "Just a bit of the empty-nest syndrome," she lied. In truth, she wouldn't mind her nest being just a bit emptier right now. "How do we go about looking for the problem?"

"Well, first, let's see what your control panel says and then, if nothing shows up there, we can check the main box—these things are usually easy to track down. The last time we had a false alarm, the problem turned out to be a nest of mice sitting right on top of the fire detector in the ceiling of a house on the other side of town."

"Oh, good. More pets," Susan muttered, leading Brett into the hallway to show him the control panels.

Brett didn't explain why he wanted to be alone with her until they were removing winter clothing from the attic cedar closet to peer into the control panel placed in the wall there. "I don't suppose you've had a chance to talk with Erika tonight?" he asked, dropping Susan's favorite Calvin Klein cashmere peacoat on the dusty floor.

Thank goodness, this had nothing to do with the murder. "She left a message on the answering machine, but I haven't had time to respond yet. Why? Is something wrong? Frankly, I don't remember what she said."

"She called me about two hours ago. I guess you were eating dinner at the Inn then."

"Well, I was there, at least," Susan agreed. There was no reason to explain that she was still starving. "What did she want?"

"Would you mind if I asked you a few questions first?" Brett asked, trying to aim his flashlight at the box while opening it with the other hand.

Susan took the flashlight from him and pointed it in the right direction. "We've talked about adding a light fixture in here for years," she muttered. "Go ahead and ask," she added.

"Did you notice anything unusual about the rehearsal?"

Susan was silent for a few moments.

"Susan, this has nothing to do with Chrissy or Stephen—or probably even with their wedding," Brett said, apparently thinking he was easing her mind. "In fact, it's probably nothing at all."

"The rehearsal was a little odd," Susan admitted. As long as he didn't want her to tell him about the body, she was happy. "In the first place, the minister who is sharing the service with Dick—Dick Price, our minister—didn't show up until it was over. We thought she was stuck at O'Hare Airport after having missed her connection, but it turned out that she had been in town the entire time." Now that she thought about it, this whole thing was very odd. She had been so surprised to find out that the Archangel wasn't the dead woman, that she hadn't stopped to wonder who had called claiming to be stuck in Chicago. "And the best man was drunk," she continued, realizing Brett was waiting for more.

"A little early in the day for that, wasn't it?"

"I'll say. I sure hope he doesn't do something stupid—like lose the ring." She frowned. "I should have suggested that Jed keep it here overnight. Although Stephen probably has it. He really is remarkably responsible."

"Susan? What are you thinking about?"

"Just something Stephen said earlier—it's probably nothing—and it doesn't have anything to do with the rehearsal," she added.

"Anything else?"

"No. Chrissy didn't rehearse, which isn't all that unusual. And some flowers fell on Alice Gordon—she's going to be the flower girl tomorrow."

"That didn't strike you as at all unusual?"

"No, but I can see the connection with Erika. She was concerned that it would happen during the service tomorrow. Not that I think that would be a disaster, either. There's almost something magical about flowers falling from above. Of course, Erika's such a perfectionist. She probably doesn't see it like that." Susan realized Brett had stopped looking for the problem with her alarm system and was sitting back on his heels, staring at her with a concerned expression on his face. "Is that what she called about? Is there something going on here that I don't understand the significance of?"

"It may be just what you say—Erika's tendency to be a perfectionist."

"But?"

"But she thinks it's something more serious."

"Brett, Erika isn't the hysterical sort. If she's worried, there very well may be something to worry about."

"I don't want to worry you the night before Chrissy's wedding, and Erika doesn't want to either."

"Brett, am I going to have a nervous breakdown right here or are you going to tell me what's worrying Erika?" She realized she was becoming slightly shrill.

"She thinks . . . She's sure, in fact, that someone tampered with the decorations and caused the flowers to fall."

"What?"

"Erika says she found one of those tiny Swiss Army knives on the floor near where the cord holding up the flowers broke."

"So?"

"She thinks it was intentional."

"Brett, we're talking about a small part of a swag of lilacs. What reason could anyone have to intentionally cause them to fall on the flower girl? Or fall at all?"

"Believe me, Susan, I asked the same question. But Erika has a point here. The other side of this is, why would someone— anyone—go to the trouble of unclipping the cords holding up the swag?"

Susan, realizing Brett was serious about this question, thought for a few seconds. "Maybe a prank?"

"Susan, do you know anyone who might not want this wedding to take place? Someone who might have been hoping Chrissy would marry him instead of Stephen?"

Susan blinked; this was the last thing she had been thinking about. "I . . . I don't really have any idea. Chrissy's always been popular. There have been boys hanging around since she was fifteen. And she's been away at college for the last four years—who knows how many young men she dated there—or how serious she was about them. Or they were about her." She paused, remembering the succession of men who had been brought home on vacations. One had dyed his hair orange and purple. The next had shaved all his off, and made up for his lack of locks by growing a long beard. Then there had been the anarchist. . . . She must be crazy to worry about Stephen. But she realized Brett was expecting a response. "Why are you asking? Do you think someone wants to interrupt her wedding? You don't think anyone wants to hurt her?"

"Look, I don't want to worry you," Brett said. "It was something Erika suggested. She thought . . . "

"What did she think? You can't leave it hanging like that," Susan insisted.

"She was concerned about that Tom Davidson—the photographer who is helping her at your church. You must know him—I just saw him downstairs right now."

"Of course, I know him. He's always struck me as a nice young man."

"Well, that may be. But Erika seemed to think he was paying an awful lot of attention to Chrissy. And then, when the flowers fell and Erika found the knife, she began to wonder if maybe he, or someone else, wanted to interrupt the rehearsal for some reason."

"To keep Chrissy from getting married?" Susan asked, incredulous.

"Well, it is just one explanation for something that is worrying her," Brett suggested.

"You think it's something more serious."

"I don't think it's anything. As far as I know, the flowers falling was an accident, and the fact that Erika found the little Swiss Army knife was just a coincidence. After all, it could have fallen from someone's pocket or purse during church last Sunday."

"Is that what you really think? You don't seem particularly worried."

Brett chuckled. "Frankly, yes. I'm nuts about Erika, but she really hates it when anything goes wrong, and she sure doesn't like to admit that she's made a mistake."

"Then—"

"But don't tell her I said that, please."

Susan, passing up an opportunity to learn a little more about a relationship that had interested her since its inception, merely nodded. "So you don't think I have to worry," she said.

"I think—" But it would have to remain a mystery. There was a loud crash as if someone had fallen into one of the many boxes and trunks that lined the attic walls and then Chrissy appeared. She was crying and slightly hysterical.

"Mother! You won't believe what's happened. . . . Someone has stolen my wedding dress!"

TWENTY

"WHAT? BRETT, SOMEONE STOLE CHRISSY'S WEDDING GOWN! You have to do something! Call someone . . . We should search the area. . . ." Susan, excited, grabbed Brett's sleeves in both hands. She did, however, have some idea of how silly she sounded.

"Susan, calm down. Were there diamonds on this gown? Was it made of something so valuable that a thief could turn it over to a fence and make some sort of profit?"

"Valuable? Of course it's valuable! What else is Chrissy going to wear tomorrow?" Susan cried, impatient with his male attitude.

"You're thinking this is some sort of prank, aren't you, sir?" A calm (inappropriately so, Susan thought) voice asked the question.

Susan was surprised to find Stephen standing beside her daughter. "What are you doing here?" she asked, immediately realizing just how rude she sounded. "I don't mean . . ."

"Please don't worry about it. I can understand your surprise. It's awfully late. It's just that I tried to call and explain, but someone hung up on me, so then I thought I'd better come right over and explain in person what's going on. Or what we think might be doing on." He amended his statement as he wrapped an arm around Chrissy's shoulders.

"We think? You mean, you and Chrissy?" Brett asked, taking an unreasonable amount of time to call out his officers and inform them about this crime, Susan thought.

"Yes. We think someone is trying to keep us from going through with the service tomorrow," Stephen said.

"You mean that's what *you* think," Chrissy said.

Susan, pleased to see her daughter standing up for herself,

smiled for the first time since she had arrived home. "What do you think is going on?" she asked the young woman.

"I don't think anything's going on—"

"Then where do you think your dress has gone? It didn't just get up, put itself in its box, and walk away," Stephen interrupted.

"A box? What box?" Jed had joined them.

"The box the dress was shipped from Italy in," Chrissy explained. "I was worried about the dress becoming crumpled— you know how silk chiffon is, and that fabric is so fine"—Susan took note of the gown's material—"so when I saw that Stephen had the box it arrived in, I asked if he would give it to the Archangel so she could put the dress back in it—if that makes any sense," she ended, biting her lip. "It's sort of late."

But not too late for Susan to notice that someone must have emptied the box before it was turned over to the Archangel. Had Stephen done it? She glanced over at him. The young man was looking at her daughter in a manner she would have approved of before she found herself questioning his part in this murder—or its cover-up. There were too many questions here. What had happened to the body? Had Stephen mentioned finding a dead woman to anyone? If he hadn't, why hadn't he? Certainly, he must have been shocked to find her. . . . Unless, of course, he had known the body was in the box. And who would know that except for the person who placed it—her—in there?

She frowned. Jed's expression was equally grave.

"Now, I know it's late, but just let me get this straight," Brett said. "Who had the gown?"

"The Archangel," Susan said, then realized she would have to explain. "That's the woman who was the commune's minister . . . or not exactly a minister, more like a spiritual leader—"

"Actually, she sewed in whatever it was that she thought was important and gave the dress away to—" Chrissy started to explain.

"To my parents. Well, my mother actually." Stephen picked up the story.

"Where is your mother?" Brett asked.

"In her room at the Hancock Inn, I assume . . . Oh, you mean where did she have the dress."

"Exactly."

"In her room. She was going to bring it over here in the morning."

"Why was the dress at the Inn?" Jed asked.

"I took it over there to show Stephen's parents," Chrissy said. "Then it came back here, but later the Archangel wanted to sew some sort of small talisman in it. She said she would give it to Stephen's mother when she was done with it. And she did."

"And why they had it—" Stephen began.

"They had it because your mother wanted to bring it over here in the morning. She asked for it," Chrissy cried, sounding outraged. "I did it to be nice to your parents! Your mother insisted. Said she'd never had a daughter and wanted to share in the morning before the wedding with me."

"So why didn't you just ask her to come over for breakfast or something? Why did the dress have to stay with her overnight?"

"I did!" Chrissy's eyes flashed. "I said I'd bring the dress home and that she was welcome to come over first thing in the morning and help me dress. And the Archangel offered to bring it over tonight, but your mother almost insisted on bringing it in the morning. What else could I do?"

"I—"

"Everyone's tired . . ."

"Maybe we should worry about this later."

The three adults broke in at the same time. But it was Stephen who stopped the argument from escalating. He clasped Chrissy's hands in both of his and apologized. "I'm sorry. What isn't my fault here is my parent's fault. I should have warned you about my mother's need to get intimately involved in the lives of everyone around her."

"No, it's my fault. I should have insisted on the dress coming home with me. My own mother hasn't even seen my dress. . . ." Chrissy's maturity was short-lived, and tears started to seep from the corners of her eyes. "And now no one is going to be able to see it. I don't know what I'm going to wear tomorrow. I was . . . I thought . . . All I wanted to do was look beautiful for you . . . for our wedding."

The last words were wailed into Stephen's shirtfront and, as his arms closed around her daughter, Susan offered a prayer that this young man had nothing to do with the body in the box.

"You don't have to worry about that," Stephen insisted, gently kissing the crown of Chrissy's head. "You don't have to worry about anything."

"Maybe the Henshaws should all go to bed," Brett suggested. "Stephen can tell me where the dress was last seen and I'll call out some of my men to talk to the staff at the Inn and search the area if it turns out to be necessary. That dress didn't walk away by itself, after all."

"But—" Susan began.

"What about the fire alarm?" Jed interrupted.

Brett sighed. "Maybe you should put a call in to your alarm company. Who do you use?"

"It's one of the smaller companies—they took over Kathleen's business when Alex was born. I'll call Kathleen," Susan said, inspired.

"At this hour?" Stephen glanced down at his watch.

"Mother is always calling Mrs. Gordon. I told you," Chrissy explained, sounding like her old self.

"That's right. You said they had solved crimes of some sort together, didn't you?" Stephen gave Susan a long look. She couldn't decide if he was wondering about the genes that might be passed on from a woman with such a peculiar hobby or . . . or if he was wondering if she and Kathleen might know about the body . . . or if he was wondering how much she knew about his part in the disappearing body . . . "You know, I *am* going to call Kathleen," Susan said. "Maybe she'll know what to do here."

"I think—"

"I think it's time for you to go to bed," Stephen interrupted Chrissy. "You don't have to worry. I'll find your gown before tomorrow morning."

"Oh, Stephen . . ."

Susan thought for a moment that her daughter was going to swoon in her fiancé's arms. But she didn't have time to be irritated by the girl's unliberated behavior; what, she wondered, was Stephen going to do now? And how could she find out?

"Maybe everyone should go to bed," Brett repeated. "I can call when we find the dress."

"Wonderful," Jed said, starting down the attic stairs. "Coming, Susan?"

"We'd better give them some time to say good night," Brett said.

But Susan was rushing down the stairs and didn't bother to reply. She hoped Stephen and Chrissy's good-nights took a good long time—or, at least, time enough for her to change her clothing, drive out of the driveway, and park down the street. She had no intention of letting Stephen leave here without an escort. To be safe, she would call Kathleen. After all, the mother of the flower girl and ring bearer might as well be as tired as the mother of the bride—if there were a wedding, she thought, closing the bedroom door behind her and heading straight for her closet.

Black. If she was going to be snooping around in the dark, she needed black clothes. She dressed in leggings, a long sleeved black T-shirt, and, alas, dirty white Keds (she had decided to trade consistency for traction), and was pulling stuff off the top shelf of Jed's closet when he entered the room.

"What are you doing?"

"Looking for a flashlight. Don't you keep one in here?"

"I keep two of them in there." Her husband squatted down and pulled a box off the shoe shelf near the floor. "Which do you want?" He offered a choice of a foot-long Maglite or a Coleman torch.

Susan chose the Maglite. "Heavy, isn't it?"

"Yes. Now, are you going to dash out into the darkness this minute, or can you take the time to tell me what you're planning on doing?"

"I'm going to call Kathleen." She grabbed the phone. "I just hope I'm in time . . ."

"For what?"

"To find out where that young man is going tonight."

"Susan, you're not telling me that you're going to follow him?"

"What else?"

"Susan—"

"Jerry. It's Susan. I know it's late, but I have to talk to Kathleen for a moment." Susan ignored her husband and spoke into the receiver. "Hi, Kath, I need your help."

"I—"

Susan impatiently put a hand on her husband's arm. "Stephen is going to leave here in a few minutes—I'll explain later," she continued into the receiver, "and I think he's going to head over to the Inn. Would you drive over and see what he does when he gets there? Without him knowing that you're watching, if possible. I know it's late. But he gave the box to his parents—and I assume the dress wasn't in it at that point."

Kathleen understood immediately, and with a few more words, Susan hung up.

"I can—" Jed began.

"You need to stay here in case Brett calls," Susan said.

"Susan, you'll be running around in the dark and there's a murderer loose somewhere. I think I should be with you."

"Jed, you're right about the murderer. Which is why I'll feel better if I know you're here with the kids." She headed out the door.

"Are you going to tell me where you're going?"

"I'm going to follow Stephen—he might not go to the Inn, after all," Susan said, as the bedroom door swung closed behind her.

"But—"

"Jed, I have my phone with me. I'll call you as soon as I know anything . . ." Susan called the last words over her shoulder as she ran down the stairs, through the hallway, and into her kitchen. She was taking the time to mentally applaud her foresight at not tripping over any of the boxes in the hallway, when she smashed right into the largest dog crate she'd ever seen.

Naturally, she startled the puppies inside, and just as naturally, the poor things began to bark their heads off.

"Damn! Shhh! Shhh!"

"Susan? Jed? Something wrong?"

Susan was horrified to see Brett stick his head in the kitchen door. "It's me, Brett. I . . . I just . . ." She looked around the room and an answer came to her. "I'm having Jed's and my relatives in for brunch tomorrow . . . and now it appears as though the Canfields will be here. I . . . I was just making sure I have everything organized before I go to bed." She noticed that the skeptical expression remained glued to his face. "Maybe you'd like to come over, too? You can bring Erika. I'm planning on starting to serve food around nine. . . ." She felt something strange seeping into the sides of her Keds and, looking down, discovered that she was standing in a puddle of puppy pee. "Shit."

Brett chuckled. "That, too." He nodded. "Over there in the corner by the refrigerator. I guess one of them made a pit stop on the way to its crate and no one noticed."

"I thought I smelled something. I guess I have more to do than just worry about breakfast," Susan said, relieved to be honest for once, but wishing Brett would leave so she could be on her way. "Of course, the dress is worrying me more than anything else," she hinted broadly.

"I'll go to the Inn and see if I can track it down." He paused. "You don't know any reason why your future in-laws might have hidden the dress, do you?"

"Heavens, no. Do you?"

"No. But obviously something strange is going on here."

"Brett, they're California people. It's probably just something New Age or Millennium-ish or something like that," she ended weakly. What could she say to get this man to leave? How was she going to follow Stephen if he left before she could get out of here?

"Well, I'll leave you to your cooking and cleaning," Brett said, turned, and left the room.

Susan heard the front door slam as the kitchen door swung closed behind Brett. Without a thought for what she was now tracking across her quarry tile floor, she ran across the kitchen to the garage. If she hurried, she might just manage to see where Stephen's car went. . . .

TWENTY-ONE

So much for going to the Hancock Inn. Stephen was obviously heading to the Yacht Club from the time he pulled out of the Henshaws' driveway. Good thing his direction stayed so consistent, Susan thought grimly. In the fifteen minutes it took them to travel from home to the club, it was difficult not to come to the conclusion that Stephen was avoiding the police. More than once on their joint jaunt across town, he had turned abruptly and Susan, following as closely as she dared, had noticed a patrol car traveling slowly down the street they just left.

Tailing the navy Volvo had been more difficult than she would have imagined, and Susan hadn't had the energy to think much about what Stephen's unwillingness to run into the police might mean until she was sitting on the ground underneath the bottom porch of the Yacht Club listening to Stephen's footsteps on the boards above her. He was carefully trying all the windows and doors.

Perhaps, of course, his avoidance of the police wasn't surprising, considering his apparent determination to break into the building. It might have nothing to do with the body. On the other hand, he certainly must have done something with the body; it couldn't have fallen from the box without his noticing, could it?

The tinkle of breaking glass followed by a string of expletives informed her that Stephen had discovered an entrance to the building. She heard him scramble through the opening he'd made. After waiting a few moments, Susan slung her purse over her shoulder and, wincing with pain, climbed up on the porch and peered in the window.

Apparently Stephen also had come equipped with a flashlight, and she watched its beam travel around the large room, noticing that he took the time to check under the long linen cloths that covered the buffet tables. Whatever he was searching for wasn't small—his inspection was cursory, and apparently satisfied that he wasn't going to find what he was looking for here, he started for the stairs.

Much as Susan wanted to follow him, she restrained herself. If he found what he was looking for, she was in position to watch him cart it off when he left the building. She found a stuffed porch chair in a dark corner and settled down to wait for his appearance.

The full moon's wide smear of light shimmering on the water was beautiful enough for Susan to forget for one moment that there was a dead woman—and a missing wedding dress—and that there were heaven knew how many people coming to brunch tomorrow and she had no idea what she was going to feed them.

She glanced at her watch. It was almost one o'clock. Those guests would begin arriving in less than eight hours. Chrissy would be stepping into the car that would take them to the church in little more than fourteen hours. She took a few moments to wonder what her daughter would be wearing. And if Jed had remembered to polish the shoes he was going to wear with his morning coat. And whether or not Chad . . .

She might have begun to fret seriously if a police car pulling up in front of the Yacht Club hadn't focused her attention elsewhere. Following Stephen's lead, Susan had parked on a side street and walked to the club, so there was plenty of room for the patrol car directly in front. The driver left his flashing lights on and got out of his vehicle, training the beam from his powerful flashlight over the outside of the building. A two-way radio hanging from his belt began to chatter as he made his way down the path to the Yacht Club.

Susan held her breath as he (she could see well enough to identify the sex of the officer, but not much more) carefully moved the barriers in front of the awning and walked out of sight. She wondered what would happen when the two men met.

There was little time to speculate. Within moments, the officer reappeared from under the canopy, a handcuffed Stephen by his side. "If you'll just let me explain," Stephen was saying. "I'm the groom. I have a reason to be in there. All I have to do is make a few phone calls—"

"If you have such a good reason to be lurking around the Yacht Club in the middle of the night, why didn't you turn on the lights? Why were you wandering around with a flashlight like a common burglar?"

Those were, Susan realized, excellent questions. She would have liked to hang around and hear the answers, but it occurred to her that someone needed to do something about this situation immediately. She tiptoed to the back of the building and scrounged around in her purse for her phone—before remembering she hadn't taken the time to charge the batteries. She cursed and looked around, wondering if there was a pay phone about. But she didn't have time to call—something else was going on. Or else she had fallen asleep and those screams and shrieks were merely a feature of another nightmare.

As quietly as possible, she ran around the side of the building and peered around the corner.

She need not have been so careful. None of the three people standing on the sidewalk before the building was the least bit interested in what she was doing.

Blues Canfield was doing an extraordinary imitation of a hysterical mother. "Get your filthy handcuffs off my son! Don't you know he's a Phi Beta Kappa graduate of an Ivy League university? That young man got perfect scores on his boards less than a year ago! He was offered fellowships at three of the best graduate schools in the country. Why, this young man could have attended Berkeley for free!"

That bit of news stopped Susan dead in her tracks. Chrissy and Stephen could have been moving to California? Almost did move to California? There would have been no family holidays! Probably she and Jed would have had to travel across the country to see their daughter. And when . . . if . . . there were grandchildren, how could she possibly manage to spoil them long-distance? And what about . . . ?

"Look! There's another prowler! Why isn't that prowler being dragged off in handcuffs?" Blues had changed her theme.

Another prowler? Susan spun around, peering into the darkness for the person—until she realized Blues was talking about her. Then, "I'm not a prowler," she called out. "I'm the mother of the bride. Susan Henshaw."

"Susan! Thank goodness, it's you! You must do something.

This dreadful man . . . this officious police person . . . he's threatening to lock up Stephen and throw away the key! There'll be no wedding tomorrow. Unless, perhaps, a jailhouse ceremony. Something for them to be ashamed of forever . . . Starting their married life in such a manner would certainly carry bad karma—"

"Mother! You are being ridiculous!" Stephen roared into the night.

Susan had enough presence of mind to be amused—but for only a few seconds. Then she had to act.

"Is there anything I can do for you, Officer?" she asked, walking up the sidewalk to the trio. Even to her own ears, she sounded a little strange.

But the young officer seemed too relieved to notice. "Are you the mother of the young woman who is going to be married at the Presbyterian church tomorrow? It's Henshaw, isn't it? You're a friend of the police chief's."

"Yes, I—"

"Stephen, have you noticed just how well known to the police the family you're marrying into seems to b—"

"Mother! Shut up!"

"Is that the way you were brought up to talk to your mother?" Blues asked, almost curiously.

"Mother! That is exactly the way I was brought up to talk to you!" Stephen shouted.

That seemed to slow her down just a bit. "Well, yes. Well, we believed in raising a child to stand up for himself . . . to question authority . . . to . . ."

"Lady, it's late. If you're going to start quoting bumper stickers, we'll be here all night. And I'm busy even if you aren't."

"Not busy! Until your beloved child gets married, you don't know what being busy is, young man."

Susan thought Blues's statement was right on target, but the police officer was mumbling something about not even being married to say nothing of having children, so she politely let him get on with it. The only thing she was interested in hearing was Stephen's explanation of what he was doing wandering around the Yacht Club in the middle of the night—as long as it had nothing to do with the dead body. She didn't need the police meddling in that particular matter right now. "You know who I am," Susan said calmly. "And this is the young man my daughter is going to marry tomorrow, Stephen Canfield. And his mother, Bl—"

"Barbara Canfield, Officer." Blues held her hand out to the policeman. Susan noticed that the other woman was taking special note of the badge number on the man's chest. "Now, why don't we all take a few moments to find out just what's going on and then we can be on our way."

"I was here looking for something," Stephen said, trying, Susan assumed, to start the ball rolling.

"What?" the officer asked.

"What do you mean?" Stephen asked.

"What were you looking for here? At the Yacht Club. In the middle of the night. With a flashlight."

"Heavens, Stephen, were you doing that?" his mother asked. "How did you get in?"

Susan cringed. She had hoped that knowledge of the broken window was going to remain her little secret.

"I . . ." Stephen paused and glanced at Susan. Was he wondering just how long she'd been hanging around outside of the Yacht Club, she wondered.

Next Stephen glanced up and down the street, the frown on his face deepening.

"Stephen, your entire upbringing should prevent you from being intimidated by this type of puppet of petty local government. . . . Speak up!"

"Mother, I can handle this myself." Stephen sounded tired and angry, and suddenly, Susan felt sorry for him. This was, after all, the young man her daughter had chosen to share the rest of her life.

"If Stephen will let me, I'd like to explain, Officer." Susan added swiftly, seeing he was about to interrupt, "Stephen was here on an errand for me. I'm afraid this whole misunderstanding is all my fault."

All eyes turned toward her and Susan thought quickly. "You see, I was worried about . . . about . . ." It was late. It had been one of the longest days of her life. She was completely exhausted. Her brain, normally capable of creating a legitimate-sounding excuse under trying circumstances, seemed to be failing her.

And then Stephen chimed in, finishing her sentence and solving the problem. "Her notebook. I came here looking for the notebook Mrs. Henshaw has been using to keep track of the wedding plans. You see, I was just over at the Henshaws' house, saying good night to Chrissy—"

"That's my daughter," Susan chimed in, appreciating the story Stephen was weaving.

"And by this time tomorrow night, she'll be my wife," Stephen said, never missing a beat. "But when I was dropping Chrissy off, Mrs. Henshaw mentioned that she had misplaced her notebook."

"Isn't it a little late to be worrying about wedding plans?" the policeman asked. "Isn't everything all set and ready to go by now?"

"That just shows how little you know about planning something like this," Susan said, thinking of all the last-minute details that were still worrying her.

"And I thought I had seen the notebook here earlier in the day when Chrissy and I were checking out the decorations, so I offered to stop on the way home and see if I could find it. I . . ." Here, for the first time, he paused, as if doubting whether he should tell this part of the story. "I thought I might be able to get in through an open window, but I'm afraid . . . I'm afraid I broke one around in back of the building."

"You entered the Yacht Club through a broken window?" The police officer sounded solemn.

"Yes, but—"

"But my family has rented the Yacht Club for the entire weekend," Susan interrupted, suddenly seeing a loophole in the direction the policeman was traveling. "So don't I have to press charges if you are going to arrest this young man?"

"I don't know about that," the policeman answered slowly. "I think—" The walkie-talkie on his belt interrupted him. "Excuse me."

"I—"

"Mother, please, just don't say anything at all until we have this worked out," Stephen said quietly.

But it all worked out much more quickly than Susan would have expected.

"I'm going to have to take Mrs. Henshaw's word for it and let you go," the officer said, reaching over to unlock Stephen's handcuffs. "But I think someone should hang around here until that window gets fixed," he added, starting toward his car.

"You're leaving?"

Susan thought Blues seemed remarkably nonplussed by the fact. She, herself, was overjoyed.

"Got to, ma'am. The burglar alarm just sounded over at the Presbyterian church. Say," he added, calling back over his shoulder as he ran toward his vehicle. "That's where the wedding is supposed to take place tomorrow, isn't it?"

"If we all live that long," Susan answered grimly.

TWENTY-TWO

"WELL . . . UH . . ."

"So . . . uh . . ."

"I think . . . that . . . uh . . ."

It was obvious that no one wanted to be the first to finish a sentence. Susan suspected neither of her companions had any idea what to say. Susan, however, knew what she wanted to know. "Why are you here?" she asked quietly.

"What do you think my son is doing here? He's looking for your notebook—he just told that policeman—"

Susan heard the indignation in Blues's voice and quickly stepped in to placate her. "It's not that I think Stephen was lying—"

"Actually, I was. There is no notebook—at least I didn't see one," he interrupted.

"You lied?" His mother gave the impression that she could not imagine such a thing. "Stephen, how many times have I told you that it doesn't matter what you do as long as you tell the truth about it? You know I'll understand. You know I'll always love you. You know your father and I value truth above everything else. As the poet Keats said—"

"Mother, I know all that. I appreciate it. And, if you want to hear the truth, you'll have to stop talking and listen."

"You know, I feel strongly that listening is really a creative activity. And one I'm very good at, if I do say so myself." Even in the dim moonlight, Blues looked self-satisfied.

Susan didn't believe a word of it, but there wasn't time to go into it. "So why are you here?" she asked Stephen. "What were you looking for when you broke into the Yacht Club?"

Stephen glanced at his mother and Susan before speaking. "The wedding ring."

"Chrissy's ring?" Susan wondered what would get lost next.

"The symbol of the love the two of you are going to share together forever?" His mother was less succinct.

"Yes."

"You lost it?"

"David lost it."

"David? The best man? The one who's always drunk? You trusted him to keep the ring overnight?" Susan was too upset to consider whether or not she was being unforgivably rude.

"David and I are best friends," Stephen protested. "It never occurred to me that he wouldn't take care of it. He's never done anything like this before—and he's not always drunk."

"Stephen is right, Susan. I've known David since he was a child, and he's usually very responsible. Things are a bit difficult in his life right now. His parents . . . well, that's not important. But poor David is a lost soul. However, he'll find himself someday."

"Mother . . . it's late. I'm exhausted and I'm sure you are, too. Father is probably wondering what's happened to you."

"Father is here. You know my motto. Action, not reaction."

All three of them turned toward the voice.

"I thought it better to wait in the shadows until the police presence had been eliminated." Rhythm seemed to think that was an explanation rather than the lead-in to a rather obvious question.

"Father, what are you doing here?"

Susan heard exhaustion, exasperation, and something else in Stephen's voice. Whatever was going on here, and she suspected it was more than the loss of a wedding band (why break in if Stephen had a reasonable excuse to enter the building?), it was beginning to take its toll on the young man.

"When my wife gets up, gets dressed, and sneaks out of our bedroom in the middle of the night, I consider it my duty to see just where she is going," he answered.

"Excuse me?" Blues was obviously outraged. "Are you suggesting that I can't take care of myself?"

"Of course not. I just thought you might like to share your adventure," her husband answered smoothly.

Blues frowned and Susan noticed that no one except Stephen had explained—either honestly or not so honestly—what made it necessary for them to be at the Yacht Club in the middle of the night. One of the most interesting aspects of this, she suddenly realized, was that her presence seemed to be accepted as perfectly normal. Was it possible that the Canfields thought it was the mother of the bride's duty to check out the place where the wedding reception was to be held the night before the big event? After midnight?

"So where were you going?" Blues asked her.

Susan didn't know what to say. She didn't want to admit that she had been following Stephen, and she didn't want to say anything that might lead to questions about how she happened to be here. She glanced at Stephen, who was staring intently at her.

"I think Mrs. Henshaw and I should be leaving," he said firmly. "After all the wedding is tomorrow, and I think I'd better get busy coming up with something to put on Chrissy's finger tomorrow."

"You know," Susan said, suddenly inspired, "Jed's mother offered you two her mother's wedding band, didn't she?"

"Yes, but we refused it. So I don't suppose she brought it with her—and she doesn't live nearby, does she?"

"No, but Claire rarely takes no for an answer. I'll bet she brought that ring along just in case," Susan answered.

"In case?"

"In case Chrissy changed her mind," Susan explained. Although the truth was that Claire would undoubtedly be working to make the girl see her point of view—at least, she would if past experience meant anything. Susan's mother-in-law had never let a *no* dampen her enthusiasm for one of her own ideas.

"Is Claire staying at your house?" Stephen asked.

"No, the Inn. Why don't we both head over there and we can ask her if she's brought it along?" Susan suggested. "I'm sure she won't mind being awakened for something so important."

"Okay, why don't I follow you—I don't know my way around town all that well . . ." Stephen's voice seemed to dwindle off. Susan wondered if he was remembering all those twists and turns he'd made between her house and here—could unfamiliar ground account for them all?

"Great! Well, good night, all. See you at my house for breakfast tomorrow."

"You mean today, don't you?" Rhythm joshed.

"I'm sure Susan knows what time it is," Blues stated flatly. "And I'm sure she's as exhausted as we are. Let's get going, Robert."

"I . . ."

"Now, Robert!"

They went.

Susan and Stephen exchanged looks—as much as that was possible in the darkness. There was a pause, and then . . . "You followed me here, didn't you?" he asked.

Why lie? "Yes." After a shorter pause, she said, "Did you actually lose the ring?"

"No, of course not. It's in the safe at the Inn. When I asked if I'd be able to get it out tomorrow morning, that nice man who owns the place, Charles, said he would come in and open it up just for me. I'd never lose that ring. Chrissy loves it. We designed it together. Her favorite instructor at RISD cast it for us. I'd never misplace anything that meant so much to her. I just couldn't think of anything else on the spur of the moment when Mom asked why I was here."

Susan was more than a little glad to hear it. But, she realized, that didn't answer most of her questions.

"So why did you say David had it?"

"Poor David's been taking the rap for things that went wrong in our group for such a long time that I automatically blame him," Stephen said. "And, don't worry. He wouldn't—won't—mind at all. He may be drinking too much this weekend, but it's not like him. He's usually a responsible son of a bitch—more responsible than his parents or my parents would ever believe."

Did every word out of this young man's mouth have to bring up more questions? But this wasn't an ideal place to interrogate anyone. "We told your parents that we were going to the Inn . . ." She left the statement unfinished.

"And they will expect us to be there. So I guess we'd better go."

"You think they'll check?"

"I know they'll check. My parents talk a lot about trust and claim to believe in my honesty, but they'll want to see for themselves that I'm doing what I said I was going to do. Of course, you can do what you want."

"Actually, I'm supposed to be meeting someone at the Inn . . ." Susan began slowly, remembering Kathleen should be waiting there for her.

"Now? Do you have any idea what time it is?" The response was automatic, and almost immediately Stephen recanted. "I'm sorry. I'm tired, but there's no excuse for being so rude."

Too bad, Susan thought, that she had to include Stephen in her mental list of murder suspects. As the night wore on and became insanely more complicated, she found herself liking this young man more and more. "You weren't. In fact, you've been very . . ." She paused and looked around her tired brain for the correct word. "Sweet," was all she came up with. Apparently it didn't offend him in the least.

"Thank you. I think you're going to be a wonderful mother-in-law," Stephen said, and surprised her with an awkward peck on the cheek. "Now, what are we going to do about that body?"

Susan gasped. "You . . . you know . . . you . . . I . . ." Words failed her. Completely.

"I know about her. I know where she is. I don't know who killed her, though."

Stephen seemed amazingly calm. "Do you . . ." Susan asked the first question that came to mind. "Do you know *who* she is?"

"I think so."

"You *think* so!"

"Shhh! Chrissy said you tend to get emotional, but we don't want to draw more police attention, do we?" Stephen asked.

Maybe she wasn't going to like him quite so much. Susan insisted on sticking to what she thought was the primary question. "Who is the dead woman?"

"I said I'm not sure. Listen, why don't we drive over to the Inn and I can explain all this on the way?"

Susan agreed without giving more than a quick thought to her own car still parked around the corner. She could pick it up later. "Fine." She started for the car she had followed here less than half an hour ago.

"Does she have something to do with why you're here in the middle of the night?" she asked.

"Yes. Since she was in the box the dress was delivered in, and since David told me that he brought the dress straight from the airport to the Yacht Club, I thought this might be the place to start finding out what's going on."

Susan thought that sounded sensible. And she had some questions she wanted to ask. The first being, "So who do you *think* the dead woman is?"

"I think she's David's mother." He climbed into the driver's seat, but Susan wasn't going to wait one moment more.

"Didn't I just meet David's mother today? Wind Something is what she calls herself. . . ."

"Wind Song isn't David's mother—she's his stepmother."

"Okay, but still . . . David's your best friend and you're not sure what his mother looks like?" She hoped that didn't sound too undiplomatic. She was old enough to understand that family relations came in many shapes and sizes. And women do change their hair colors, have facelifts and tummy tucks, all sorts of things that might make recognition difficult.

"She didn't raise him. I don't think I've seen her more than a few dozen times in my entire life. And as far as I know, David hasn't seen her all that many more." He put the key in the ignition and then paused and looked straight at Susan. "You probably already realize that I didn't have a very normal upbringing."

"Well, I've never known anyone raised in a commune before."

"It wasn't as interesting as it sounds—no group sex or wild, illicit drug use. At least, I don't think there was," he concluded with less assurance. "What I'm saying is that it was unconventional, but . . . well, my parents—all the parents—weren't irresponsible."

"Except for David's mother?"

"She wasn't there. David was raised by his father and his step-mother. You met them both this evening. High Hopes and Wind Song." He glanced at her and started the car. "Yeah, the names were already pretty ridiculous when I was a kid and they were young. Now they've become absurd."

"But you said you had seen David's birth mother. Did she come to the commune to visit?"

"No, she wasn't welcome there. I don't know why. The details of the relationship between her and David's father were never discussed openly in front of us kids," he added quickly.

"So when . . . where did you see her?"

"The first time I actually saw her, to talk to, was when we were all together . . . living in the commune, actually." Stephen stopped. "Do you think we have time to go into this now?" he asked, taking his hand off the steering wheel to glance at his watch.

"It seems to me that we have no choice but to do this. The woman was murdered, Stephen. That means there's a murderer loose. And . . . and . . ." She didn't know quite how to continue.

"What you're trying to say is that you need to find out if your daughter is marrying into the family of a killer. Or marrying the killer himself."

TWENTY-THREE

"I . . ." Susan didn't know what to say.

"Don't worry. I'm not offended. I care about your daughter. I only want the best for her, too. So I understand that we'll all rest more easily if the identity of the murderer is discovered before the wedding."

"I feel like I'm wandering around in the dark looking for the killer. I don't even know who the potential murderers are—" Susan stopped, embarrassed, as she realized that he understood exactly what she was saying.

But Stephen seemed to be a young man who was completely comfortable dealing with reality. "Then I guess it's time for you to hear a bit more about how I grew up—and the people I grew up with," he said.

"If you think it has to do with the murder. Yes, I think so."

"Well, you already know my parents were members of a commune, and in some ways it was exactly what you think of when you think of a Sixties commune."

Susan remembered his assurances about drugs and sexual activity and decided that she doubted it—but she didn't say anything.

"And in some ways it wasn't," he continued.

"I know it wasn't rural," Susan said.

"It was in an old hotel near Union Square in San Francisco, in fact. It was torn down a while ago, and now a large luxury hotel fills most of that block. But, when I was growing up, it was a pretty seedy neighborhood. In fact, when we moved in, we displaced the winos and the hookers—they had to travel all the way to the next block to find equally cheap and filthy accommodations. Of course, for a group of hippies, overcoming that squalor was just another challenge to be met. I was barely two years old when we moved in, and my first memories are of lots of loving adults wearing brightly colored clothes hugging and kissing me, saying 'far out' and 'groovy,' and smelling of paint."

"They redecorated?"

"That's one way of looking at it. You know those painted VW buses which seem to have become an enduring image of the Sixties?"

"Sure."

"They turned a six-story, twenty-four-room hotel into a large landlocked version of a VW bus, psychedelic colors and all. The room I grew up in was wonderful, actually. The walls were covered with a sort of Day-Glo zoo. The floor was painted to resemble a topographical map of Yosemite National Park, and the ceiling had images of the sun and a cloudy sky that changed at night to realistic constellations—one of the commune members had been an astronomy major at college."

"Sounds fantastic."

"It was. It was also noisy and disorganized—except for my schooling. My father insisted on the importance of that."

Susan made a mental note that perhaps this indicated a less than enthusiastic embracing of this lifestyle by Rhythm, but didn't ask about that. "You went to public school?"

"At first, but children who have been raised to put their creative needs first don't really thrive in most public schools. So the group decided that home schooling should be part of the commune, and we were all taught that way for a few years. They built a schoolroom on the top floor of the hotel where an old ballroom had been, back at the turn of the century. It wasn't large, but it had these wonderful plaster angels on the ceiling, and even a small stage. All the adults tried to teach us their specialties. There was some quite inspired teaching—I still think of Freedom when I have to memorize material. He showed me a bunch of actor's tricks that came in very useful in college. But I . . . I sort of outgrew the teachers, and I ended up spending my junior high school years at a Catholic school. It was run by the Jesuits, and it was an excellent school. I was sorry when I had to leave."

"Why did you?"

"Oh, well, the commune disbanded and we moved."

"Why?"

"Well, the hotel was being sold, so we couldn't live th— Oh, you mean why did the commune break up?"

"Exactly."

They were arriving at the Inn's parking lot and Stephen turned in carefully, found a spot, and turned off the engine before he answered. "I'm not actually sure if there was any one reason. The times changed. People's lives changed. Some of the couples broke up and a few individuals left to get on with their lives elsewhere." He shrugged. "I think it was just one of those things. Very little lasts forever, I guess."

"You sound like you miss it." Susan was surprised. Stephen was so conservative, so unlike anyone she would expect to come out of a communal upbringing.

"You know, I didn't at the time. I'd wanted to live a more normal life, and I did when my parents moved out. The best thing about growing up in a commune was the shocked looks on the faces of my friends in high school and college when I told them about it. But somehow, everyone being here for my wedding— it's the first time we've all been together again in years—well, I guess it's just making me sentimental for that time again."

"It sounds like it was very special," Susan said, wondering how she could return the topic to the identity of the murdered woman. Luckily, Stephen was more directed than she was.

"It was. But David's mother wasn't a part of it. She and David's father—"

"High Hopes." Susan identified the man.

"Yes, but we usually call him Art these days," Stephen said. "Everyone seems to have taken on their old identity at this wedding."

"You mean the group doesn't usually use their . . . their commune names?"

Stephen chuckled. "No way. They're respectable people now— with real professions, and living in the suburbs, likely as not. And really, no one past the age of twenty-five should call themselves something like Red Man or Moonbeam."

"I won't argue with that. You were telling me about David's mother," she reminded him.

"Well, she left his father right after David was born—just abandoned the baby and left town—so you can see why David's father was sort of bitter."

"Bitter?"

"Well, he didn't want David to have anything to do with his mother. In fact, he insisted that she not be allowed to visit him at the commune."

"You knew this then? When you were young?"

"Not in so many words . . . at least I don't think so. I didn't talk about David's mother—I remember that I had the impression that it would make him unhappy to mention her . . . at least, that's the way I remember it. You know how you forget what it was like to be young."

Susan smiled. If he thought he was forgetting things now, wait until he hit forty-five! "But you did see her," she prompted.

"Yes. The first time that I remember her was at the commune, in fact. She just sort of appeared in the common room one morning after our family focus moment."

"Would you mind translating?"

"Well, the common room was the lobby—with the front desk removed, lots of pillows strewn on the floor, and, I must admit, a lava lamp or two on the windowsills. The members of the commune met there every morning right after breakfast for announcements and what were called focus moments."

"What were they?" Susan's image of this commune was sending her right back to her college days—although she had always thought lava lamps particularly ugly.

"The commune members believed that if everyone focused on a problem, they could solve it mentally."

"Some sort of brainstorming?" Susan was familiar with the concept from Jed's work at an advertising agency in New York City.

"Not really. More a positive energy-flow type of thing."

She had no idea what he was talking about, but it probably wasn't important. "And what does all this have to do with David's mother? Was she the problem the group was trying to solve?"

"Oh no. I don't remember what the problem was that day—probably something small like accomplishing world peace. That was when I first saw her. She sort of snuck in the front door of the building, and sat down on the floor. Probably no one paid all that much attention immediately."

"How strange . . ."

"It wasn't, actually. The hotel had been decorated with big

swirls of Day-Glo paint outside as well as inside. We were always attracting stoned hippies off the street. They wandered in, sat down, and sometimes stayed for a few days. Not that we were a flophouse or anything like that. And if anyone had heavy drug problems, they were directed to the free treatment center over in the Haight. But this time was different, of course. When Art recognized his ex-wife, he just blew up."

"How?"

"He screamed and yelled and ranted and raved. It was amazing. One of the major tenets of the group was peaceful action and nonviolence. There was not a lot of yelling and screaming in the commune—or what there was went on behind closed doors. I remember David's mother's visit mainly because I was stunned by seeing one of the adults I'd come to depend upon acting like that."

"What about David?"

"He burst into tears. He told me years later that he was scared to death."

"Why?"

"Well, first, because his father was acting so . . . so out of character. And second, because he had been told for as long as he could remember that his mother was an evil person—although a person with bad karma was probably closer to the exact wording his father used—and David worried that she might do something awful."

"And did she?"

"No. Not that she was given much chance. First, there was all this shouting, and then David crying, and then the poor woman was surrounded by the adults and rushed back out onto the street. We kids were hustled up to our schoolroom and told that it would be insensitive to the needs of others if we asked a lot of questions."

"Wow! That's quite a statement."

"Doing the right thing was raised to an art form in the commune—of course, for us kids, the right thing was defined as whatever our parents wanted us to do."

"Just like kids outside the commune," Susan suggested.

"Except that it's one thing to rebel against your parents' wishes, and another to act in a manner considered to be immoral."

Susan could see his point, but this wasn't the time to discuss child-rearing techniques with her future son-in-law. "So David didn't get to know his mother."

"Not until later."

"And did he like her then—or would liking her have been insensitive to the needs of others?"

"He loved her," Stephen said simply. "He said she was a warm and loving person."

"But why did his father say differently?" Susan asked the next logical question.

"He has no idea."

Susan heard the present tense. "Has no idea?" she repeated. "He still doesn't understand?"

"That's right. His father refuses to talk about it. *Still* refuses to talk about it—at least, that's what he told me, the last time the subject came up."

"And when was that?"

"I think about two years ago."

Susan was glad it was dark, because she had a hard time not smiling. Her daughter was marrying a man who was a dreadful liar. She decided not to press the issue then. Identifying the dead woman was the important thing. "Let's go back to those years you lived in the commune. How much time passed before you saw David's mother again?"

"Not long after that first time. I was walking down the street alone and she approached me."

"Do you remember what she said?"

"No. Although I've wondered since then if she thought I was David—after all, she hadn't seen him since he was a baby and we're the same age and have similar coloring. I do remember that she seemed very nice—interested in what I was doing at the commune, how I liked living there. Stuff like that. Not the usual stuff, like what do you want to be when you grow up, that grown-ups always seemed to want to know back in those days. We started meeting fairly frequently after that. And then one day I ran into her when David was with me."

"You hadn't told him you were seeing his mother?"

"I hadn't told anyone. I knew I wasn't supposed to like her, but I didn't know why exactly." He shrugged. "So I just kept it a secret."

"So what happened when David met her?"

"That's when the fun began," Stephen said warmly. "She became something of a fairy godmother—she broke all the commune rules. David was allowed to call her Mother and I called her Aunt Ginny—in the commune we were supposed to be all one family, so no one was singled out like that."

"So you didn't live in family groups?"

"We did, actually. My parents and I had a small suite of two rooms with an attached bath. Wendy's and David's families had the same arrangements."

"So you saw David's mother a lot?"

"Probably twice a month for a few months."

"And then what happened?"

"And then she disappeared."

"You haven't seen her since you were a kid?"

"Not until today . . ."

"And David?"

"I . . . I don't know."

"But David is here now. You can ask him yourself." A dark figure sagged against the car's windshield.

"David. Man . . ." Stephen jumped out of the car and put an arm around his friend's shoulders.

"I really am drunk this time, Steve. But I have a good reason. My mother's dead. Ginny's dead." And the young man leaned across the car hood and began sobbing loudly.

Susan jumped out, anxious to do anything she could to comfort the young man. "Can I help?"

"Don't worry. He'll be fine. He's already thrown up twice." Kathleen appeared from the shadows.

"I should get him to bed," Stephen said.

"Wait. We need to know where—" Susan stopped. "How do you know your mother is dead?"

"His mother." David waved a shaky finger at Stephen.

"What does my mother have to do with it?"

"She told me. She told me my mother was dead."

TWENTY-FOUR

"How does she know?"

Susan knew Stephen regretted the question the minute it was out of his mouth.

"You mean you knew?" Apparently David wasn't too drunk to realize what Stephen had just said. "Your mother told you before telling me?"

"Well . . ." Susan understood Stephen's reluctance to tell his friend any more. The fact of her death obviously was more than enough for this young man to deal with right now.

David's shoulders drooped. "It doesn't matter. Nothing matters. My mother's dead. And the last words I ever said to her were angry ones." He swayed and began to sob.

"Maybe you should go to bed?" Stephen suggested, grabbing his friend's arm.

Kathleen was doing the same thing to Susan. "She's his mother? The murdered woman is his mother?" she whispered in Susan's ear.

"Maybe we should all go inside—now," Susan said loudly. She didn't think this was the way David should find out that his mother had been murdered.

"Good idea," Kathleen agreed enthusiastically. "I have more than a few things to tell you," she added in an undertone.

"Okay . . . Is that someone yelling?" Susan asked, realizing that the sounds she had been hearing in the distance were voices.

"It's more than someone yelling. That commune may have had a political base, but it was filled with party animals. Poor Charles is having quite an evening," Kathleen explained.

"You're kidding!"

"Come on in and see."

Susan looked over her shoulder at the two young men heading for the Inn's main entrance. "What about them?"

"They'll be fine. I don't think David is capable of doing much more than passing out on his bed."

Well, probably lots of weddings had a best man who was nursing a hangover. Susan followed Kathleen along the sidewalk toward the back of the Inn where the restaurant was located. The noise increased as they got closer. The music and the voices reminded Susan of *Laugh-In* reruns. Then she opened the door.

She was still napping. This couldn't be real. She closed her eyes and opened them again. It was real.

Or possibly a hallucination?

Maybe she had unknowingly taken something in the Sixties and was only now waking up to reality? Perhaps her entire life with Jed and the kids had been a hallucination and this was just the grand finale?

"Susan? Are you okay?" Kathleen put a hand on her arm.

"Just a little tired, I guess. I thought for a second . . ." But she decided there was no reason to sound like she was in the middle of a breakdown—even to her best friend. "How long has this been going on?" The two women stood and stared at the scene. It was the "don't trust anyone over thirty" nightmare—they were older and they were more foolish than their parents' generation had been. Earlier in the evening, the elegant dining room had been filled with flowers and candles—a tribute to the daughter of the woman who had kept the owner of the Inn out of jail for murder, Susan knew—and now it was filled with over-aged hippies doing what had once been called "getting down and partying."

"That's exactly what I asked Charles," Kathleen answered. "He said they all went upstairs after you and Jed left, but in just a few minutes couples started drifting back into the bar and they'd just been getting rowdier and louder ever since—remember, most of them have flown in from the West Coast, and in California it isn't all that late."

"Good point." Susan thought for a moment. "So they haven't been together in this room since dinner?" she asked, realizing that the information might be important. After all, someone had moved the dead woman—whose name, she realized, she still didn't know.

"I sure doubt it. With all the drinking going on, I suspect each person must have made at least a few trips to the rest room, if nothing else."

"They were probably alone, too."

"If you're trying to keep track of everyone, it's not going to work," Kathleen said. "I think—"

"I don't believe it!" Susan interrupted. "How long have *they* been here?"

"Claire and her boyfriend?" Kathleen asked, glancing at a table by the window where Susan's mother-in-law was laughing and drinking as though she were twenty-one and it was early in the evening.

"No, them!" Susan pointed to her parents. Her mother was giggling at something Freedom was saying and moving just a bit closer. Susan wondered if she was aware of the man's sexual preference. Her father was leaning toward the redheaded woman (Susan had to think for a moment before she remembered the name Havana Rose) who was strumming a guitar, her long hair fanned out over her shoulders. Havana Rose may have been well over thirty, but she was a fabulously exotic-looking woman.

"Your parents? I think they've been here ever since the rehearsal dinner. They're having a wonderful time."

Susan just shook her head. "Do you think everyone at the wedding tomorrow is going to be suffering from a hangover?"

"I'm sure your parents will be fine. Where are you going?"

"I need to talk with Claire for a moment." She knew Stephen was going to need her to back up his story about the ring—or rings.

Kathleen grabbed her arm. "Susan, you don't exactly look festive. Why don't I ask Claire to come over here and talk to you."

Susan, who had been unaware, until now, of the dirt that had attached itself to her during the evening's travels, agreed readily. "Fine. Tell her it's important and that I don't want anyone else to know I'm here," she added, glancing over at her parents. She knew it was stupid, but she had a feeling they would send her off to change her clothing if they saw her like this. She moved back into the shadows at the edge of the room.

But she didn't move quickly enough, and the group was in one of those mellow, jovial moods where a newcomer is always welcome.

"Hey, look, everyone, the mother of the bride is here!"

She was swept into the party, and if anyone noticed her filthy black attire, they were too polite to comment. A chair was pulled up to the largest table for her and a glass of champagne placed in her hand. She found herself between Freedom and Hubris—the gay theater owners. They were, she realized immediately, reminiscing about their own wedding.

"We got the most incredible gifts—maybe it was because gay men back in those days seemed to be thought of as a group: domestic, artistic. We got handwoven dish towels, I remember. And the most remarkable Chinese teapot with small cups made from dark brown clay. A Waring blender—still going strong making margaritas and daiquiris in the summertime! And my favorite gift was the cookbook by a Spanish poet—it was written entirely in verse . . ." Freedom said. Susan's mother looked startled by his revelations, and muttering something about it being late, moved off to join her husband.

"Hey, my best recipe for cioppino comes from that book," Hubris cried. "Did you ever think we'd be making the same recipe, only on the opposite coast, almost twenty years later?" The men exchanged fond looks.

"You were . . . uh, married . . . when you were at the commune?" Susan asked, unsure of the terminology.

"Yes, by the Archangel," Freedom replied.

"We actually met at the commune. We had both joined for different reasons. I was feeling guilty about getting out of the draft for what were then called psychological reasons—not that I wanted to end up a combat soldier in Vietnam, but I did think that my sexual preference shouldn't mean that I wasn't contributing to the antiwar movement in some sort of significant way," Hubris said. "The commune's ideology and emphasis on action were exactly what I was looking for."

"And I just sort of wandered in, not knowing what to do with my life after every agent, director, and producer in L.A. had told me I didn't have what it took to be a movie star," Freedom explained. "What they meant was that I wasn't macho enough, of course."

"And we met and fell in love," Hubris said simply.

"Well, it wasn't quite that simple. First we had to come out to each other and then to the rest of the commune—and we sure weren't sure of their reactions, I can tell you," Freedom said.

"But the Archangel was wonderful then, do you remember?" Hubris asked his companion. "She saw exactly what was going on between us and offered to marry us—something fairly unusual back in those days."

"Although, remember, there was already a gay church in San Francisco, and people were just beginning to talk about ceremonies to celebrate permanent relationships—even that far back," Freedom reminded him.

"But you must have appreciated the Archangel's offer," Susan said.

"Yes, we did," Hubris said.

"And we still do," Freedom added with a smile. "But I've often thought it was interesting that the Archangel, who was and is so liberal, encouraged us to consider a step as traditional as marriage. Even our service was pretty traditional—especially by Sixties' standards. We eliminated things like who gives this woman to be wed, but, other than the fact that all the references to husband and wife were changed to life partner, it was the service most of us had grown up with."

"Did Chrissy and Stephen write their own vows?" Hubris asked.

"No, they've opted for the traditional service also," Susan answered.

"I think that's nice," Hubris said. "There is something wonderful about joining the long line of couples who have been making the same promises to each other for hundreds of years. It adds something."

"You know, I agree," Susan said, and then asked, "Were all the services at the commune traditional?"

"No way. At least, a few of the services the Archangel performed were way out even for those days, remember!"

"You mean Dot and Brad or Wind Song and High Hopes?" Freedom asked, grinning.

"Well, Wind Song and High Hopes had a pretty typical hippie service. They wrote their own vows and walked down the aisle to Grateful Dead music—except that, of course, there wasn't an aisle since they got married on the top of Mount Tamalpais—they kind of skipped across the grass, as I recall. And everyone was barefoot, of course. And the women all wore granny dresses and ribbons in their long hair. . . ."

"And the men wore bell-bottoms and streamers in their long hair, too, if I remember correctly," Freedom reminisced. "And we had a picnic afterwards. That may have been the first time I baked bread. Dozens of loaves all shaped like wreaths. They were a little dry. . . ."

"But they looked beautiful," Hubris insisted. "When you think about it, it wasn't very odd that they would choose to have that type of service—they were almost the definitive hippies—why else would they have talked their parents into letting us all live in their building?"

"Because it was such a slum in those days that no one else would have even considered living there," Freedom reminded him.

"Yeah, that's true. And we did improve it. When the commune closed, no one would ever have had any idea what a wreck the place was when we moved in."

"Were there any other weddings at the commune?" Susan asked. "You said something about . . . about . . . the couple with the normal names. I can't believe I can't remember their names."

"They are less than memorable names," Freedom said.

"They are less than memorable people," Hubris agreed, and then supplied their names. "Dot and Brad Morris. They were Peace and Love at the commune. Now they're dull suburbanites—then they were unimaginative hippies—at least, when it came to choosing their names."

"But you sure couldn't say that about their wedding," Freedom argued. "That was far out—as we used to say."

Susan was exhausted, but the tale Freedom and Hubris told about the Morrises' wedding was one that would keep almost anyone awake. Apparently the Archangel and the couple conceived of combining a wedding ceremony with street theater. The results were amazing, starting with a "no chauvinist pigs allowed" bachelorette party for the women, continuing on to a "celebration of twoness" on the beach near the Golden Gate Bridge, and ending with a naked love/be-in at the entrance to the Presidio, the army's residence in San Francisco. The bride, groom, and everyone else in the commune spent the first night of the marriage in jail.

At the end of the tale, Susan realized they had been joined by her mother-in-law. Claire was standing behind Freedom, a glass of wine in her hand and a smile on her face. If she noticed Susan's appearance, she didn't seem to feel that a comment was necessary. "Kathleen says you need my help," she said immediately.

"Did you bring the ring you offered to Stephen and Chrissy?" Susan was equally abrupt.

"Yes. I know the kids refused, but I thought they might change their minds—it's a beautiful ring."

"I'm so glad you brought it."

"Why? Why have they changed their minds?" Claire was suddenly suspicious. "Don't tell me something is wrong with the ring they had made—Chrissy described it to me—she was so enthusiastic."

"It's lost," Susan lied. "Where is your ring?"

"In the Inn's safe. Do you think I should go get it? I could give it to Stephen tonight if he's still up."

"No, it's safe where it is. Let's just leave it there until morning." She looked back at the room. "It looks like everyone is having a good time."

"Fabulous. You've sure learned how to give a great party."

Susan was as aware of the fact that this party had nothing to do with her planning as her mother-in-law was, but she graciously accepted the compliment, deserved or not.

"You look like you should be home in bed," Claire suggested.

"I know. There are just a few last-minute details to clear up and then I'll be able to leave."

"Well, I have to hand it to you. Everything is going fabulously well."

"Thanks," Susan said. If only you knew, is what she thought. "I'd better get going."

"What time do you expect us in the morning?" Claire asked.

"Anytime after eight-thirty," Susan answered. She resisted looking down at her watch. No matter how few hours it was until that time, she had things to do. She ran a hand through her messy hair.

"Are you two finished?" Kathleen asked, rejoining them.

"We sure are. Good night, Claire."

"See you in the morning, dear." Claire leaned over and kissed Susan's cheek. "And try to get some sleep tonight."

"I will," she answered, hoping it wasn't a lie.

"Shall we go?" Kathleen asked.

"Yes. How about a ride back to the Yacht Club? I left my car there."

"No problem. And you can tell me more about Stephen on the way."

"Yes. He's really been wonderful about all this," Susan said.

"Susan . . ." Kathleen opened the door for her friend and followed her out into the night.

"What?"

"Look, Stephen is going to marry Chrissy. I understand that you might be in a difficult position here . . ." Kathleen stopped again.

"I know what you don't want to say. That Stephen might be lying. That he might have more to do with David's mother's body disappearing than he's willing to admit."

"You know it could be true."

"Yes. That's why I have to find out who the murderer is before the ceremony tomorrow. And Stephen brought that up himself— that proves something, doesn't it?"

Kathleen paused to unlock her car door. "I suppose so, but . . ." She stopped, leaning across the seats to open the door on the passenger's side.

"If you're going to ask me what I'm going to do if I discover that Stephen had something to do with the murder, don't. Because it's not going to happen. Period."

Kathleen started her car and smiled. "I'm glad you feel so confident about him."

Susan only wished it were true. She leaned back in her seat and closed her eyes. Surprisingly enough, she wasn't tired. Her heart was racing and her brain seemed to be processing information fast and efficiently. First, she would check out things at the Yacht Club. Or had she better pick up her car and return to the Inn and spend more time with Rhythm and Blues? And had anyone at home taken those damn puppies for a walk?

Her next thought was that someone was punching her shoulder rather roughly. "Wha—?"

"Susan, wake up. We're at the Yacht Club. Listen, maybe you'd rather I drive you home and you can send someone to pick up your car in the morning. You probably shouldn't drive if you're this tired."

Susan sat up so straight that she bopped her head on the roof of the sports car. "Ow! No. No, I'm okay. It's a short drive to my house. I won't have any trouble making it. You've done more than enough tonight. You'd better get home to bed, too. Or has Alex outgrown getting up at the crack of dawn?"

"The day he started sleeping late, Alice decided to become a morning person," Kathleen said. "Jerry says we can't win."

"It doesn't get easier as they get older," Susan muttered, and then perked up. "On the other hand, for teenagers, sleeping until noon is the norm."

"Well, at least we have that to look forward to. You're sure . . . ?"

"I'm going to be fine," Susan said, not giving Kathleen time to finish her sentence. "And, if I have any problems, I can always call home."

"Then I guess I'll see you in the morning. And be sure to call me if you need anything else—even before daylight."

"I will." Susan got out of the car and, slamming the door behind her, marched over to her Jeep. She had things to do. And the first thing was to plug her phone into the battery in her car and call Jed. He could check on the puppies—and clean up whatever they had done on the kitchen floor while he was at it. She plugged in her phone and dialed, while wondering how much time she'd have to straighten up the kitchen before her guests arrived tomorrow. Perhaps she should put in an early-morning call to her mother at the Inn—even if she had to listen to comments on how disorganized she was—surely her mother would come to the rescue and help arrange things before the rest of the family appeared. Wouldn't she? Susan wondered, listening to the familiar ring. Why wasn't Jed answering? Where could he possibly be at this time of the night?

"Susan?"

"Jed? Jed, you sound strange . . . Where are you?" Susan shook the receiver. How did the phone manage to make her husband's voice sound as though it were coming from behind?

"Right behind you."

Susan whirled around and almost fell into her husband's arms. "What are you doing here? What's wrong?"

"The puppies escaped."

"They what? Where did they go?"

"Well, the last time we saw them, they were running down the road in this direction."

"Who's we?"

Her husband seemed to understand her question. "Chad and me."

"Chad's running around out here, too?"

"Yeah, he got out of the car and has been running—cutting

through yards and such. The puppies haven't been sticking to the street, as you can guess."

"Running around in the dark? Isn't that dangerous?"

"Not really. The only other people around now are the police. They're really patrolling a lot tonight."

"Do you think they know about the body?" Susan asked quietly, looking over her shoulder, afraid of being overheard by her son.

"I have no idea. There was some problem at the church. Someone or something apparently tripped the burglar alarm, but by the time the police got there, whoever or whatever had done it was gone. At least, they were by the time we got there."

"So you were at the church, too?"

"We actually caught up with one of the dogs in the parking lot there. We both got out of the car and I thought we had it cornered, but then I tripped and fell over one of those concrete things in the middle of the lot and he—or she—took off again. I haven't seen either dog since then, but I caught up with Chad a few blocks away and he said they were back together again, and heading in this direction. He thought he knew a shortcut to the water and took off."

"But you haven't seen them yet?"

"Nope. And I'm thinking of giving up and going home to bed. But the most important thing is, have you found out who killed the woman?"

"No, but I know who she is," Susan replied. "David's mother."

"And David is?"

"The best man, Jed!"

"The young man who is drunk all the time? It's his mother who was killed?"

"Yes. But the bad news is that she's lost again."

"You're kidding. Who lost her?"

"Well, actually, I think Stephen may have. I'm a little confused by all this," Susan admitted reluctantly.

"He did? Well, that's sort of two strikes against him, isn't it?"

"Two strikes? What do you mean?"

"Well, he also lied today about Chrissy never being late. That had to mean something, didn't it?"

It was going to be a long night.

TWENTY-FIVE

"At the rehearsal," Susan said slowly. "I'd forgotten. I thought it was a little strange, too—but doesn't that just mean he doesn't know Chrissy very well?" she added, searching for a logical explanation.

"Susan, how long have Chrissy and Stephen known each other?"

"They met around Thanksgiving their freshman year of college," Susan said, remembering the first time she'd heard about the young man.

"And how long has it been since they started to date seriously?"

"Since the spring of Chrissy's junior year."

"And how long have they been engaged?"

"Since St. Patrick's Da—Jed, you know all this. Why are you asking me these questions?"

"Just answer one more question for me. How long do you think Stephen had known Chrissy before she was late the first time?"

"And how many times has she been late since then? I get the idea, Jed."

"So he was lying. And why would he lie about that if not to protect himself from something?"

"I have no idea. Absolutely none." And she certainly wished it wasn't so.

"So where do we go from here?"

"Huh?"

"You've got all the experience when it comes to looking for the murderer," Jed reminded his wife. "I figured you might have some idea what we should do next."

Susan frowned. "I was thinking of going over to the church."

"Because the alarm went off earlier tonight?"

"That, too."

"What else?"

"I don't know, Jed. I just have a feeling that there's something going on there." She hated to admit to her husband how often she followed her hunches—and how often they were wrong. But right now she was thinking about Erika's worries.

"So we go over to the church."

"Maybe . . ." she started hesitantly. "Maybe we should split up."

"What do you want me to do?"

"I don't know. The dogs need to be found, and I was thinking that maybe someone should go to the Inn and see how David and Stephen are doing, and then there's the . . ."

"Why don't I help Chad round up the dogs and then head over to the Inn? Although everyone there will probably be asleep by then."

Susan didn't argue. It had looked to her as though the party was going to continue all night. On the other hand, those people were her age. They were bound to wear out sooner or later. She was certainly beginning to feel a desperate need for sleep. "You should get some sleep yourself tonight," she reminded him.

"I will. And you?"

"I will, too." She paused. "I guess I'd better get going." Suddenly she felt sad. This wasn't the way she had planned to be spending the night before her only daughter's wedding. She had things to say to Chrissy. Important things. The fact that she couldn't remember a single one of them at this moment only meant she was tired and not that Chrissy wouldn't have benefited from her wisdom.

"Susan? I'd better get going if I'm going to catch up with Chad and those dogs," her husband suggested.

"Okay. Let's get going. Take care of yourself, Jed."

"You, too."

And they parted. Susan scrounged around in her purse for the keys to her car, surprised to find them almost immediately. Maybe her luck was changing. Maybe she'd find the murderer. It would be a stranger who had just happened to wander through town—someone with no relationship to anyone involved in the wedding. The wedding dress would be found. The wedding would go off without a hitch. . . . She stopped and shook her head. Sure, and she'd lose ten pounds before tomorrow morning and grow naturally curly blond hair. She unlocked her car and climbed in. Time to stop fantasizing. She still had some things to do before going home.

The drive to the church was short and, within minutes, Susan was pulling into the church parking lot. Her Jeep stood alone. She smiled. Nothing here . . .

If only she hadn't noticed the light. Then she could have gone home, gotten some sleep, and tackled this problem in the morning.

But someone was walking around inside the church with a high-powered flashlight. Walking around in the decorated church where Chrissy would be getting married in a little more than twelve hours. Doing heaven knew what . . .

Susan ran toward the door.

She was in such a hurry that she didn't register any surprise in finding it unlocked until she was through it and running down the long, dark hallway toward the narthex. Doors on either side led to unlit rooms used by the choirs and for Sunday school. Two of the rooms had been reserved for use by Chrissy and her wedding party before the service. Susan noticed wreaths of creamy dogwood blossoms hanging on them as she passed.

Large swinging doors stood at the end of the hallway and she pushed against them, almost falling into the narthex. Here the carpeting was replaced by polished marble and she slowed down as she heard the squeak of her shoes on the hard surface. She wanted to surprise whoever was there.

Or did she? She stopped and considered for a moment, her hand on the door to the sanctuary. What she actually wanted, she decided, was that she not be the person to be surprised. With that in mind, she opened the door slightly and peeked through the crack.

Into darkness. Whoever had been waving around the flashlight had either turned it off or had left the church. Squinting into the gloom, she edged through the door.

The scent of spring flowers freshened the air as Susan crept slowly down the long banner of silk that lined the aisle. As far as she could see, nothing had been touched. If only she hadn't left Jed's large flashlight in the car . . . Wait, maybe she did have a flashlight. Claire had given her a tiny one for Christmas. If only she could find it in her purse . . .

If only she hadn't dumped everything on the floor.

"Who's there?"

"It's me." The response was automatic. "Susan Henshaw. Who are you?"

"You're Chrissy's mother, aren't you? You're the mother of the bride. In a way, the mother of us all."

Susan didn't have to pick up the pile of things that had fallen from her purse and find her flashlight to realize that the speaker was the woman everyone called the Archangel. "Uh, yes. I'm Chrissy's mother." Susan realized this conversation was becoming redundant, but what else could she say? "Hi, Archangel" was more than a little strange, too.

"I am so glad you're here. We have a lot to say to each other, don't we?"

"We do?"

"I think so. You're here for help in easing the transition. I understand such things."

"What transition?"

"We shouldn't deny the pain. It will only go away if it is acknowledged and dealt with."

"What pain?" Beside talking riddles in the middle of the night, Susan thought, but was much too polite to add.

"Common. Common. So common. Even those prurient talk-show hosts don't bother with it anymore. Empty nest. What you are left with after the little birds have flown out into the world. A small, confining circle made of scratchy sticks. Your empty nest. What will happen to your life now that your daughter is plighting her troth to someone else?"

Susan took the time to wonder exactly what a "troth" was and how exactly one went about "plighting" it before she asked another question. The one she should have asked first of all—one more relevant and immediate than what she was or wasn't going to do in the future. "What are you doing here in the middle of the night?"

"Worshipping."

Well, in a church . . . She should have known.

"Not like you are thinking. Not with my hands folded in my

lap, trying to point my thoughts to some supreme being hiding somewhere up in the corner over the organ pipes."

Susan, remembering that, if all went as planned, this woman was going to be one of the ministers officiating at her daughter's wedding tomorrow, smiled weakly—a gesture that was probably wasted in the darkness. "Everyone worships in their own way," she muttered.

"You are acting strangely. You're worried about the wedding."

Susan wondered if this woman ever asked a question. "Yes, of course." She also wondered why this woman made her feel so stupid. Who wasn't worried the night before they gave an event to which every single one of their friends was invited? Under the circumstances, even Martha Stewart would feel a flutter of nervousness—wouldn't she?

"You should worry. There is danger."

Susan resisted a strong urge to look over her shoulder (or perhaps up at the spot in the corner where the organ pipes met the ceiling). "Here? In the church?"

"There is evil."

"In the church?"

"There is also good."

"Well, that's nice to know, but—"

"We must bond. We must gain power from our bond. We will prevail."

"Of course . . ." She didn't want to be inhospitable, but this was getting to be a bit much.

"We will prevail against the forces of evil."

"Could you be more specific about that? Exactly which forces of evil are we talking about?" The way the Archangel ranted on, Susan was beginning to wonder if she knew about the dead woman. Her next words seemed to confirm that impression.

"Death. There is death about."

"Do you know who's dead?" Well, she might as well try to get something concrete out of this weird conversation.

"Who said anything about a dead person?"

"I . . . you. I thought you said something about a dead person," Susan floundered.

"I said there was death about. There is always death about," the Archangel insisted, becoming rather prosaic. "I said nothing about a dead person."

"Well, I suppose . . . Does anyone call you anything besides Archangel? I mean, what do people call you when they're not using your commune name?"

"Everyone calls me the Archangel. I'm not like the rest of the members of our little group. I did not give up my ideals when I returned to the real world. I have carried my principles along with me. I have never forgotten my ideals."

"I . . . do you mind if I sit down next to you?"

"Of course not. We will bond. We must bond."

Susan didn't feel up to arguing. "Fine. What you said was interesting. You feel that everyone else in the group has given up their principles?"

"Compromise is the devil's name. Of course, I'm speaking metaphorically. There is no devil. It's an outdated concept. Invented to keep people in their places before mankind found grace. You understand."

"Yes, definitely." She didn't at all, actually, and only hoped being struck down by God for lying in church was also an outdated concept. "So you don't approve of what the rest of the commune members have done with their lives?" If at first they don't answer, ask, ask again.

"I would not say that. These people once came to me for spiritual instruction. They wanted guidance and I, of course, offered it to the best of my abilities. But they became lost in the wilderness. They abandoned their values. They prostituted their gifts. To put it bluntly and in terms they once would have understood, they sold out."

"Then . . ."

"Which is not to offer my approval or disapproval. That wouldn't be appropriate. I no longer hold the same position with these people, you know."

"Everyone was thrilled with your arrival." Susan got the feeling that she was supposed to protest the Archangel's claims of low self-worth.

"Yes, I suppose I do hold a place in the hearts of these people. At one time, of course, we thought we were a family, a very close family."

"Even close families have their problems," Susan suggested, hoping to hear about some of them in the commune. "And your group was made up of families within families, wasn't it?"

"What exactly do you mean?" The Archangel's voice became a bit cool, Susan thought.

"Well, there were legal families at the commune—people who were married and had children—as well as all of you trying together to be a family, if you know what I mean."

"I know exactly what you mean and you are completely, utterly wrong!" And with those surprising words, the Archangel drew herself up to her full height and swept up the aisle and out of the church.

Susan, startled into inaction for only a moment, gathered up her purse and ran after her.

Maybe the woman was more than a spiritual advisor. Maybe she was a spirit. She certainly seemed to have the ability to vanish into the night. When Susan got back to the parking lot, there was no one—and nothing—there, other than her own car. It was time, she decided, to go home.

Susan realized almost immediately that she was too tired to do anything more complicated than steer her car down the street. She yawned all the way home. And as she parked her car in the garage. And as she walked in the house, past the pile of boxes (contents unknown) on the kitchen table, through the hallway (more boxes on the side table and floor), and up the stairs to the bedroom she and Jed shared.

Clue was taking advantage of the unusual late-night activity to sleep on Susan and Jed's bed. Since the dog was on Jed's side, Susan didn't bother to object. She pulled off her clothes, put on a nightgown, set the alarm to go off in three and a half hours, crawled into bed beside the snoring dog, and fell into a deep sleep.

TWENTY-SIX

SUSAN WOKE UP WITH A START, ACUTELY AWARE OF THE FACT that it was Chrissy's wedding day. She tried not to remember the image she'd been carrying of this day: the understated elegance, the calm, the celebration. Even her wildest nightmares hadn't come up with a murdered woman and a lost wedding gown, to say nothing of those damn puppies. She rolled over in bed to consult with her husband.

Only Clue was there, still snoring gently (or as gently as a golden retriever can snore). Susan sat up. Jed, still in his clothing, was asleep, crumpled up on the small love seat in the corner of the room. He'd found the puppies. They were lying on the floor, apparently as exhausted as he after their midnight-and-beyond run.

Susan glanced at the clock radio. It was almost six o'clock. Maybe a nice hot shower would wake her up. Certainly, she decided, passing a mirror, it couldn't help but improve her appearance.

Susan had always believed she did some of her best thinking while bathing. But today the invigorating spray was merely cleansing. There was, quite simply, too much to do, too much to worry about. She must get organized. But how? And in what order? Did she worry about feeding breakfast to the unknown number of guests who would start arriving at her door in two hours before figuring out how to talk to David about his mother? Should she tell her daughter that the wedding gown was still missing? Should she take the time to blow-dry her hair just in case this was her last moment of peace and quiet all day long? These were just some of the questions jamming her mind as she toweled off and dried her hair.

Clue, as usual, made the decision for her owner. The golden

retriever, whose eyes were capable of melting the strongest human being, stood in the middle of the bedside rug, a bright red leash hanging from her mouth, tail wagging expectantly.

"Okay, Clue. First we walk. Maybe the fresh air will clear my mind." Susan pulled on an old pair of sweatpants, a T-shirt, and sneakers and followed the dog's swaying hips down the stairs and out the door. As she passed through the hallway, she wondered if the pile of presents had grown overnight.

Then the front door slammed behind her, the sun gleamed off Clue's now clean (for the wedding) golden coat, the scent of late lilacs filled her lungs, and she realized it was going to be a beautiful, golden day—just what she had always dreamed of for Chrissy's wedding.

She smiled and followed her dog to the sidewalk.

Clue was the Henshaws' first dog, bought after years of envying neighbors running beside their animals as the sun crept over the horizon. But Clue just wasn't a marathoner; the sprint was the event in which the dog excelled, dashing from one interesting smell to another, but demanding long examination periods before starting off again. Anyone walking this dog had lots of time to think.

So Susan thought. She thought about brunch and decided she could rely on Kathleen to bring enough food and on her mother to find fault with whatever was brought. She thought about the wedding dress she hadn't even seen and decided she could rely on Chrissy's taste and determination to insure its appearance at the proper time, as well as its undoubted appeal. She thought about the bull mastiff puppies and wondered briefly where they were going to stay while Chrissy and Stephen were on their honeymoon in Bermuda. But that led on to thoughts of Stephen and his strange family, and then to David's murdered mother and how little time she had to make sure her daughter wasn't marrying into a family of murderers. Or a family containing one murderer, she corrected herself.

The place to start, she decided as Clue finally did what they had left the house for her to do, was with David. True, she didn't want to begin Chrissy's wedding day by announcing to the young man that his mother had been murdered, but she just didn't see that she had another choice. She tugged on Clue's leash and they headed back to the house.

Her purse was up in her bedroom, and she smiled as she saw that Jed had awakened long enough to get into bed. The smile faded when she realized that the puppies had followed him. There was a long string of drool being exuded by one of the animals onto her pillow. She grabbed her purse and, wincing from pain as she swung it over her shoulder, left the room. A wet pillow was the least of her problems.

After making sure Clue had fresh water and after leaving a note (she was tempted to address it "to whom it may concern") on top of the coffeepot so the first person to wake up, at least, would know where she had gone, she got into her car and drove to the Inn.

Chrissy's wedding guests had booked the Inn solid and, even this early in the morning, workers were bustling around getting ready for what was bound to be a busy day. Susan wandered into the bar, hoping to find Charles. The owner was, she thought, more likely to tell her David's room number than any of his staff. Instead of Charles, she discovered the young man she had been looking for.

David was sitting at a corner table, grasping a large cup of coffee with both hands. Susan hoped he wasn't so hungover that he couldn't comprehend what she had to tell him. She approached slowly. To her surprise, he glanced up at her and smiled.

"Hi. Want some coffee? There's a pot behind the bar and no one seems to mind if I help myself," he offered cheerfully.

"I . . . uh . . . well, sure. Thank you," she added, remembering her manners.

"Milk? Cream? Sugar? I can get you anything. This place is amazingly well equipped."

"I know," Susan said, sitting down at the table where he had been sitting. "Black, please."

"There's coffee cake and doughnuts, too."

"No thanks." She was hungry, but didn't think she should tell him with her mouth full that his mother had been killed.

"It's good." David sat back in his chair and took a huge bite from the food on the plate before him.

Susan sipped her coffee. Oh, to be young again. No one over the age of twenty-five would be feeling as good as this young man apparently was after being so drunk the night before. Or as happy after just learning of a relative's death. She swallowed and plunged in.

"I'm really sorry about your mother . . ."

He put down the doughnut he was bringing up to his mouth and frowned. "Yeah, I appreciate that. I suppose I'm going to miss her."

"You suppose so?" Susan resisted an urge to reach out and smack this young man—what way was this to talk about your mother? All those Little League games . . . the drives to and from soccer practice, the swim team, those hockey leagues . . . the late-night trips to the library to get information for reports due on the morrow . . . carpools to Cub Scouts . . . that horrible camping trip with the sixth grade . . . the sick feeling when he came home late at night . . .

"My mother was not exactly an integral part of my life," David stated flatly.

Susan waited, but he didn't continue. So she did. "Stephen was telling me last night about your youth in the commune."

"Yeah. We spend a fair amount of time reminiscing whenever we get together, too."

"I . . . you mean you don't go to the same college?"

"We didn't even go to college on the same coast. I've spent the past four years at UC Berkeley—where I still have at least another year to go. Unlike Stephen, I didn't know what I wanted to do when I started. And every time you change your major, you add another semester—I'm registered for classes this summer, too. I'm flying back tonight. Classes start on Monday morning."

"What is your major?"

"Psychology. It's where I started and where I seem to have ended up. I was brought up around so many strange people that becoming a therapist was just too obvious to avoid, I guess."

"You mean in the commune?"

"Where else? In a state known for its kooky personalities, that commune made everyone else look normal."

"It didn't sound awful when Stephen was talking about it," Susan said.

"It wasn't. It was fun, actually. There was always something going on. Demonstrations. Rehearsals for the street theater presentations. Writing the scripts was even a blast. When everything is done by consensus, there are always lots of loud discussions. I was the type of kid who loved it all. Probably because I'd already had to adapt to so much in a short period of time," he added.

"You mean, moving into the commune with your parents?" Susan asked, assuming, in fact, that he was referring to his mother's desertion, but she didn't want to be the one to bring it up.

"That and other things. How much did Stephen tell you about my mother?" he asked suddenly.

"Not much. What about her?" Susan had the sense to ask.

"About how she left my father and then reappeared in my life a few years later—during the time we were living at the commune," he explained.

"He did mention something about it . . ." Susan intentionally left the statement vague. He certainly didn't seem terribly upset about his mother's death.

"Yeah, we were talking about it last night. My mother was like some sort of fantasy to us back then."

"What do you mean?"

"Well, she didn't exactly see eye to eye with my father and the rest of the commune family about a lot of things."

That didn't surprise Susan, since the couple had been divorced. "Like what?" she asked, sipping her coffee.

"Meat."

"What about it?"

"The commune was vegetarian. My mother used to sneak Stephen and me out for hamburgers and hot dogs. And she took us to the zoo and the circus—it was considered politically incorrect to pen up animals by most members of the commune. I know these are the things most kids take for granted, but, for us, it was a real treat—spiced up a bit because we knew we were getting away with something. In fact, Stephen and I used to worry that Wendy would crack and spill the beans to the adults in the commune and it would all come to an end. It's hard to believe we were so guilty over things as innocuous as going to the circus and eating meat."

"Wendy is the daughter of Havana Rose and Red Man?" Susan asked, trying to get all the guests sorted out.

"Yup. Our trio of redheads."

"So Wendy went along?"

"Yup. She was a year younger than Stephen and me, but we didn't dare leave her behind for fear she would tattle—you know how kids are."

"Yeah." Susan thought for a moment. "So no one knew you kids were seeing your mother?"

"No one I knew about at the time. I found out later that my stepmother was aware of what was going on."

"Really? How did you find out?"

"She told me."

"Recently?"

"A few years ago." David stopped talking and looked at her curiously. "Why are you asking me all this? Don't you have other things to do this morning?"

"Mrs. Henshaw is meeting me for breakfast this morning. Good morning, Mom." And, to Susan's great surprise, Stephen, who had just appeared at their table, leaned down and kissed her on the cheek.

David got up hastily. "I guess I should leave you two alone."

"No. We'd love some company," Stephen insisted. "Don't let me interrupt. What were you talking about so intently?"

"I was just telling Mrs. Henshaw how my mother took us to the zoo and the circus and bought us all hot dogs and stuff like that," David explained, before Susan had a chance to say anything.

"You're hearing lots about the good old days," Stephen commented, helping himself to a cup of coffee from the bar.

"Were they?" Susan couldn't help but ask.

"Were they good old days?" Stephen repeated her question slowly. "You know, I think they were. Life was simple. One thing about living in a politically active environment—you know who the enemy is."

"That wasn't so true for me," David said.

"No, I suppose with your mother and your father . . ."

"To say nothing of my stepmother," David interrupted, a rueful expression on his face.

"Your stepmother is the woman everyone calls Moonbeam?" Susan asked.

"No, my stepmother's commune name was Wind Song."

Susan resisted the urge to wonder aloud why someone would name themselves after a kind of perfume, although she supposed that Wind Song was better than Chanel No. 5 or White Shoulders—two other prominent scents from her youth. "I don't remember which woman she was," she admitted.

"The shrill one."

"David, they were all pretty shrill last night. You know how these reunions go."

"I thought this was the first reunion," Susan said, remembering a comment someone had made.

"This is the first in . . . in how long?" David paused and looked at Stephen.

"Almost a dozen years. Everyone got together two years after the commune disbanded—when the building was demolished, remember?"

"Who could forget," David answered, a wide smile on his face. "I loved every moment of it."

Stephen saw the confused expression on Susan's face. "Sorry. Of course you couldn't know what we're talking about. The commune lasted for a little more than ten years. But the building it was in wasn't demolished until two years after everyone had moved out and moved on. There was a reunion the day of the demolition. That was the last time the group was all together—until now."

"And you all watched the building you had lived in being torn down?" Susan thought it was a fairly strange way to spend a day—and maybe, despite what David said, just a bit sad.

"Yup. We had a huge picnic lunch first. Everyone contributed something. It was just like old times."

"Except that one or two people were actually eating meat," David reminded the other man.

"Yes. I remember Wendy getting a big kick out of that," Stephen said. "And then we all went over to the building and watched it implode."

"And then?" Susan asked.

"And then everyone went home and tried to pretend that the only reason they'd ever joined a commune was that they were young and foolish," David said.

"And that isn't the reason?"

"I think my parents and some others joined so they could justify some pretty nasty life choices they'd made."

"What do you mean?" Susan asked, curious.

"When I was a kid, my father claimed that my mother had left him because he had a political awakening, as though she couldn't bear living in the same house with someone with his radical convictions. She told me later that she left him because he was having an affair."

Well, Susan thought, "a political awakening" was an original way of describing falling out of love with one person and into love with another. "So you were saying that you became close to your mother while you were living in the commune. . . ."

"Not really. I mean, I thought I was close to her. But then she just up and left me and continued on with her own life."

"How awful!" Susan blurted out.

"It was, actually. Really awful. So awful that I broke down and told Red Hair about it. I wanted an adult to help me find her, you see, and I didn't know who else to ask."

"We thought about telling my parents," Stephen interrupted, "but then we decided it might become a commune matter, discussed over and over and—"

"And I wanted to keep it private," David explained. "That was the worst part of living in the commune: Every personal experience was the common property of the commune members. Every problem became what was called a concern and it was discussed over and over by the entire group. That was very hard on us children."

"Yeah," Stephen agreed. "Remember when Wendy wanted to join a Brownie troop? There were weeks and weeks of meetings about whether the group was too structured . . . or sexist . . . or I don't remember what."

"It didn't matter what," David said, chuckling. "Wendy just went ahead and joined and then there wasn't all that much anyone could do about it." He smiled warmly. "Wendy has always been a person with a mind of her own—thank God."

"Still?" Stephen asked, leaning across the table to his friend with a concerned expression on his face.

"Still," David answered.

"Wendy and David are engaged to be married, but her parents don't approve," Stephen explained.

"What business is it of her parents?" Susan asked, with the confidence of someone who was pleased with her daughter's choice.

David shrugged. "They're a little flighty, I guess—they seemed to think it was a fine idea and then, all of a sudden . . . I'm really sure I didn't do anything wrong."

Susan, wondering if the drinking had anything to do with Wendy's parents' decision, was silent, trying to make sense of everything she was learning about life in the commune and about David's mother.

TWENTY-SEVEN

Susan, OF COURSE, HAD MANY MORE QUESTIONS THAT SHE wanted to ask, and she would have if her mother hadn't appeared, demanding her attention.

"Susan! What in heaven's name are you doing here this morning? Something's wrong, isn't it? Is it Chrissy? What's happened? Has the wedding been called off?" She looked anxiously from her daughter to Stephen, a worried expression on her face.

"No, Mother. Stephen and I were just chatting." It wasn't much of an excuse but, then, it had been many years since she'd been a teenager accustomed to concealing bits and pieces of her life from her parents.

"You're just chatting? So early in the morning? On the day of Chrissy's wedding? What could you be thinking of, Susan?"

"Well, I—"

"Half the people staying in this inn are planning on going over to your house for breakfast. Shouldn't you be home setting things up?"

"I—"

"Or doing something with your hair? You know, a trim this week would have been a good idea."

"Mother, I went to a new hairdresser just yesterday—"

"You tried a new hairdresser the day before your daughter's wedding? Didn't that disaster on the night of your senior prom teach you anything?"

"Mother, I—" Susan tried to head off what she knew was coming.

"I'll never forget it! Why, the way you cried and carried on, you would have thought that man had shaved your head."

"Mother, I asked for a trim. I just wanted him to snip off the split ends."

"And he simply evened out the back."

"He scalped me! And anyway, Mother, you're talking about high school—" Susan began, becoming aware of the fact that both young men were trying hard not to grin. "Besides, I like my hair this way," she insisted, changing the subject.

"Well, if it's what you want. It is your head, after all, isn't it?"

It had been years since Susan and her mother had fought over hairstyles. For that reason, she suspected, it made her feel young—and just a little rebellious. "It is, as you say, my head," she agreed.

"God, how dreary. I hope my mother and I won't be repeating the same conversation forty years from now." Wendy, wearing crumpled linen slacks and an equally mussed shirt, appeared at their table.

"Maybe you should sit down," Stephen suggested, standing up to offer his chair to the young woman. Susan's mother aleady had seated herself in the last spot available. "You look like you had too much champagne last night."

"Too much champagne and too many margaritas. Too bad you talked me into being part of the wedding party, isn't it?"

Susan opened her mouth and then stopped, allowing Stephen to answer the question in his own way. Wendy, in fact, was acting the way she had expected David to be acting. It was obvious she was as unhappy as she was hungover.

"You're one of my oldest friends; I wouldn't have wanted to get married without you present," Stephen said, reaching across the table and putting his hand over Wendy's.

"I knew I shouldn't have come here," Wendy said. "I should have followed my instincts. Nothing good ever comes from these people getting together again. Nothing."

"Family relationships can be very difficult."

Susan and her mother spoke the same phrase at the same time.

"You can say that again," Wendy agreed.

"But can you do it simultaneously?" Stephen asked, grinning.

"Probably not twice in one morning," Susan said agreeably; she had noticed that David seemed to have dropped out of their conversation. He was looking at Wendy, an expression she didn't understand on his face.

"You three were raised together, weren't you?" Susan's mother took the conversation in exactly the direction Susan had been wishing it would go.

"Just for the years we were in the commune together," Stephen explained.

"And you've stayed friends all these years?"

"Well, pretty much. We were taught together in the commune, and then David and I were educated in the same parochial junior and senior high school."

"It was for boys only," Wendy explained. David had brought her a cup of coffee and a plate of doughnuts and she appeared to be relaxing. "I was sent to an alternative school for those years. While they were wearing jackets, rep ties, and chinos, I was in the middle of the last bastion of tie-dyed clothing outside of Grateful Dead concerts in the country."

"But we stayed friends," David pointed out.

"Probably the oddness of our early years formed a bond not many have an opportunity to appreciate," Stephen suggested, choosing a vanilla frosted doughnut from the plate and taking a taste.

Susan was interested in his choice—it was her daughter's favorite, too. "Of course, not many children ever live in a commune—"

"Most children are luckier than we were," Wendy stated flatly.

"You know, I'm not sure I'd agree with that," Stephen said.

"David would." Wendy seemed sure of her statement.

Everyone looked at David to see if this was true.

"At least that's what he's always told me," Wendy insisted.

"There are days when I think that," David admitted. "You have to agree, it was weird. I mean, most kids are taught to sing 'The Farmer in the Dell' and 'Bingo,' not 'We Shall Overcome' and 'Give Peace a Chance.'"

"True, but most kids don't live in a place where there are so many adults around who sincerely care about them and the way they're brought up," Stephen pointed out.

"Most kids don't have a whole shitload of adults looking over their shoulders and spying on them every minute of the day, is what you mean," Wendy surprised Susan by stating bluntly.

"Certainly too much attention can be almost as damaging as too little," Susan's mother said—surprising her even more. This was the honest opinion of a woman whose hovering abilities astounded all who were related to her? What would come out of her mouth next?

"I know I've tried to keep from interfering in Susan's life even when I knew my opinion was correct or my advice would lead her in a better direction."

What the . . . Susan opened her mouth to speak.

"Besides, I knew my daughter had the good sense not to listen to me anyway."

Susan snapped her mouth shut and reached for another doughnut.

"Of course, I've always believed junk food is a very poor way to get the day started." Her mother reached out and snagged the last doughnut on the plate. "On the other hand, sometimes I don't listen any better than my daughter does." She grinned and took a huge bite.

Everyone chuckled. The tension was broken, but Susan had no idea how—or if—she could return the conversation to the commune and then on to David's mother.

"Well, I guess I'd better go upstairs and . . . and do something," Wendy said, standing up.

"Yeah, I think it's time I got going, too," David said. "We've got to find that man . . . what's his name? Charles? . . . and get the ring out of hock this morning, don't we?" he reminded Stephen.

"Don't worry. I already spoke to him. Everything's taken care of. I should give Chrissy a call."

"On your wedding day?" Susan was astounded. "Isn't that bad luck?"

"I think it's only bad luck if you actually see the bride before the wedding," David suggested.

"My, you young people today certainly are conservative. Susan's father and I had breakfast together the day we got married. Of course, we'd spent the night together, so—"

"Mother! You'd what?" Susan's shriek could have awakened the dead.

"I knew that would wake her up. Well, I don't know about the rest of you, but it's almost eight o'clock and I've got things to do."

"Mother, you didn't . . . it's . . . it couldn't be that late," Susan sputtered, glancing down at her watch. She was wrong. It was later than that. She got up and headed for the door. "I've got to get going," she informed anyone who was interested, and left without waiting to hear more.

She ran toward her car, wondering if Kathleen was at her house and if she had found everything necessary to set up for company. Then she stopped running and wondered just what the Archangel was looking for in the back of her Jeep Cherokee. Maybe she'd slow down just a bit and give her a chance to find it. . . . But the woman seemed to be looking in each and every car in the lot, and Susan suddenly wondered if perhaps this was the Archangel's way of searching for the missing murder victim. She was just trying to think of something to say when the Archangel, apparently spying what she wanted, reached into the large bag she had slung over her shoulder (larger even than the one Susan carried), pulled out a long, thin piece of metal, and, sticking it in the edge of a window of the Honda station wagon she was looking into, proceeded to unlock the car, pull something out the door, and slam it shut—all in a matter of seconds.

Susan was astounded. Without thinking, she ran toward the woman.

"Why it's Susan Henshaw, isn't it? You seem to have this wedding well organized. Most mothers of the bride would be pulling out their hair over some detail or another at this point," the Archangel said pleasantly, as though she hadn't been caught breaking into a car in the Inn's parking lot.

"I . . . I . . . You took something out of that car," Susan sputtered.

"Yes, my makeup bag. I'd left it there last night." She looked carefully at Susan. "You seem upset. Is there something wrong? It *is* my makeup bag that I got out." She reached in her purse and removed a multicolored silk sack. "See? This is it."

"Oh, I guess I was just surprised." Susan took a deep breath. "You didn't use a key!"

"I guess I left it up on the dresser in my hotel room." The woman looked at Susan. "This *is* my rental car, you know. You didn't think I was breaking into someone else's car, did you? Gods in the heavens, you did! It's been years and years since anyone thought I was doing something illegal. Although back then, I probably was. Thoreau called it civil disobedience, you know."

Thoreau called breaking into a locked car civil disobedience?

Well, it had been many years since she'd read Thoreau, but she was fairly certain—

"Weren't you on your way somewhere?" The Archangel interrupted Susan's train of thought.

"Yes. I . . . In fact, yes I was," Susan said. "I . . ."

"You were going to get into your car."

"Yes, I'm needed at home," Susan insisted, as though anyone was going to dispute the fact.

"Then you'd better be on your way. May the goddesses bless you on this most auspicious of days." Instead of making the sign of the cross in the air, the Archangel waved both hands, delineating an elegant hourglass figure.

Susan just smiled weakly and headed over to the car. She was damned if she was going to worship someone with a better figure than her own.

TWENTY-EIGHT

WHAT EVERY WOMAN NEEDS MOST IN LIFE IS A GOOD FRIEND. If that good friend can find her way around your kitchen, she's a gift from heaven, Susan decided, looking at the lavish buffet spread out on the cherry sideboard in her dining room.

"Does everything look okay?" Kathleen's voice came from behind her.

"It's wonderful! How can I thank you?" Susan spun around and hugged her friend, squashing the pile in Kathleen's arms between them.

"Just promise you'll help out when Alice gets married," Kathleen said, placing the large damask napkins next to the sterling silver laid out on the table.

"Tell her to wait until she's thirty. I may be rested enough to tackle a project like this one again in about twenty-five years." She looked around the room. "Kathleen, this is fabulous. Are you the same woman who claimed to be completely undomestic when she came to town over a decade ago?"

"Let's just say that hanging around you, one learns how to put on a good party."

"Thanks for the vote of confidence. I sure hope everything goes well today."

"I'm sure it will. You're such a planner."

"But I didn't plan on a dead body, or bull mastiff puppies, or a missing wedding dress."

"Oh, Susan, the dress isn't missing anymore and it's beautiful—really the most beautiful dress I've ever seen."

Before Susan could get excited over this bit of good news, they were interrupted.

"What dead body? Mother, you haven't gone and gotten involved in another murder! Not on my wedding day!"

The bride had arrived.

And she looked dreadful. Chrissy's fabulous long blond hair was wound around more than a dozen gigantic chartreuse plastic curlers. Her face was smeared with something that looked like a mashed avocado. Her hands were encased in large cotton sleep gloves printed with dozens of idiotically happy naked cherubs. Her feet were stuck into slippers embroidered with feline faces. And she wore a large, faded black T-shirt with the words SKI YELLOW-STONE emblazoned across the chest. Instead of a bouquet, she carried a box of Kleenex (at least this was printed appropriately with a selection of delicate spring flowers, Susan noted).

"Oh, no, is your hay fever acting up?" Susan asked, noticing her daughter's red nose for the first time.

"Don't change the subject. Why were you talking about a dead body?"

"Oh, you know us. We just always talk about murder," Susan said, attempting to be gay.

It didn't work. "On my wedding day? You talk about murder on my wedding day? Mother, I cannot believe—"

"God, Chrissy, you were yelling so loud, you didn't even hear the phone." Chad appeared in the doorway. "Your fiancé is on the line. Good thing you have those tissues. You'll need them to mop up the tears. He's probably come to his senses and wants to call off the wedding."

Chrissy, apparently deciding that didn't call for a comment, swept from the room with as much dignity as her ridiculous costume allowed.

"There goes the bride," Chad commented, pilfering a succulent slice of smoked salmon from a platter.

"Since when do you eat smoked salmon?" Susan asked, astounded. In her experience, Chad and seafood simply didn't go together.

"I've been eating it for a while," he replied self-consciously. "You don't seem to realize I'm growing up. I like it. It's salty— sort of like potato chips."

So much for sophistication. "Is your father up yet?" Susan asked.

"I don't know. Someone was showering earlier, but it might have been Chrissy. Has anyone given the puppies their breakfast?"

"I don't think so. Are they in the kitchen?"

"No way. They're in Clue's pen out back—at least, I hope

they're there. Dad said he'd put them out as soon as it was light. I'm sure as sh— as hell not going to spend any more time running all over town after them."

"I certainly hope not. I know your grandmother is anxious to spend some time with you this morning," his mother said, smiling.

Chad narrowed his eyes at his mother. "Then I guess I deserve first choice of the Danish on the platter in the kitchen."

"But—"

"Go ahead and enjoy yourself," Kathleen interrupted. "He can eat all he wants. There are two full platters waiting on the pool table in the basement," she explained, as Chad bounded from the room.

"Excellent planning. You're thinking like the mother of a teenage boy. Now tell me about the wedding gown."

"Not until you tell me about the body."

"I think," Susan said, sighing, "that I need another cup of coffee."

"We both do. Why don't I bring two mugs up to your bed-room and you can dress while we try to get our allotted amount of caffeine."

Susan grinned and looked down at the clothing she'd thrown on earlier. "That bad, huh?"

"Didn't we spend an afternoon in the city about a month ago buying an outfit for you to wear this morning?"

Susan slapped herself across the forehead. "Of course, the red flower-print linen skirt and the white shirt. Where is my head? I know it's right at the top of the list I made for today."

"You included what you were going to wear on your list for Chrissy's wedding day?"

"I was afraid I'd be too busy to think—what I didn't know was that I'd be too busy to check the list," Susan admitted, hurrying from the room.

Jed was coming downstairs as she went up. She smiled. He patted her on the shoulder as they passed. So much for romance, for those tender moments she had expected when they would lie in bed as the sun rose over Hancock and exchange memories of their own wedding day . . . of Chrissy's birth . . .

"Mother. What could you possibly have to say to Stephen?" Chrissy asked.

"Stephen?" Susan repeated the name as though she'd never heard it before.

"Stephen Canfield. You remember him. We're getting married today. He didn't call to talk to me. He wants to talk to you!"

"He . . . I . . . we have a surprise for you," Susan improvised.

"Oh . . . I . . . I guess that's very nice of you, Mother. Very nice," Chrissy repeated, as she turned and wandered back toward her room.

Susan resisted reminding her daughter that there were going to be people arriving any moment now and hurried to pick up the extension in the hallway. "Hi, Stephen," she said.

"We have a problem," he announced abruptly. "I think my mother has guessed that David's mother was murdered. And I'm afraid she's going to tell David."

"And what do you think will happen then?"

"I don't know for sure. David's not real upset about his mother's death—well, you saw that. She had pretty much moved out of his life and they hadn't spoken in years, but I don't think David will keep quiet about a murder until after the ceremony."

Susan sighed. "No, I guess we can't expect him to. Isn't there some way to head off your mother?"

"I've been trying to find her. I'll keep trying. It's just possible that she's already on her way to your house for brunch. If she arrives—"

"I'll try to convince her that nothing can be gained by making this public too soon," Susan said quickly. "Stephen, I think I hear someone at my door."

"Okay. I'll let you know if I find out anything more." And he hung up.

Susan hurried into her bedroom. The outfit she planned on wearing was hanging in the closet and she yanked off her clothing, pulled on the long flowered skirt, and was adjusting the fitted white linen shirt when Kathleen arrived. "Thank goodness. Can you help me tighten the ties in the back of the shirt? And I'm going to wear the gold inlaid necklace Jed gave me for our twenty-fifth anniversary and it's almost impossible to fasten. Oh, and which shoes do you think go best? The red sandals or those light yellow strappy things? And is Stephen's mother here and does she look like she knows David's mother was murdered?"

Kathleen placed the mugs of coffee on the dresser and reached out for Susan's jewelry box. "Let me find the necklace first. And I think the shirt is tight enough—it just skims your waist and makes you look so thin. Blues isn't here. Your mother and father are and they don't look like they know anything. And wear the yellow shoes—they're adorable."

Susan beamed. The perfect friend!

"So what about David and his dead mother? Has something changed?" Kathleen asked, as she fastened the necklace around her friend's neck.

Susan explained Stephen's phone call.

"Why does he think his mother knows anything at all?"

"He didn't explain and I didn't ask him," Susan admitted. "I'm just not thinking. . . . You know, maybe Blues knows she was murdered because she murdered her herself!"

"I suppose that's as likely as anything else—but wouldn't she be quiet about it if she was the one who killed her? . . . What was that?"

Susan listened for a moment and then chuckled. "Sounds to me like the entrance of the bridesmaids."

"Do they always giggle and squeal?"

"These young women have been friends since Chrissy was in elementary school. Whenever they get together, they sound like that," Susan explained as the noise level rose.

"What do they sound like separated?"

"To be honest, I've always thought of them as a group."

"Why are they clucking like that?" Kathleen asked.

"I have no idea. That's a completely new sound. And I think it's coming from outside. Can you see anything out the window?"

"Just one of Erika's vans in the driveway."

"That must be the topiaries! Trust Erika to be right on time. Do you think we have a minute to peek at them?"

"Topiaries?"

"They're the decoration for the house. They're made of peonies—and they go on either side of the front door. Erika thought they would be a nice touch, but they had to be refrigerated overnight."

"But Erika didn't know you were going to be putting balloons on the mailbox down by the street." Erika herself appeared in the doorway of the bedroom.

"That's just so the guests can find the house," Susan explained, smiling. "A little tacky?"

"No. Practical. I should have suggested it myself. We could

have used balloons like the ones at the Yacht Club." Erika stopped and ran both hands through her dark cap of hair. "I've been thinking. I don't want to worry you right before the wedding, but I couldn't sleep last night."

"What's wrong?" Maybe no one had remembered to water the bouquets at the church. Susan had visions of wilted flowers. Or perhaps vandals had destroyed the wonderful arches outside the Yacht Club.

"Erika, tell her what's wrong before she gives herself a heart attack imagining dreadful things," Kathleen, who knew the way Susan's mind worked, insisted.

"It's probably nothing. . . ."

Or maybe she had realized that all the flowers were giving Chrissy hay fever.

"It's about the rehearsal last night," Erika continued, bursting that particular bubble of worry.

"About the flowers falling down? You said that wouldn't happen today." Susan's brain, ever agile when it came to panic, leapt from one possible disaster to the next. She was imagining the weight of the flowers bringing down the entire church balcony when Erika started to explain.

"I think the flowers were tampered with."

"They looked beautiful." Susan remembered that Brett had told her about this very thing yesterday evening.

"You mean they didn't fall accidentally?" Kathleen asked.

"Exactly." Erika nodded seriously.

"What difference does it make? What could that have to do with the murder? She was already dead at that point," Susan protested.

"What she means is—" Kathleen started, realizing that Susan had just let the cat out of the bag—and, possibly, set it off running in the direction of Brett Fortesque and police interference.

Erika raised her hands. "I don't want to know what Susan means. Because if we're talking about a real murder here and I knew about it, I would have to tell Brett, and I think I can assume that if anyone wanted the police involved in a possible murder investigation, they would call him themselves."

Susan and Kathleen exchanged looks. "Thank you," Susan said.

"Look, it wasn't so long ago that you kept me from being arrested for murder. I owe you one," Erika said. "But you should know about the flowers, just in case there is something more serious going on here."

"You really think they were meant to fall during the rehearsal?" Susan asked.

"I'm sure of it. I invented the hanging system myself: the flowers are attached to heavy nylon cording. An even heavier cord is attached to whatever the flowers are to be hung from, in this case the railing on the balcony, and then the two are clipped together at intervals. The clips are either open or closed; there's no halfway. And I had checked the clips myself. Someone had pried them open with a little Swiss Army knife that I found on the floor nearby."

"They couldn't have become accidentally unclipped?" Kathleen asked.

"No."

"If someone had just brushed them the wrong way when they were walking by? They would stay attached?" Kathleen persisted.

"Absolutely. They're designed that way. Those clips don't unclip unless someone pinches them—one finger has to be on either side of the clip. And they're tight. I've had workers who use pliers to do the job."

"That's interesting." Susan frowned.

"What do you think it means?" Kathleen asked.

"I haven't the foggiest," Susan admitted.

"I just thought you might like to know. I'll head over to the church and check out everything there before the wedding, so you won't have to worry about it happening again," Erika said.

"Well . . ." Susan stopped herself from saying anything. She didn't understand what this could possibly have to do with David's mother's death. But what other reason could there be for someone to try to disrupt the wedding?

"You know, those flowers couldn't possibly do much damage to anyone they fell on," Erika said slowly, wandering over to the window and looking out.

"That's a good point," Kathleen said.

"Yeah . . . what's wrong?" Susan asked, not understanding the expression on Erika's face.

"I was wondering why Brett is walking up your sidewalk."

TWENTY-NINE

"MAYBE HE SAW YOUR VAN OUT FRONT AND IS DROPPING IN to see you," Susan said to Erika. She sure hoped that was the truth.

"I don't think so. This wedding seems to be putting a strain on our relationship," Erika answered slowly. "I think he thinks I want to get married."

"Do you?" Kathleen asked.

"No. I had one rotten marriage. And I don't want children. Why would I want to get married?"

"Maybe because it's time you experienced a good marriage?" Susan suggested gently. She knew how badly Erika had been burned by her first husband. Being an optimist and a romantic, she had hoped Brett and Erika would decide to take the plunge and live happily ever after. But it sounded as though Erika had other ideas.

"Actually, I was hoping we could just live together," she was saying. "But every time I try to approach the topic, Brett changes the subject. I'm coming to the conclusion that we're on the verge of breaking up."

"At Chrissy's wedding?" Susan realized she sounded horrified—and that she was being more than a little self-centered.

"I sure hope not," Erika said, as the doorbell pealed. "That's probably Brett now. I could go open the door for you," she offered.

"Great. And if you see Jed, would you tell him I'll be right down?" Susan asked, looking in the mirror. When was she going to find the time to do something to her hair? she wondered. And what was she going to do with it anyway? But apparently she wasn't even going to have time to think about it now.

"Susan? Honey? Brett's down here. He'd like to talk with you a minute." Her husband's voice sounded unusually sweet.

Susan realized the house was full of relatives. "I'd better get down there."

"I'll head down, too. I hardly had time to do more than say hello to your parents yesterday," Kathleen said.

"I may need to talk with Brett alone," Susan suggested.

"Don't worry. I'll run interference if you need it."

"Thanks. I don't know what I'd do without you," Susan said sincerely.

"Just remember that if I'm not home for at least an hour before the wedding, I don't guarantee the cleanliness of the ring bearer and flower girl—and Jerry is a disaster at styling his daughter's hair."

"That's okay. Alice and I will match," Susan kidded, hurrying downstairs with Kathleen close behind.

Brett was standing in the hallway, reading the tags on yet another pile of presents—delivered, apparently, by hand. The last-minute present givers seemed to have descended. Susan paused one moment to admire a package wrapped in silver metallic paper and tied with what appeared to be dozens of brightly colored ribbons. The handwriting on the card seemed familiar.

"It's from Erika. I recognize the writing," Brett said.

And now so did Susan. She had paid enormous sums for bills made out in that elegant penmanship.

"She was just here," Brett continued.

"Where did she go?"

"I'm not sure. She opened the door and said hello, and then Jed arrived—and Erika said she had to do something . . . somewhere. She headed off in the direction of the kitchen."

"I'm serving an impromptu breakfast this morning. You're welcome to stay if you'd like," Susan offered graciously—as though Brett were here on a social call.

"I'm pretty busy, but thanks."

Susan took a deep breath. She had to ask—he'd said he was busy. "So why are you here?"

"I got a confusing message from one of my officers. Something about you running around the Yacht Club last night, with Chrissy's fiancé and her future in-laws. I just thought maybe there was something going on that I might be able to help you with?"

"No, I—"

"And then there was something about some sort of activity at the church in the middle of the night—"

"Oh, that. Have you met the woman who calls herself the

Archangel?" Susan asked, deciding to throw her out as a red herring. Let Brett spend some time trying to figure her out!

"I don't believe so. Does she have another name?"

"I guess she must, but she sure doesn't share it. All anyone ever calls her is the Archangel—I swear you can hear the uppercase letter when the old members of the commune say it."

"She was a member of the commune that everyone is talking about?"

"Yes, their spiritual leader, apparently."

"What does she have to do with the Hancock Presbyterian Church?" Brett insisted on sticking to the point.

"She was there in the middle of the night."

"She broke in?"

That stopped her for a moment. "You know, I'm not sure how she got in. I suppose Reverend Price might have given her a key. They are performing the service together today."

"This woman who calls herself the Archangel is a minister and she was in the church late last night? Is there something unusual about that?"

"Well, it was very late. And she's a little strange."

"Susan, the last wedding I went to was my cousin's. He was marrying this much younger woman. . . . Well, that doesn't matter. But the minister who officiated thought the service was an appropriate time to lecture the congregation on the sin of eating meat. The sermon lasted over an hour and then we all headed off to the reception, where the main course was prime rib. Ministers aren't necessarily the dull, tactful people of my youth anymore."

"I guess. But she is more than a little strange." Susan realized she was sounding silly. Since Brett didn't know about the murder, he couldn't understand that she was looking at everyone as a possible suspect.

"Are you concerned about her for any particular reason?" Brett looked at her curiously.

Susan hesitated. "Well, I hope she doesn't decide to bore my guests with a long sermon against seafood at the service today— we've invested heavily in shellfish for the reception this evening." She hoped she sounded casual.

Apparently not. "Susan, if there is anything going on here that I should know about—"

"You'll be the first to know," she lied to him. "Believe me."

She didn't know what she would have said next, but, fortunately, Clue appeared and threw herself at Brett, her habit in greeting the couple of dozen people whom the golden retriever currently considered the loves of her life.

"Hey, Clue. Good to see you." Brett bent down and rubbed the soft fur on the dog's upturned stomach. "There was also something about a dog or dogs in the report," he added, as though it were just coming back to him. "Did Clue take off last night?"

"Just for a short run. The Canfields—Chrissy's future in-laws— gave them a pair of bull mastiff puppies as a wedding present and they got out last night. Clue ran after them but Chad happened to see her, and they all came home together."

"So the puppies are boarding with you until the honeymoon is over?"

Susan blinked. She had been trying not to think about that. The puppies sure couldn't be packed up and put on the plane to Bermuda. Did kennels board puppies? "Well, I guess they'll have to stay somewhere." On the other hand, if Jed was right, the Henshaws were going to be in jail for obstruction of justice. She'd better get busy checking out those kennels.

"Susan, someone seems to be calling you from upstairs," Brett broke into her reverie.

"Oh, it sounds like Chrissy." Clue rolled over and, apparently deciding that there were other people in the world willing to offer attention, scrambled up the stairs. "I guess I'd better see what's going on. I'll see you at the wedding."

And she ran up the steps, hoping that the next time she saw Brett, he wasn't leading one of the wedding party off to jail in handcuffs.

"Oh, Mrs. Henshaw, we have such a problem. Chrissy, your mother is here." One of the bridesmaids, hair in curlers even larger than her daughter's, wearing holey jeans and a white T-shirt, turned and headed back to Chrissy's bedroom at Susan's appearance.

"What's wrong? What's happened?"

"Chrissy can't find the box Blues gave her."

"What? What box?"

Chrissy stood in the middle of the room, dressed in a skimpy white silk teddy, a worried expression on her face. "Oh, Mother,

Blues gave me this very special present—she said it was something very important. And I promised I'd open it as soon as I woke up this morning."

Susan and Chrissy both glanced toward the alarm clock that usually sat on the nightstand by her bed. A black bra was draped across its face, keeping the time a secret, but they were both aware of the fact that Chrissy had been up for hours, showering, doing her hair. Susan suddenly realized Chrissy was no longer topped by a bevy of curlers. In fact, her hair was wet, dripping onto her bare shoulders. "What did you do to your hair?" Susan asked.

"What's wrong with it?"

"It's wet. The last time I saw you it was full of curlers."

"I took them out and it was too fluffy. Mindy is going to do it for me."

"Maybe I could help, Mrs. Henshaw," a young woman named Mindy volunteered. She was probably qualified to do the job—the shy, stringy-haired brunette Susan remembered from Chrissy's first-grade class had been transformed into a very attractive frizzy redhead.

"Thanks. I'd appreciate that," Susan admitted.

"So would Grandma. She was down in the kitchen telling Nanny that she just didn't see how you could look so terrible on my wedding day."

Susan, familiar with family nomenclature, realized her own mother was trashing her to her mother-in-law, smiled weakly, and returned to the original subject. "Do you have any idea what was in the box Blues gave you?"

Chrissy shook her hair energetically. "None. But it may have been something that Blues wanted me to wear today."

"Like pearls," one bridesmaid breathed in an excited tone. "Did you know that Courtney Gottfried's mother-in-law sent her a string of absolutely priceless pearls to wear on her wedding day—and then demanded them back immediately after the reception! Poor Courtney had already packed them up and was planning on taking them on their honeymoon!"

"That's better than what happened to my college roommate," another bridesmaid said. "Her future mother-in-law absolutely insisted that she wear the family veil. It seems that every bride since the *Mayflower* landed had worn the damn thing and it was supposed to bring the marriage luck, so how could she refuse? Unfortunately, it was made from old, heavy lace. She had this beautiful Anna Sui gown and had to drape this hideous thing over her head and smile bravely all day long. I would have died!"

"The box wasn't more than four inches square," Chrissy said. "It couldn't possibly have held a veil."

"You're sure it was up here? You didn't leave it downstairs, did you? There are so many presents and boxes around—" Susan started.

"Mother, I remember bringing it up here! You may be going nuts running around doing heaven knows what in the middle of the night, but I'm organized. I know what I brought to my room!"

All seven bridesmaids as well as Susan looked around the messy place. Every single surface was covered with stuff. There was a moat of clothing around the bed that Chrissy had displaced last night. Susan realized something was missing. "Where are your suitcases?"

"In the guest room. I've been putting everything for Bermuda in there and—" Chrissy jumped off the bed. "That's it! I put Blues's box in there! I was afraid it would get lost in here!" She was running out of the room, all the bridesmaids following her, squealing as they went, before Susan could think of something to say. (At least something that wasn't sarcastic.)

Then, suddenly, the entire female bridal party streamed back into the bedroom, screaming loudly.

"There's a man out there with a video camera!" Chrissy shrieked, hands held over her barely covered breasts. "Mother, what have you done?"

"I haven't done anything," Susan insisted as she stamped out the door to see what was happening.

The first thing she saw was a large camera lens—stuck straight in her face.

"Who are you and what are you doing in my home?"

"Smile, mother of the bride! I'm capturing this moment for posterity!"

She was tired. She was worried. And now she was angry.

Susan kicked the cameraman in the shins. If she'd been a bit more dedicated in regard to her aerobics classes, she'd have hit what she was aiming for.

THIRTY

"LADY, WHAT THE HELL ARE YOU DOING? YOU COULD HAVE hurt me!"

"What am *I* doing?" Susan realized she was shrieking, but she didn't care. "What the hell are you doing?"

"I'm doing my job. Just doing my job."

"It's your job to scare people to death in their own homes? You . . . you're probably trespassing. In fact, you *are* trespassing this very minute!"

"Lady. Calm down. I'm not here because I want to be here, or because I ain't got no place else to go. I'm here because someone paid me to be here. To tape the wedding."

"The wedding isn't until four o'clock this afternoon."

"And before the wedding. You know, the bride and her bridesmaids giggling while they put on their makeup."

"But—"

"And after the wedding, at the reception."

"I—"

"And the bride leaving the reception with her groom. You know, the throwing of the rice and all that shit."

"What I want to know—" He opened his mouth and she waved her hand to stop him. "Don't interrupt! What I want to know is who hired you?"

"Lady, how the hell should I know? Do I look like an executive? Do I look like the type of man who would be running a company as large as U Luv Ur Pix?"

"What's the name of your company?" Susan asked.

He spelled it.

"I've never heard of them." It certainly didn't sound like a company that would be located in the part of Connecticut where the Henshaws lived.

"We're nationwide. Look in any wedding magazine. Look in any Yellow Pages. Look—"

"I get the idea. So who do I call to find out who paid for you to be here?" Susan asked. She needed to know; she didn't want to kill the wrong person.

"There's an eight hundred number. Just look it up. Not that you'll get anyone on a Sunday. Tomorrow morning's the earliest you get anyone to talk to, besides a machine."

"You're kidding . . ." She stopped. She was wasting her time. Besides, it had occurred to her that maybe this photographer was a gift from someone—possibly even the Canfields. "Look, who tells you what to photograph?"

"Hey, lady, this ain't brain surgery. I do the normal stuff, like I told you. The bridesmaids . . . the blushing bride going to the church . . . the walk down the aisle . . ."

"No way. Chrissy and I talked about this months ago. We do not want any filming in the church."

"It's taping, lady. And who the hell is Chrissy?"

That did it. "Chrissy is my daughter and the bride. And you are to listen to me . . . to every word I say."

"I—"

"Listen! You may film—or tape—all day long, but from a distance. Do you understand? I don't want to see you in my house. I don't want to see you in the church. I don't want to see you in the Yacht Club. You may fil—I know, it's videotape. You may tape everything—but from afar."

"But—"

"That's all there is to it. If you come close or get in anyone's way, I will have you arrested for trespassing! Do you understand?"

"Yeah, I—"

"So go!" Susan pointed.

He went—muttering something about mothers of the bride that Susan chose to ignore.

She leaned back against the wall, feeling energized and awake. Apparently yelling at someone was just what she had needed. And it was a good thing she'd done it already, because the next person coming down the hallway was her mother. And, much to Susan's surprise, Wendy was following her.

"Mother! Wendy! I . . . I didn't know you'd arrived already.

It's so earl—" She glanced down at her watch. "Heavens! You're right on time."

"You know I've always prided myself on my punctuality, Susan," her mother said.

Wendy merely sniffled.

"Hay fever?" Susan asked, thinking of her own daughter.

"A broken heart," her mother announced. "Wendy is in love with David. And her parents refuse to allow her to marry," she added.

"No, that's not exactly true, Mrs.—"

But Wendy would learn it was a mistake to try to speak for yourself when Susan's mother was around. "She has loved him since they were childhood sweethearts in that commune thing they were raised in."

Susan was impressed that her mother had managed to make commune into a dirty word. "Childhood sweethearts?" was all she said.

"Torn apart by their families. Very *Romeo and Juliet*," was her mother's reply.

"Oh." Susan had no idea what to say to this. After all, it didn't have to do with either the wedding or the murder—it would just have to wait. "Are either of you hungry? Have you seen the breakfast Kathleen has laid out in the dining room?"

"Susan, we're here to help this young woman, not eat."

"I . . . Actually, I could use some breakfast," Wendy said hesitantly. "At least some coffee, and maybe some granola?" She looked at her hostess with raised eyebrows.

Oh, great, she'd failed to anticipate the needs of her out-of-town guests once again. "I don't think there's granola. But I'm sure you'll find something. Smoked salmon, bagels, cream cheese with olives, muffins, Danish pastry, cheese strata?"

"Well, I suppose so," Wendy said slowly.

"Honeydew, cantaloupe, mixed berry compote with mint." Susan could see her mother was impressed with the selection even if Wendy was not.

"Maybe you would feel better if you ate a bite," she suggested to Wendy.

"I . . . I guess so. David . . . David has never liked me to be too thin." This last was accompanied by loud sniffling and, Susan thought, imminent danger of a fresh burst of tears.

"You go on down and fill a plate. I'll join you in a few minutes. I need to talk with my daughter."

"Okay. You don't think I'm going to run into my parents, do you?"

"If you do, you just keep your chin up. Young love always wins the day. And weddings are very romantic, you know. Sometimes they give people ideas. Your parents may see my granddaughter walking down that aisle and begin to think of you and David just a bit differently."

"That's true, isn't it?" Wendy seemed to brighten up at the thought and almost had a spring in her step as she started down the stairway.

Susan watched her leave and then turned to her mother. "You know—"

"We don't have time for that now," her mother interrupted. "I need to talk with you a moment."

"Mother! I hope it isn't anything pressing. I have enough on my mind today! And I don't have a second to spare. Not a second!"

"I can see that, dear. So why don't I explain what's going on while you put on your makeup?"

"I . . ."

"You were planning to wear some makeup this morning, weren't you?"

"Yes, of course. It will just take me a minute."

"Good. I thought your cheeks were just a little pink last night, dear. Maybe you have something more . . . brownish? Maybe something plummy or bronze? It would go better with your sallow coloring."

Sallow? Susan decided she'd better change the subject before she started leaving the house with a bag over her head. "Tell me about Wendy and David . . . besides the fact that she claims she's always loved him," she said, heading for her bathroom with her mother close behind.

"And he loves her, remember."

"Mother, the young man has hardly stopped drinking since he got to Hancock. He's probably not all that reliable." Susan paused, remembering how alert and helpful this same young man had been just a short while ago.

Her mother, apparently believing that Susan couldn't talk and apply eyeliner at the same time, took this opportunity to explain her concerns. "You don't know the entire story, dear," she began. "David and Wendy were not only raised together in the commune, but they remained friends when that damn thing split up—as they always do. Young idealists think they can change the world and they can't even manage their own lives—"

"Mother!" Susan grimaced. Maybe she couldn't do two things at once anymore—a large splat of midnight-brown liner was much closer to her eyebrow than it should be. She rummaged around in the medicine chest for eye-makeup remover while her mother continued rather complacently.

"And, you know, of course, that they went to college together. Berkeley. She started in English lit and then changed to something more practical—health administration or something. Some people seem to realize how ridiculous it is to major in something totally impractical like—"

"Mother!"

"I wasn't necessarily speaking about you, dear. In fact, I could have been talking about David. He seems to be a young man who had a difficult time figuring out what he wanted to do with his life. Four majors! Can you imagine? Probably the result of the uneven upbringing he had. And then he decides that he wants to be a therapist. Not even a doctor, but a regular therapist—and work in the school system. Just like a teacher."

"Mother, that's a wonderful goal! We need good teachers. In fact, this country needs good teachers more than any other profession."

"I'm not arguing with you. But you can see how it would make Wendy—and, more importantly, her parents—concerned about how he's going to make a decent living."

"Mother, one of the things about people in communes is that they don't base their lives on the acquisition of material possessions."

"Maybe some people, but according to Wendy, her parents have become serious materialists. And recently, she said, they had become very worried about David's ability to support her, and any children they might have."

"So . . ." Susan leaned closer to the mirror. A pimple? She was getting a pimple on her daughter's wedding day? What did her medicine cabinet hold that might take care of a pimple—or maybe she could search in the drawers in the kids' bathroom? There were probably a bunch of half-used tubes of Clearasil, Oxy500, and the like still hanging around from their high school years.

". . . so, of course, they refused to accept the engagement and Wendy felt she had to explain why to David."

"Wendy refused to be engaged to David because her parents didn't approve?" Why hadn't she thought of that? Then she might be spending a nice relaxing Sunday around the pool at the Field Club instead of smearing the eye shadow she'd just applied.

"No, she just told him her parents didn't approve, and he told her they should wait to get married until they had convinced her family it was a good thing."

"You're kidding!" That certainly didn't sound like David. He didn't seem like a young man who would let others make his decisions for him.

"I'm not kidding. She said, one day he was enthusiastic about getting married and then, almost overnight, he changed his mind. And Wendy's been heartbroken ever since."

"Well, maybe the wedding will make him feel romantic. Or maybe her parents will see how happy Chrissy and Stephen are and change their minds about what's important. What do you think?"

"Well, I suppose either one of those things is possible."

"I meant about my makeup." She figured she might as well ask since her mother probably wouldn't be able to resist telling her anyway.

But apparently it wasn't even worth a glance. "Nice. I suppose you'll get the color right when you change into your mother-of-the-bride dress."

Susan opened her mouth and closed it again. Her mother wasn't paying attention to her; she had pulled the crisp white pique curtain aside and was staring out the window. "Something wrong?"

"There's a strange man outside. He seems to be filming the house."

Susan smiled. Here she had the advantage. "It's a video camera. He's taping, not filming."

"Why isn't he inside? Considering the amount we paid, he certainly should be getting some personal shots."

"You hired him?"

"It was your father's idea. He has always regretted that we didn't hire a professional to take photos at your wedding."

That stopped Susan—she hadn't thought of her father as so sentimental. "Oh, well, I thought . . . I told him . . . Why don't you go see if Wendy is okay and I'll just run out and make sure he comes inside to fil—to tape."

It took Susan only a few minutes to explain to the cameraman that she was sorry, she had been mistaken, she hoped he would understand—the tension of giving a wedding, and so on. He did understand, didn't he? (She got the impression that he didn't but he figured he had nothing else to do, so he might as well tape.)

"Besides," he added, as Susan walked him back to the house, "the police keep stopping me and asking what I'm doing hanging around outside."

Susan, remembering Brett's concerns about burglaries during the wedding ceremony, wasn't surprised by this. "Well, it's their job, after all.

"Why don't you stay on the first floor of the house and fil—tape the guests at our brunch," she added, hoping her parents would appreciate his industriousness. "I'll call you when the young ladies are ready upstairs."

"Lady, I've seen more bridesmaids in their bras than you could shake a stick at. Nothing upsets me."

"It wasn't you I was worried about upsetting," Susan assured him. "I'd better get going. There are dozens of things to do . . ."

"Always are, lady. Always are."

But Susan was ignoring him. Her attention had been drawn to the line of creamy yellow antique Bentleys turning the corner and making their way down the street. They had been hired to drive Chrissy and her wedding party to the church. But they were an hour early!

THIRTY-ONE

Susan returned to the hallway, having assured the chauffeurs that coffee and Danish would be delivered to the curb momentarily. The door was barely shut behind her when the mayhem began.

"Mother!" Chrissy appeared at the top of the stairs, wide-eyed, wearing a short white slip that revealed shimmering silver stockings attached to narrow blue garters. Her silky blond hair was teased straight up into the air. "Something has happened to the gloves the bridesmaids are wearing. I'm sure they were in a long gold box on my dresser last night, but now they've just disappeared!"

The gaggle of bridesmaids who had appeared in her wake fluttered, giggled, and muttered.

"Did you look—" Susan began, but Jed pushed to the front of the crowd of young women, seeming to think he had a more immediate problem.

"Hon, I can't find my studs. They're not where they usually are in the top drawer of my dresser. And don't tell me I don't know how to look, I dumped the damn thing out on the bed. They are not there!"

"Jed, I—"

But her mother, coming into the hallway from the direction of the kitchen, interrupted. "Susan, I've been thinking. Wouldn't it be better if your father and I drove over to the church in our own car? Then we'd have it available if . . . if there was an emergency of some sort. And you might be able to send one of those dreadfully expensive limos home. They must cost a fortune to rent—to say nothing of the gas. . . ." She stopped and turned around. "Is that Wendy yelling?"

Wendy answered that particular question herself, appearing at the top of the front steps behind Susan, a leather leash (one end chewed to a pulp) in her hands. "Mrs. Henshaw. Back in the commune, the animals used to attend all services, even weddings. Freedom and Hubris were wondering if you wanted them to bring along the puppies—or your dog."

"I really don't think—"

"Susan, you just got a call from the Inn. The boutonnieres for the ushers have arrived and they're the wrong color!" A voice Susan couldn't identify was yelling from the living room.

"Mother—" her daughter began again.

But the photographer was back. "Lady, where do you want me to stand while the service is going on? Just a still picture of the church for half an hour or more—and it's usually more, you know how these men of God like to blab when they finally get a good-sized audience—well, a still picture ain't going to be real good. Not many memories there, lady."

"Susan, I know you're busy ..." This time she recognized Kathleen's voice calling down the hallway. "... but that woman, the one who calls herself the Archangel, is on the phone. She wants to talk with you. She says it's urgent."

"I—"

"Susan—"

"Mother—"

"Sue—"

Susan's mind was racing. Wrapped packages, misplaced clothing, people going off on their own regardless of her careful planning, life in a commune years ago, problems with the flowers, the Archangel's hysterical urgency over things that simply didn't make any difference ... didn't matter. Suddenly it all came together for her.

"Shut up!" Susan was astounded by the loudness of her own voice. "Everyone just shut up. You can all take care of your own problems. Chrissy, the gloves are still in their box on the windowsill in the guest room. I saw them last night. Jed, I bought you a present—antique studs—they're in a wrapped package in the top drawer of the nightstand on my side of the bed. Mother, we've already paid for the cars, we might as well use them, don't you think? We don't want to be wasteful," she couldn't resist adding. "Wendy, no dogs. Do you hear me? *No* dogs at the church. And tell whoever called from the Inn that any questions anyone has about flowers should be directed to Erika Eden. Her beeper number is on the bulletin board next to the phone in the kitchen. And you," she added to the photographer, "you tape outside of the church only. Hear me? Outside only. And, Kathleen, hang up on the Archangel and call Brett. Tell him we have an emergency and I have to see him immediately!"

"But—"

"A serious emergency! I'll be in my bathroom and I don't want to be interrupted by anyone other than Brett!" And she turned and marched up the stairs. But she had one last thought, and she turned to face her family and friends as she arrived on the second-floor landing. "There will be a wedding today. And—" she glanced at her daughter's worried face and smiled "—and it really will be the loveliest wedding Hancock has ever seen."

She went to her bedroom, stomped through it without even pausing to pat Clue's head, comfortably cradled by her own down pillow, and on into the bathroom, closing and locking the door behind her. She had, she realized looking in the mirror, two important tasks ahead of her. She had to have a murderer arrested and gotten out of the way before the service began. And she had to do something about her hair!

First things first, she decided, and reached for her hairbrush.

She was just beginning to feel satisfied with the result of her work when there was a knock on the bathroom door.

"Susan? Are you in there? It's Brett Fortesque. I understand you have some sort of problem. . . ."

She opened the door. "Come in. Yeah, I know it's a rather odd offer," she added, noticing the surprise on his face. "But I want to talk with you privately and this is as private a spot as we're likely to find in this house today. Besides, I think I need to do something with my eyebrows. . . ."

"Susan, what's going on?" Brett asked. "I know you've been running all over town in the middle of the night and it's pretty obvious that it's not just because you're giving Chrissy a wedding."

Susan, standing so she could see Brett's reflection in the mirror over the sink, took a deep breath and plunged in. "A woman was murdered, Brett."

He was, she decided, one of the most amazing men she'd ever

met. "Who? When? Where? And where is she now?" was all he said. And he said it quietly.

"I . . ." She stopped. "You know, I don't actually know her name. Stephen called her Aunt Ginny. And David . . . I guess David just called her Mother."

"So she is David's mother? And Stephen's aunt? We are talking about the Stephen who Chrissy is supposed to be marrying in a few hours, aren't we?"

"The Stephen Canfield who . . . whom . . . she is *going* to marry in a few hours," she corrected him. "And oh, Brett, Chrissy doesn't know anything about this—nothing. And I sure don't want to tell her. Okay?"

"Susan, I don't know enough to tell anyone anything. Yet."

"I am trying to tell you, Brett. You see, Chrissy's wedding gown disappeared yesterday and then the box—the box it was shipped from Italy in—the box was at the Yacht Club in the ladies' room . . ."

"Okay, I get it. You found her in the stall you were trying to keep the plumber, or anyone, from entering?" Brett asked.

"Well, I found her in the box on the couch. I put her in the stall so no one else would find her."

"Susan, if you had told me about this yesterday—"

"Brett—"

"Okay. I'm sorry. Let's not argue about that now. Just tell me what you know. How exactly did this woman die?"

"First, I should tell you that she is not Stephen's aunt. He just called her Aunt Ginny when he was young. And she is not the woman who is here with David's father—she is his stepmother. The dead woman never even lived in the commune they all spend so much time talking about. David's father and she broke up before the commune was founded."

"And how did she die?" Brett asked patiently.

"Well, Kathleen said it looked like someone had strangled her."

A crumpled grin appeared on Brett's face. "I should have known Kathleen was involved in this. Anyone else?"

"No, there's just the one woman. . . . Oh, you mean, does anyone else know about the murder."

"Yes."

"Just Jed. And the murderer, of course." She stopped and

thought for a moment. "And Stephen. And David—well, he knows his mother is dead, but I'm not sure he realizes it was murder. And Stephen's mother seems to know that David's mother's dead—but she might not know how. And Tom Davidson might have looked in the box—although I really don't think he would do that when he thought it was a wedding present. And whoever has it now may have looked in—"

"Susan. Stop for a moment. I hope I didn't hear what I think I just heard."

She knew exactly what he was talking about. "The body is missing. Well, not exactly missing. I just don't know where it is."

"Which amounts to the same thing right now."

"Sort of—"

"Susan, a woman you invited to your daughter's wedding was murdered—"

"That's not right, Brett. She wasn't invited to the wedding. Although she did get hold of an invitation. I think that may have to do with Stephen's parents, too, but I'm not sure."

"So she lives around here and just happened to stop by to see old friends—or her son?"

"I . . ." Susan was beginning to realize how many questions she still didn't have answers to. "I don't think so. Actually, I got the impression that she was still living out on the West Coast somewhere."

"So she just came here to be murdered."

"I . . . ah . . . well, that's not exactly what I think," Susan said. "But, you know, you may have a point. Do you want me to tell you what I think?"

"Susan, I would love to know what you think. Especially if you think you know who killed the poor woman and why—and where her body is right now."

"Well, this took me a while . . ."

"Susan—"

"I know what you're thinking. I found the body less than twenty-four hours ago, so I'm exaggerating the time, but, believe me, it's been a very long and eventful twenty-four hours."

"I'm sure, but—"

"Of course, I asked the same questions you're asking now. Who is she? Why was she here for the wedding? Why would someone kill her? Who killed her? I am getting to some of the answers," she added, recognizing the impatience on his face.

"And I'm waiting for them."

"Okay, do you want to know the entire process I went through? I mean, I didn't realize who the dead woman was at first—"

"Do you want to see your daughter get married?"

"Brett! Of course I do! How could you ask such a question?"

"If Chrissy is going to walk down that aisle on time, you'd better fill me in on all the details. Unless your solution has something to do with the wedding?" He raised his eyebrows, a serious expression on his face.

"It has to do with a wedding . . . but not Chrissy's."

"You are going to explain before I'm old and gray?"

"I'm going to explain this minute. And then we're both going to join our family and friends and see my daughter get married to the love of her life."

"Good."

"But first I have a few things to say to Chrissy on her wedding day. And I absolutely must make one phone call."

"Susan . . ."

"Just fifteen minutes, Brett. That's all. I promise."

"Well, you've waited this long, I suppose another fifteen minutes won't make any difference. But, Susan . . ."

"Yes, Brett?"

"Fifteen minutes, and that's all."

THIRTY-TWO

"It was nice of Brett to let you have that time with Chrissy. I know it meant a lot to her," Jed said, picking up his wife's hand and giving it a squeeze.

She smiled and squeezed back. "It meant a lot to me, too." She felt tears at the corners of her eyes and reached into her purse for a handkerchief. A tiny beaded Judith Liebner bag had replaced her vast satchel. She peered into the pristine silk interior; she was, it seemed, carrying three tubes of bronze lipstick, black mascara, a twenty-dollar bill, a small pot of solid perfume, and a broken toothpick.

"Here. I brought an extra." Jed offered his wife a clean linen square.

"You did? Oh, you are so sweet . . ." She grabbed for it and dabbed at her eyes.

"Being married to a woman who tears up at the sight of the Christmas tree every year has taught me to be prepared—especially on the day her only daughter gets married."

Susan smiled again, sniffled a few more times, and continued her story. "Well, I explained to Brett that it finally dawned on me that the only reason for David's mother to be here was that she knew all the members of the commune would get together again for Stephen's wedding—everyone kept mentioning that this was the first real reunion the group had had. And David's mother had some people she wanted to see."

"And when she saw these people?"

"Then she had to be killed so the wrong people didn't find out what she knew."

"You know, this still isn't making a lot of sense." He leaned forward to peer from the backseat of the Bentley out into the traffic in front of them. "And it isn't all that long until we get to the church."

"Well, the story isn't very long either. I was right about my first hunch. It all hinged on the Archangel. Of course, she wasn't the victim, but she was the most important player here."

"Don't tell her. She's self-important enough as it is."

"Boy, you're right about that. And she loves attention. Look at the way she arrived here yesterday. First, she was supposed to be stuck at O'Hare Airport, then the story went that she was testifying at a congressional hearing. But it was all garbage. She was here earlier in the day, just visiting old friends like everyone else. She seems to be one of those people who needs to be the center of attention—and when she isn't, she makes up stories. But, to give credit where credit is due, she was still the pivotal person in this story."

"Because she married all those people?" Jed asked.

"Just the opposite. Because she couldn't legally marry anyone. She may have been an ex-nun. And she certainly was a self-proclaimed spiritual leader. But not an ordained minister."

"Then were the marriages that took place in the commune legal?"

"Nope. I should have realized that when I first heard about them. After all, the first couple she married was Freedom and Hubris. . . ."

"I hope it doesn't matter which couple you're talking about. I'm still having trouble connecting the names with the faces," Jed admitted reluctantly.

"They're the ones who own the theater up on the Cape."

"The gay men?"

"Exactly."

"Then . . . what you're saying is that their marriage couldn't be legal—even if it was performed by a minister."

"Yes, but the rest of the services the Archangel performed weren't legally binding either. She may have been well-meaning and sincere (although I doubt it). But she can't legally marry anyone."

"What about Chrissy?"

Susan heard the alarm in her husband's voice. "Chrissy and Stephen are going to be quite legally married by the Reverend Richard Price. Don't worry. I called him this morning right before

I spoke with Chrissy. Everything is going to be nice and legal. He's known about the Archangel's limitations the whole time. Apparently she knew better than to hide her lack of accreditation from him. Dick is going to do the standard service and when it comes time for a short sermon, the Archangel will say a few words to the couple and then to our guests. That's the way it was planned from the beginning." Susan frowned. "I think he's just hoping the few words she wants to speak won't turn into a long soliloquy."

"He's not the only one. So finish telling me the story—and how you figured it all out."

"It wasn't at all difficult after that. Who in the commune benefited from being married?"

"Or not married, as the case may be . . ."

"Exactly, Jed! That's what I'm trying to explain."

"Susan, in ten minutes I hope I'm going to be walking our daughter down the aisle of the church. And I sure hope you're going to be finished explaining by that time. . . ."

"I'm trying, Jed. It's not that complex a story really. It's easy. Let me tell you what I know . . ."

"Please."

"Well, the commune was located in an old crumbling hotel that David's stepmother had inherited. The neighborhood was run-down; it probably wasn't worth an awful lot at the time the commune moved in. But, years later, after the commune broke up, the neighborhood had become more desirable—enough for a major corporation to pay big bucks to buy up that hotel, tear it down, and build a gigantic hotel and convention center on the site."

"So?" The line of limousines was stopped at a light and Jed peered out the window while listening to the story his wife was relating.

"So anyone who thought about it would have assumed that half of the profit belonged to David's father—because of California community property laws—and at least some of that would be passed on to David, making him a very rich young man."

"Who thought that?" The limo slowly started again.

"Everyone, I guess. David surely did—why would he have assumed anything else? And I'm sure Wendy's parents did."

"You think that's why they encouraged the marriage in the beginning? They wanted their daughter to marry money?"

"I'm sure of it."

"Why?"

"Because one—or both of them—killed David's mother so no one would ever find out that his father and the woman he had assumed was his stepmother weren't legally married."

Jed thought for a moment. "What about a common-law marriage? What about all those celebrities who are always suing for massive amounts of money in California even though they've just been living together for years—without benefit of any legal document?"

"That might be fine—except for the fact that David's father and mother had never gotten a divorce. That's why David's father and stepmother were thrilled to have the Archangel perform a service for them. Like Freedom and Hubris, it gave them a validity they couldn't get legally."

"So that's also the reason that Wendy's parents, after encouraging the relationship, began to discourage it—"

"It's not quite that simple, Jed. You see . . . What's wrong? You keep looking out the window."

"There seems to be something happening on the road. We're slowing down for more than lights and stop signs."

"It's the photographer, sir." The uniformed driver made the statement without looking around.

"Excuse me? What photographer?"

"There's a man with a video camera outside the church asking each driver to wait in a line by the sidewalk. Then each group is to leave their car separately so he can get a good shot of them going up the stairs and into the church."

"Does this always happen?" Jed asked.

"Standard practice. There are probably MTV videos with less production time than some weddings these days."

"How do you know what's going on?" Susan asked.

The driver picked up a small phone from the seat beside him. "We're in constant contact. Want me to tell them to get the show on the road?"

"Ye—"

"No, Jed." Susan put her hand on his arm and, looking down, realized that most of her nails were either chipped or broken. How long had it been since she'd left that manicurist? "This is fine. It gives us a chance to talk before the service—and if it goes on too long, you know Dick will come out and speed things up."

"Okay, I guess you're right. So keep going. Explain. How did you figure all this out, for heaven's sake?"

"Well, a lot came together for me when I spent some time with Wendy this morning. She was so distraught over her parents' disapproval of her marriage with David; she simply didn't understand why it had happened. At first I thought she was just being upset and slightly hysterical. But she claimed to have no idea why her parents didn't approve of their marriage. And then there was the fact that she seemed to be surprised by David's heavy drinking."

"Really? I'd gotten the impression that he was an alcoholic, that his behavior this weekend was normal for him," Jed said.

"Exactly what I thought. But apparently it wasn't true. Remember, Wendy and David have not only dated for years, but they've been living near each other all their lives. She seemed to be genuinely upset and shocked by his behavior."

"And that doesn't make sense, right?"

"And the only way it makes sense is if his behavior was an aberration, not the norm. Wendy claimed that was true. And I decided to believe her. But then, I began to wonder whether David was drinking because he knew his mother was around and he was afraid she might be planning on making an appearance at the wedding."

"And that made sense."

"No, not at all. I saw him right after he discovered his mother was dead. He was shocked—and said at the time that he'd had no idea she was around. It was a genuine moment. He was too distressed to be thinking of providing himself with an alibi." She paused and pursed her lips. "Poor kid. He was so upset. So, anyway, I was pretty sure he hadn't killed his mother. And I was pretty sure that the drinking wasn't normal in his life. So the next question was, why was he drinking?"

"Good question."

"No, wrong question. There is no way the young man I saw early this morning was drunk for hours and hours last night. Even youth has its limitations. So I realized that we only thought David was drinking."

"If he was acting, he was pretty convincing," Jed said.

"Acting drunk is the easiest thing in the world. In the first place, we all know how drunks act, and in the second place, we've all been partying pretty heavily since yesterday afternoon. I'm not sure if any of us was capable of picking up on the finer nuances of anyone's behavior."

"Why would he pretend to be drunk?"

"Well, I wondered about that. And it brought me back to something that's been bothering me since yesterday afternoon. Something Stephen did."

"Stephen? What does he have to do with this whole thing? Chrissy's not going to be marrying a man who might be a murderer, is she?"

"No, no. You don't have to worry about that. In fact, she's getting a young man who's a terrible liar. . . . What did you say?" Susan stared at her husband. It had sounded very much like Jed had insisted that Stephen would become a better liar once he was married.

"Sorry, just making a stupid sexist joke—not even a funny one. Somehow weddings seem to bring out the worst in men."

"I've noticed," Susan said. And she was not amused.

"So what was Stephen lying about?"

"Chrissy's lateness."

"And why was he lying about something so . . . so trivial?"

"It wasn't trivial to him. At that time, Stephen thought Chrissy might be involved in the murder of David's mother."

THIRTY-THREE

"WHY? WHAT REASON WOULD CHRISSY HAVE TO KILL ANY-one? Especially David's mother! She didn't even know David's mother, for heaven's sake!"

"Jed, don't get so upset. He was trying to protect Chrissy, re-member." Susan glanced at the driver, who was rather ostenta-tiously concentrating on the road ahead of him. "And he was trying to protect his parents, too."

"His parents? Where do they come in here?"

"That's where the wedding gown comes into the story. You see, David picked up the wedding gown at Kennedy Airport and brought it to Hancock. Not knowing the area, he got lost looking for our house. When he passed the Yacht Club, he dropped it off there and called me."

"I remember you told me that. What does it have to do with Stephen's parents?"

"Well, Blues saw the box and realized what was inside, opened it, and took the dress out."

"Blues? Blues Canfield took Chrissy's wedding gown? Why, in heaven's name?"

"I have no idea. Maybe she wanted to sew something on it like the Archangel did. So when David told Stephen what he had seen—"

"Which was what?"

"Rhythm and Blues going into the Yacht Club right after he had walked out, leaving the dress in its box near the front door."

"But—"

"And Chrissy being dropped off at the curb by a friend and calling out to his parents."

"As though they had planned to meet," Jed said, nodding.

"They did plan to meet, in fact. Rhythm was taking Chrissy to visit a friend of his who just happens to own an art gallery in Philadelphia. Oh, Jed, did she tell you she might be getting a job at a gallery?"

"Susan, don't get off the subject. I'm getting confused again. If Rhythm and Blues didn't have anything to do with the murder—and they didn't, did they?"

"No."

"Good, I don't want to think of our daughter marrying into a family of murderers—although it would give you something to do in your declining years, other than mourn your empty nest." He grinned.

"They are not. And I am not. I have plans, in fact . . . but we won't go into that now." She knew Jed wasn't going to agree to an expensive and extended vacation until all the bills for the wedding were paid. "Now, all that matters is that the only reason Blues wanted the dress was to sew in these little amulets she claims will bring Chrissy and Stephen good luck. It was a little devious of her and more than a little odd. But she is that way, and I think the best we can hope for there is that the Canfields stay on the West Coast and the kids stay here in the East."

She took Jed's nod as enthusiastic agreement with her statement, and she continued.

"So Stephen, who knew something was up, was trying to protect our daughter when he claimed she was always on time. He didn't want anyone to think some of Chrissy's time might be unaccounted for."

"Well, that's good of him." Jed peered out the window. "We're almost there, hon."

"I've really told you the entire story, Jed. It was greed, pure and simple greed. That's why David's mother was killed. If she hadn't been hidden in the box the gown arrived in—"

"Why was she?"

"I think anyone would realize that the more time that passes before the body is found, the more likely one is to get away with . . . well, with murder. But I'd bet that whoever killed her—whether it was Havana Rose or Red Man or both of them acting together—thought hiding the body there would at least confuse the issue."

"Which it certainly did," Jed agreed.

"Especially because the gown itself kept moving from one person to the other."

"Why was that? Why didn't Blues just return it to Chrissy after she was done with it? It was in our house and out again like some sort of strange jack-in-the box."

"Because great—or mediocre—minds seem to run in the same direction."

"You mean—"

"Blues wasn't the only commune member who decided that Chrissy should have more than something old, something new, something borrowed, and something blue on her when she walks down that aisle. Three other people sewed in tiny amulets as well," Susan said, nodding.

"Heavens, could the dress support everything?"

"Not very well. I mean, it was dragging a little around the hemline. Luckily, these hippie types spent a lot of time doing hand sewing in the Sixties—all those embroidered jeans—and they didn't do any damage. And then Mom took over."

"Your mother?"

"Yup. You see, she brought a little momento of her own that she felt Chrissy should wear today."

"What?"

"The blue garter that I wore when we got married."

"You wore a garter? I don't remember tossing it to the single men or anything like that."

"That's because you didn't. I thought it was a tacky, sexist tradition. But I didn't want to argue with my mother at the last moment so I wore the damn thing."

"And you saved it?"

"No way. I must have left it in the hotel room when I changed for our honeymoon, and my mother picked it up. She's been saving it all these years."

"But I don't understand what that has to do with all the . . . the amulets . . . or good luck charms, or whatever we're calling them."

"My mother very carefully cut them all off the gown and stitched each one around the garter. If you notice anything lumpy on Chrissy's thigh as you two walk down the aisle, just ignore it. Young couples these days can use all the luck they can get."

"Well, I won't argue with that. So everything is all set for the service? No one is going to be pulled out of the congregation in handcuffs?"

"No. Brett and his men have already picked up Red Man and Havana Rose. Last I heard, he even expected to be back here in time for the service. At least, I hope he makes it," she added, remembering her plans for him and Erika.

"Wendy decided that she didn't want to be a bridesmaid under the circumstances," Susan continued, looking sad.

"And David?"

"He's going to be best man. I think he felt he owed it to Stephen. Chad, on the other hand, volunteered to give up his position as usher and even out the numbers."

"Susan, you didn't let him—"

"Not at all. One of the other ushers is not going to be walking up the aisle. It's all been worked out." The car had come to a halt and she peered through the window at the green lawn cheerfully sprinkled with bright yellow dandelions, the fluffy white clouds in the deep blue sky, the arch of flowers hanging over the glossy double doors, and then sat back in her seat with a sigh.

"Everything looks beautiful, hon," Jed assured her.

"It does. Oh, look, there's Chrissy."

Their daughter had just joined her bridesmaids on the sidewalk in front of the church. Her attendants wore simple floor-length sleeveless princess gowns in varying shades of delicate pastel silk. Their lush bouquets were tied with wide ribbons over two feet long, a mix of the many colors of their dresses. They all looked beautiful.

But even in such illustrious company, Chrissy stood out. Her gown was worth every single one of the faxes, the phone calls, and the panic. Like her bridesmaids' gowns, it was sleeveless, with a scoop neckline, fitted through the bodice, then flaring gently to the ground. It was the fabric that astounded. The dress had been fashioned from layers of the thinnest silk chiffon, each layer a slightly different shade of white, just barely washed with shimmering pastel tints. The total effect was incredible. As Chrissy moved, it was as though iridescent rainbows floated around her. Her bouquet was huge, tied with five-inch-wide watered silk ribbons of bronze, silver, and gold. Those same ribbons (antiques, discovered in a small shop in Florence by the young designer) had been sewn into a large bow that supported the white gossamer veil that hung down to within an inch of the floor.

"Of course, every mother thinks her daughter is beautiful—" Susan began.

"In this case, it's true," Jed said, and leaned over and kissed his wife. "Almost as beautiful as her mother."

"I love a man who can tell a good lie," Susan said, and laughed.

"I'm not going to respond to that," he answered. "Shall we join the ladies? I see your parents. I see my mother. I think we're almost ready to have a wedding."

Susan took a deep breath, offered a prayer, and joined her family in church.

THIRTY-FOUR

"Susan, I don't know how you do it. It was a beautiful wedding. And you seemed to have done it all absolutely effortlessly." Susan's ebullient neighbor leaned closer and whispered in Susan's ear, "And I'm so impressed with your hair—so casual and unpretentious. I wish I had the confidence to be as relaxed about my appearance."

Susan just smiled and passed the last guest in the receiving line on to her husband. "I," she said to anyone listening, "could use a drink."

"Champagne, ma'am?" A tray covered with glasses of pale gold elixir appeared by her side.

"Thank you!" Susan smiled at the young waiter. She took a crystal flute, started to drink, and then noticed that the young man had not yet moved on. "Are you waiting for something?"

"Jamie Potter said . . . well, she said you might need more than one glass."

"What? Is something wrong?"

The waiter started to laugh. "She said you'd say that, too, and to tell you that everything in the kitchen is right on schedule and for you to just have a good time and enjoy the party."

Susan drained the glass, returned it to the tray, and chose another. "I'm planning on doing that very thing," she assured him.

"Me, too." Jed reached out and captured a glass for himself.

The receiving line was dispersing. Stephen put his arms around Chrissy and led her away as Susan watched.

"Feeling a little sad?" Jed asked quietly.

"Nope. Just hoping our daughter made the right decision when she chose that young man. His family is so strange."

"But he's not. He's everything you would want in a son-in-law:

intelligent, responsible, interesting, full of surprises . . . What do you think about their honeymoon plans?"

"Two weeks in Bermuda? You think that's interesting?"

"Actually, it sounds good to me—just what you and I need. A lounge on a nice pink beach, an icy rum swizzle by my side, nothing to do but smear sunscreen on my nose . . ."

"Maybe fun for old folks like us, but it doesn't sound like Chrissy."

"Sure doesn't. Which is why I was so impressed with Stephen's plan."

"But I thought—"

"They're spending one night in Bermuda, then being picked up by a chartered yacht. They're going to sail down to the Caribbean on an antique sailing sloop. Just the two of them and a crew of three for twelve days."

"Jed! How fabulous! Does Chrissy know? She'll be thrilled."

"She does and she is. I gather Stephen was not going to divulge his plan until they arrived in Bermuda, but he had second thoughts and realized Chrissy might want to pack differently for sitting on a boat than for hanging out in Hamilton."

Susan smiled. "Wow."

"Maybe our daughter really has got the perfect husband," Jed said, taking his wife's hand and leading her toward their table.

Susan wondered if maybe that wasn't an oxymoron—at best. "I hope so. . . . What's going on over there?" she asked, as her attention was drawn to a crowd on the porch.

"The flower girl and ring bearer are tossing crumbs to a flock of seagulls," Erika said, coming up to the Henshaws, a glass of champagne in one hand and a plate of shrimp in the other. She was smiling. "The food is wonderful, Susan. Everyone is talking about it. Fabulous Food is sure living up to its name."

"I'm glad to hear that. But the flowers . . . Erika, the flowers are incredible." She stopped and looked more closely at her companion. "Erika? Is something wrong?"

Erika's expression had changed as Jed left Susan's side to greet a business colleague standing near the long buffet table. "Susan, I just wanted to explain—"

"About the flowers at the rehearsal last night?"

"How did you know?"

"I wouldn't worry about it anymore. It was probably Tom Davidson."

"How in heaven's name did you know?"

"It made sense. He was up there. He's the type of young man who would always have his Swiss Army knife close by. Have you talked to him about it?"

"Yes."

"And did he explain anything?"

"He said he was trying to get Chrissy's attention. He seems to have had some sort of ridiculous notion about talking her into running away with him before the ceremony."

Susan just shook her head. "That was never going to happen. Chrissy is really in love with Stephen."

"I know. And while we were cleaning up this morning, I overheard Tom asking out one of the young college girls who's working for me this summer, so I think he's going to survive."

"So much for a broken heart," Susan commented, and then looked more closely at Erika. "You certainly seem to be happy."

"Yes. Well, I should be. I'm engaged."

"Erika! How wonderful!"

"I know it's foolish for a woman as old as I am to really be engaged. I mean, Brett and I won't announce it in the newspaper or have an engagement party or anything—"

"Why not? It's wonderful. You should celebrate!" Susan found herself sipping champagne and wondering what her husband would think about their throwing a surprise party for the happy couple. "When did this happen?"

"During the service, actually. The church was so beautiful—if I do say so myself—and Chrissy and Stephen looked so happy up there at the altar. And when that woman minister started talking about the place of marriage in the modern world, I sort of drifted off and began to remember how I had played at being a bride when I was a kid—in fact, the first flower arrangement I ever made was for a pretend wedding I had with the boy next door—and then Brett leaned over and whispered in my ear, and . . . and I said yes!"

"And a good thing she did, too. Don't you think?"

The chief of police had joined them.

"I think it's a wonderful thing, Brett. Congratulations."

"And congratulations to you, too. A beautiful wedding, Susan.

And I don't think anyone here knows better than I do what you've been through in the past twenty-four hours."

"I'm just glad the service went okay."

"Went okay? Hon, it was better than okay," Jed said, returning to his wife's side. "The band is starting to play, Brett. Aren't you and Erika going to dance?"

"Just as soon as Chrissy and Stephen have begun, we'll be on our way," Brett said, offering his arm to his new fiancée and leading her to the dance floor.

That happy couple was replaced by Rhythm and Blues. They also seemed happy, giggling and carrying on like teenagers. "Hey, the kids really are married!" Rhythm announced needlessly. "We're related!" And he flung his arms around Susan and hugged her so hard it took her breath away. But she had oxygen enough to see that Blues was attempting the same movement with Jed—to his obvious discomfort.

"Great wedding! Great day!" Rhythm continued in his usual hearty manner. "Brings back many a memory for Blues and myself. Many a memory," he repeated a bit less enthusiastically, possibly remembering the weddings that weren't marriages, and the resulting tragedy.

"Tell them what we've been thinking, dear," Blues urged, as Susan tried to tactfully disentangle herself from Rhythm's embrace.

"We have a plan. A wonderful plan. A great plan. A . . . a remarkable plan."

"Why don't you explain what it is," his wife suggested.

Jed, who had been more successful than his wife in detaching from their new relations, made encouraging noises.

"Well, you know how important we think family is," Blues began.

"Most important thing in the world!" Rhythm boomed.

"And . . . well, I guess we didn't exactly get off on the right foot," Blues added, her cheeks turning pink. "I'm afraid I was a little suspicious of you last night, and . . . Well, it's been a difficult time for some of us who were together in the commune."

"That's all in the past," Susan hurried to assure her. "Today is a new day. And the beginning of a new life for our children."

"And for ourselves! Don't forget the old folks!" Rhythm

insisted. "Although I always say, Blues and I are just a couple of kids."

"You certainly are," Jed agreed, peering through the crowd that was surrounding the dance floor.

"We think the two families should get to know each other better."

"Of course . . ." Susan didn't see that she could do anything but agree.

"No time like the present. That's what I always say. No time like the present."

Susan and Jed exchanged looks.

"So we've decided to spend more time in your lovely town—just a few weeks. Then we can bond. You know?"

Susan did. And she saw her visions of a long week resting and trying to catch up flying right out the window. But she certainly couldn't be rude and refuse to see them. In fact, she really should offer the hospitality of her own home. She opened her mouth, but Jed jumped in before she could speak.

"Well, Rhythm, it's an excellent idea, but I think it's going to have to wait for another time."

"But Jed—"

"You see, I made some plans that Susan doesn't know about. I have a surprise for her."

"For me? Jed, what?"

"I have reservations at that hotel you loved in the countryside just outside of Lucca—for an entire week. Our plane leaves for Rome tomorrow night!"

"Jed! How wonderful . . . but what about Chad? And Clue? And those damn . . . uh, those adorable puppies?"

"I've thought of everything. I am paying our son an enormous amount of money to take care of all three canines while we are gone. He was thrilled with the prospect. Seems he's saving to buy a motorcycle so he can tool around town with his new girlfriend. Now, don't start worrying about him. He'll be fine. But you see that we're going to have to put your visit off for just a while."

"Of course. Of course. You'll be on a second honeymoon while the kids are on theirs!" Rhythm enthused.

"Oh, Jed. Italy . . ." Susan looked up at her husband. There were tears in her eyes for the third time that day.

"Why don't you just dance with me—and you can tell me that you have a perfect husband."

He put his arm around his wife and led her away from their new relatives and toward the dance floor.

"Well, I know you have the one thing necessary to become a perfect husband," Susan said, smiling happily.

"What's that?"

"A perfect wife."

WE WISH YOU A MERRY MURDER

Chic suburbanite Kelly Knowlson's ex-husband returns to Hancock for Christmas—shot dead in her living room. In between holiday parties, Susan Henshaw tracks down the killer.

AN OLD FAITHFUL MURDER

The Henshaw family's vacation at Yellowstone National Park is interrupted by murder when the domineering patriarch of another vacationing family is found dead near Old Faithful. Susan Henshaw, with her previous sleuthing experience, is called onto the case.

ALL HALLOWS' EVIL

When a celebrity morning talk-show host is murdered, neighborly Susan Henshaw invites his wife to stay with her. But Susan soon discovers that her houseguest has a nasty reputation for losing lovers under suspicious circumstances. . . .

A STAR-SPANGLED MURDER

Susan Henshaw and her family have been coming to their summer house in Maine for years, but when neighbor Humphrey Taylor is found bludgeoned to death in her living room, Susan's relaxing holiday goes out with the tide.

A GOOD YEAR FOR A CORPSE

All the local organizations were courting wealthy Horace Harvey—until he was found strangled in the wine cellar of the Hancock Inn. Susan Henshaw wants to know why he was murdered—and where his money came from.

'TIS THE SEASON TO BE MURDERED

Exhausted by the rigors of holiday shopping and family management, Susan Henshaw hires caterers for her New Year's bash. Unfortunately, the chef is found strangled in a van full of helium balloons, putting a dent in Susan's holiday plans. . . .

REMODELED TO DEATH

Susan Henshaw is forced into unexpected renovations when her bathroom pipes burst. Fortunately she doesn't have to deal with the town's hated building inspector, because he has just been murdered. . . .

ELECTED FOR DEATH

Hancock's heated mayoral election runs into serious scandal when one of the three candidates is found murdered. When Susan Henshaw's husband, who is running for town council, is smeared in the local politicking, Susan gets serious about finding the killer.

The Susan Henshaw Mysteries
by VALERIE WOLZIEN

Published by Fawcett Books.
Available at your local bookstore.